Winged Victory

SARAH LEVINE SIMON

"Simon tells a heartwarming tale of what it was like to be an unpopular minority in an industrial town in the middle of the twentieth century when people with disabilities were given no quarter. It's a story that will open your eyes and stay with you a long time." ~ *Taylor Jones, Reviewer*

"Winged Victory is a heartbreaking, heartwarming, and thought-provoking story of courage, strength, and the determination to succeed despite the obstacles disabled people and their families face. It gives us a glimpse into a world most of us can't even imagine." ~ *Regan Murphy, Reviewer*

Sarah Levine Simon

Black Opal Books
BECAUSE YOUR STORIES JUST HAVE TO BE TOLD

It was so unfair. But where would I find justice in a world that was always against me?

"I'm going to fly in a vaccine for the pox," Bill Rile tells me.

"Shut up!"

"Ooooh! You told me to shut up? I'm going to get you."

Mr. Lane is drawing an airplane wing on the board, and Bill Rile is smiling appreciatively at him when I feel a sharp jab in my thigh. He points under the table to the point of the compass he's holding in his hand. "I inoculated you from yourself!" he whispers.

"He poked me," I scream.

"I can't have you in my class, Miss Povich, please go down to Doctor Waldrop's office for the rest of this period. Tell Doctor Waldrop that I am giving you detention. You'll have to do it in the principal's office because I have a meeting, and please have your uncle come to see me. I think you should be considering the vocational curriculum."

All the mill girls take the vocational curriculum. Everyone knows they drop out by sixteen anyway. In my neighborhood, the mere mention of "vocational" is humiliation itself. The kids in my neighborhood are expected to go to college even if their parents haven't. No one holds it against a parent if he or she was in the war or went to work. But no one would dare drop out of high school. Sometimes the college-bound girls take vocational subjects like shorthand and typing in the summer. When you get to college, you're expected to type papers for the boys so it's acceptable to take vocational subjects in the summer.

Tears are streaming down my face.

"Why are you crying?"

I don't answer.

"I have a 'no crying' rule in this classroom."

"He poked me with his compass," I tell Mr. Lane again.

"I don't care what he did. First, you come in late and then you disrupt my class. Some of these guys are serious science students, and I have to prepare them for the AP exams." Mr. Lane folds his arms and watches as I gather my things.

In 1950, Victory Povich is a nine-year-old Jewish girl in Pittsburgh, Pennsylvania, when her father becomes ill. He is Hearing and Victory's mother is Deaf. Victory is caught between the two worlds, talking to her father and signing to her mother, as well translating for her when a speaker doesn't sign. Her father's illness—and the persecution that Victory suffers, not only from being Jewish, but also from being the daughter of a Deaf woman—causes her to do poorly in school, and she retreats into the world of books and imagination where she pretends she's Nancy Drew, solving complex mysteries. Her father's death when Victory is thirteen turns her life upside down. Her Hearing relatives want to take her away from her mother and control both their lives. To make matters worse, Victory is the target of a neighborhood bully who viciously torments and injures her every chance he gets. Now Victory and her mother must find a way to survive in 1950s Pittsburgh when the whole world seems to be against them through no fault of their own.

KUDOS for *Winged Victory*

In *Winged Victory* by Sarah Levine Simon, Victory is the hearing daughter of a hearing father and a deaf mother in Pittsburgh in the 1950s. And if having a deaf mother wasn't enough to get her bullied in school, she is also Jewish. Then when her father dies, she and her mother are on their own. Victory is also ostracized because her family doesn't have much money, so life is hard. Then a new friend moves in across the street, and Victory starts getting into trouble, but she also learns to take responsibility for her actions, no matter the consequences—a hard lesson to learn and not without its adventures. Simon tells a heartwarming tale of what it was like to be an unpopular minority in an industrial town in the middle of the twentieth century when people with disabilities were given no quarter. It's a story that will open your eyes and stay with you a long time. ~ *Taylor Jones, The Review Team of Taylor Jones & Regan Murphy*

Winged Victory by Sarah Levine Simon is the story of a young Jewish girl growing up in Pittsburgh in the late nineteen fifties. Victory Povich is nine when the story opens, and even at that age, a lot is asked of her. Her mother is deaf, though both Victory and her father can hear. Being an only child, Victory is often called upon to translate for her mother, who can only use sign language. Since people often fear what they don't understand, Victory's family is shunned because of her mother. In those days, people with disabilities had few options and were often persecuted. Victory has few friends and is bullied at school. Then when she is thirteen or so, her father dies of cancer, and Victory and her mother are left all alone. Victory's aunt and uncle try to take over and control their lives, but Victory and her mother have other ideas.

Winged Victory is a heartbreaking, heartwarming, and thought-provoking story of courage, strength, and the determination to succeed despite the obstacles disabled people and their families face. It gives us a glimpse into a world most of us can't even imagine. ~ *Regan Murphy, The Review Team of Taylor Jones & Regan Murphy*

ACKNOWLEDGMENTS

My editors Faith & Reyana at Black Opal Books and independent editor Susan Dalsimer

Peter Miller & Thomas Rodd, your high school antics inspired Victory to new heights.

At every phase of writing I had the support of friends who read and made helpful suggestions: My husband Roger Hendricks Simon, Juliet Heyer, Anne Lancellotti, Eric Somers, Julie and Al Rosenblatt, Charles Turner, Susan Sheldon, Deaf actress Jackie Roth, and, again, Peter Miller.

My high school English teacher Lenore Mussoff. You taught me to live "the writing life" during troubled times.

Winged Victory

SARAH LEVINE SIMON

A Black Opal Books Publication

GENRE: HISTORICAL YA/COMING OF AGE/AMERICANS WITH DISABILITIES

This is a work of fiction. Names, places, characters and incidents are either the product of the author's imagination or are used fictitiously, and any resemblance to any actual persons, living or dead, businesses, organizations, events or locales is entirely coincidental. All trademarks, service marks, registered trademarks, and registered service marks are the property of their respective owners and are used herein for identification purposes only. The publisher does not have any control over or assume any responsibility for author or third-party websites or their contents.

Published by Black Opal Books **http://www.blackopalbooks.com**

DEDICATION

In memory of my parents
Maita Sivitz Levine & Jules Levine

Chapter 1

In my family we have two names for everyone—one name links the person to family, the other—the snapshot impression your mind takes of that person. My mother calls my father The Red Tie Artist because he was wearing a red tie the day he met my mother in the museum—too dressed up to carry a sketchbook, she thought. He says she reminded him of a stubborn flame. She was dressed like a beatnik, all in black. Her red hair flowing about her shoulders first caught his eye. According to my father, they almost didn't meet. He had gone to the museum on his day off from the linoleum store to sketch the statue of the Winged Victory in the long marble hall.

It was my mother's day off from the factory where she painted delicate flowers on porcelain. She was sketching the Winged Victory, too. My father was very impressed by her drawing and paid her a compliment. She can't hear and didn't turn to acknowledge it. So he repeated it. My mother still didn't budge. Her eyes stayed fixed on the Winged Victory.

"Look, I didn't mean to bother you. I'm sorry okay. Your drawing is really remarkable. That's all I wanted to say." He started to walk away but when he entered the periphery of her vision, she turned and fell immediately in love with his eyes—his version of the winged victory, too. My mother says my father should have tapped her on the shoulder. But he insists that it would have been rude.

My father had to learn to sign because my mother, born deaf, never learned to speak. I asked my mother if she ever worried that I would be born deaf and she signed. *"No! Only the family worried, especially my mother."* When I was born, the first thing my grandmother did was strike a tuning fork on the side of my crib. My uncle Abe smashed the lids of metal pots together when they brought me home. I was too good-natured to cry. If these attacks didn't bother my mother, there was no reason for them to bother me. That was the first of many misunderstandings in the Hearing part of my family about the Deaf part.

Chapter 2

I am nine years old the summer of my father's first illness.

"We think we caught it in time," they tell me but not what it was they had caught.

In the beginning, I am part of that we—a co-conspirator, the brave triumvirate. I can hear the sound of Julie Kramer playing forty-fives through the wall that separates our houses. The Kramers live in number four and we live in four and a half. Our house is the mirror image of theirs. I descend our stairs to the sound of "Stella Dallas" blaring over Mrs. Kramer's vacuum cleaner.

"Just a little test," they tell me.

Our house begins to whisper with hints of my father's illness. Whispers follow me outside on to the back stairs and hover over me like an ether. The Nancy Drew book I've been reading is in my hands, always secrets and clues, this one in the attic. Each book recaps how Nancy has lost her mother. A frisson of fear jets through my heart and into my arteries and travels into my capillaries. My fingers and toes grow numb with it. What if my father were to die. I know I don't dare ask this question. I sense vague thoughts could turn into a new reality if I unleash them.

"It's only indigestion," my father says.

He has been complaining for the last three months and dragging to and from work. My mother has been begging him to call Dr. Frank. When he comes home from work, he stays in bed. They seem to have forgotten about me. I don't tell them I haven't been doing my arithmetic homework. In my satchel is a permission slip. Doctor Salk wants to test his new polio vaccine on the school children. I hide the slip.

My mother hands me the telephone. "*Tell Doctor Frank to come over,*" she signs.

I don't want to call. The other children say Doctor Frank's son, Henry, has polio and will have to wear a brace on his right leg. This past summer I wasn't allowed to swim—polio season posters are displayed everywhere of children in braces, in iron lungs. The doctor's wife answers. She's amused to hear the voice of a child on the other end of the line.

"My mother says she wants the doctor to come over."

"What's the matter, Victory?"

"My father throws up everything."

"Has he tried toast and broth?"

"He tells my mother he's not hungry."

The humidity and closeness of the air intensify. I hear a click on the line. My father has picked up the receiver on the upstairs extension. "It's okay, Victory. Tell Doctor Frank it's nothing," he tells the wife. "I'll call him in a few days if I don't feel better."

When he hangs up, he calls for me. "Victory, I can call the doctor myself."

"Then why don't you?" My eyes travel over the mahogany headboard that was my grandmother's. Ivy tendrils scroll in every direction on the yellowing wallpaper. My mother would like to put up wallpaper with roses, but my father says they don't have the money.

He sees that I am upset. "A little hug?"

Why always a hug? I want to say. *Because you smell like vomit.* Instead, I burst into tears.

"Did you draw today?"

I nod in answer. I'm too choked up to talk.

"Show me."

I go to my room, return with my spiral sketchbook diary, and hand it to him. I begin to leave.

"Wait, you have to tell me what this is." He has a page open to an elaborate tapestry of doodles, faces, animals, and plants all crammed onto the page over a long period. The pencil is smeared and the page is worn from erasing and redrawing. There are fish and birds larger than the people depicted. Buildings topple. "Can I show it to your mother?"

I shrug.

"It could be a bigger painting."

"I don't want to do a bigger painting."

"Someday you might change your mind. Can I draw you?"

I open my sketch diary to a clean page and hand it to him.

"Sit still!"

My eyes glance downward with shyness.

"That's what I would like to capture in you."

I like it when my parents draw me. It is a way of touching another person, yet you are not touching the other person. The pencil pulled over the paper caresses the lines of my face and my energy begins to flow throughout my body. My hands and feet become warm as I emerge on his page.

"Can I keep it?" he asks.

I nod and he tears the page out of my sketchbook.

Chapter 3

The week of my father's first operation, I become acutely aware of the ways our little family lacks independence. My uncle Abe and aunt Shirley come to take my father for tests. It is Uncle Abe who communicates to the doctors because my mother has to depend on my father or me to translate for her. She rides along with her notebook. Doctors in those days never tell the truth to their patients. If anyone knows the truth, it is my uncle and aunt and not my father or mother.

Uncle Abe is accustomed to assuming the paternal burdens of the family. He is thirteen-and-a-half years older than my father is and that gives him almost a grandfatherly relationship to me. I say "almost" because if Abe feels jealousy toward his younger brother, he manifests it in the lack of a filial relationship between him and me. Uncle Abe runs the linoleum store Povich Floors. My grandfather Manny Povich started the business in 1935. My father works in the store, too. In the evenings and on the weekends, however, he paints pictures.

My father's artwork does not belong to any school. He never studied art. He painted as a child and just kept up with it as an adult. Neither Uncle Abe nor my father went to college. My father served in the army during World War II, and when he came out, Abe needed him in the store. Manny Povich died when my father was eight. Uncle Abe was already married to Aunt Shirley and their daughter Marlene was already born.

The doctor schedules my father's operation for the following week and my father asks my mother and me to come with him to the museum the week beforehand. My parents often take me to the Carnegie Museum. Sometimes we look at the dinosaurs but most often we look at the paintings—Mondrian, Braque, Picasso, Corot, flat looking renaissance triptychs and whatever is currently being displayed. My father comes home and experiments with different styles. But he always seems to return to scenes of impending storms over a landscape or cityscape. He never connected to any artists or groups of artists. His tether to Povich Floors and the living his older brother permits him to take from the business keeps him from exploring possible associations. "No time," he always says. "If I socialize with all the artists, there won't be time to make art."

He has stopped trying to go into work. But despite his pain and waning strength, he drives us down Forbes Street to the gray stone building which houses the natural history part of the museum, as well as an extensive art exhibit. Andrew Carnegie gave Pittsburgh two museums in the space of one. We mount the front staircase and emerge through the revolving doors into the reception area. The signs point to dinosaurs off in one room and paintings in the opposite direction. We are alone at this hour on a weekday and can hear our footsteps echo across the marble floor. I look up at the domed ceiling coffered between skylights.

My father wants to see the Winged Victory, as always. We visit the long sculpture hall first. A new crop of young artists sits sketching before it. Then he wants to see a newly acquired painting by Edward Hopper. He compares his own style to this artist—clean realism. My father draws plain brick buildings covered with the soot of the mills. He rarely puts human beings in his paintings, except for the pictures he paints of my mother and me. Despite the lack of people in his work, there is a strong sense of human presence in them, as if the viewer is stepping into the shoes of an unseen observer. When I was very small, I used to think that if he had painted his images on the floor or a sidewalk, I could have stepped into them as if Mary Poppin's friend the sidewalk painter made them. Father's pictures seemed to want to tell stories. Maybe the stories would have been somewhat naïve, my father certainly was. But his paintings arouse in me oceans of feeling, and something would begin to churn inside of me. His paintings had a kind of presence. Maybe his impending illness guided his hand in their creation—the absence of humanity in some way a comment about our temporary place on this planet.

In the museum, we look at the Hopper painting he has come to see—an empty street early Sunday morning, building cornices in colored silhouettes against a bluing sky. We linger in front of it for a good half hour as he discusses the bold use of primary colors to portray a morning light. He is tiring and realizes that I might want to move on.

"I want to show you Bosch," he tells me. "Your drawing reminds me of his work. But I think we can only find drawings in here. We pass through several galleries going back in time from the Hopper—my mother taking brief detours to see what captures her attention.

My mother could draw very precisely and accurately from her years repeating flowers in the china factory.

Mainly women belonged to the local artist group that dubbed itself "The artists association." Every year they exhibited in the basement of the museum. My father would like my mother to exhibit with them, but she won't join.

Chapter 4

The week following our visit to the Carnegie Museum, we bring my father to Montifiore Hospital, the Jewish Hospital, for his first operation. Uncle Abe drives us there. I watch with Aunt Shirley from the visitor's lobby as he disappears with my mother and Uncle Abe through the double doors. Aunt Shirley is a member of the Ladies Hospital Aid Society. She insists on showing me the bronze plaques on the lobby walls. "In memory of," "in honor of" she reads for the benefit of my young ears. "We need to be very proud of Montifiore. This is a hospital where Jewish doctors can practice. Your father's surgeon and Dr. Frank both went to medical school in West Virginia because The University of Pittsburgh wouldn't let many Jews study medicine there," she tells me. "When you are a teenager, you can volunteer here. You might even consider being a nurse."

I say nothing and follow her into the gift shop where she knows all the volunteers. "My brother-in-law is in surgery. This is his little girl, Victory."

"What's wrong with him?"

Shirley sees a coloring book and steers me toward it.

"Would you like me to get this for you?"

"The C word," I hear her say to the volunteer.

"May the one who blessed our ancestors heal him," says the volunteer. "I will say a Misherberach in Schul this Shabbos."

"Thank you," says Shirley. "He will need your prayers."

c/ɔc/ɔ

We had a long wait until Uncle Abe came back, his face ashen but with news that my father was out of surgery and resting well.

Children weren't allowed to visit the patients, but my mother sneaked me up to his room, anyway. He's propped up in the big hospital bed swathed in white sheets, his arms blemished with purple marks where a medical army had attempted to invade his veins. My mother helps him sip liquid through a bent straw.

My father stays in the hospital for three weeks. We pick him up on the first day of summer vacation. His clothes lay on the hospital bed. In the hallway, Uncle Abe and Aunt Shirley talk with somber-faced Dr. Frank. Aunt Shirley is looking my way. "Victory, darling let me take you downstairs so you can do your homework. Daddy needs to get dressed.

"School's over," I say triumphantly. It is the first day of summer vacation. I feel in my pocket for the folded yellow cardboard in the manila envelope. My report card: It reads D-, D+, C-, etc. "I don't want to go downstairs."

"Let's get a treat in the gift shop soda fountain."

I drag my feet but follow Aunt Shirley over to the elevator banks. When we are seated in a Naugahyde booth too big for the two of us, I open another Nancy Drew book.

"What one is that?"

I shrug.

She sighs. "I want to see if it's one I read?"

I can't imagine Aunt Shirley mesmerized by Nancy Drew. My private identification with the teen detective allows me to separate myself from Aunt Shirley's world. Like any adolescent, I am blind to the possibility that Shirley was once young. However, I suspect she was more like Julie Kramer, who will someday snag an Abe of her own. While Julie is creating her nesting arrangement, I will be savoring life's adventures and coming back once in a while to regale the old neighbors with tales that they will have already heard about, but want to know personally from me.

"What would you like to eat, darling? It will take them a while to bring Daddy down. You could use a few pounds."

"I'm not hungry." My fingers touch the manila envelope in my pocket. Everyone seems to have forgotten that report cards come home on the last day of school. "I don't understand why I can't wait upstairs."

"Your father is going to have a long recuperation. And the surgeon will have a lot of instructions."

"Yes, but no one will talk to my mother."

"That's why it's best to let Uncle Abe take care of everything. Maybe I will eat something." She signals the waitress who appears at her side, holding her order pad.

"I think I'll have a scoop of vanilla, no better yet—a root beer with a scoop of vanilla." She winks at me. "Whipped cream, two cherries! And bring two spoons and two straws."

"Comin' right up."

When the waitress goes to get the order, Shirley turns my book to lay face down on the table. "When you're not writing in that diary, you're reading. It doesn't make sense that you don't do well in school."

The waitress returns with a tall fluted glass entirely covered with a cloud of whipped cream in which four maraschino cherries loll like cherubs in a bubble bath. "Help yourself," Shirley tells me, "you first." I prod the concoction with a long spoon. "Too sweet."

"Nonsense. You're young." She heaps her spoon high, careful to dig down into the ice cream, and takes it to her mouth. "Nancy Grey Ice cream. It's very good." Some trickles on her bosom. She sips from one of the straws and pulls the paper off of the other for me. I catch the reflection of an orderly pushing my father in a wheel chair. Uncle Abe joins us and Shirley offers the root beer and soda to him. "Stay a minute, Abe. Let them have a minute alone."

I run to hug my father, who says, "I'm glad to be getting back to both of my girls."

"Did the doctor say you're all right, Daddy?"

"Fit as a fiddle. I'm just going to have to work hard to get my strength back."

"We'll help you."

"I know you will, sweetheart."

It is painful for my father to sit in the front seat of Abe's Chrysler. My mother, Shirley, and I sit in the back with me in the middle. There are still cobblestones on the streets near the hospital with streetcar tracks running through them. The car rumbles over them and my father winces. I see they are not heading toward our house. We cross the Allegheny River on a stone bridge. "This isn't the way home," I say.

"We have a surprise. Right Abie?" my father says. My mother winks at me. *We are taking your father to the lake to recuperate. We rented a cottage.*

"Did she spill the beans?" my aunt asks.

"It's okay, Shirley," says Abe.

"You don't know yet," my mother signs.

Soon the two-lane country highway becomes a local road through a dilapidated town that consists of a grocery store, a gas station, and a hardware store. There is another gas station farther along that closed up a long time ago. Weeds sprout from the cement at the pump.

"Now we need to clock the miles," says Abe.

I lean over the seat and watch the odometer. At three miles, we turn at a sign carved out of wood into the shape of an arrow. Garth's Knoll is heat-etched into the surface and Uncle Abe follows the direction of the arrow.

"Who's Garth?"

"Owns the cottage. You'll see soon."

We enter the woods—the road is unpaved and narrow. Several miles in, we come to a clearing with a lake beyond. A few boats are tied to a wooden dock and clank against each other on the bobbing waves. The cottage sets back from the water around a bend—a bit dilapidated.

"Now you can be surprised, my mother signs to me."

Are we staying here?

"I thought you'd like that," says my father. "The cure that cures!" my father called it.

My parents loved the lake and the woods surrounding it and, by September, my father had regained all of his strength and color.

Chapter 5

My parents bought the lake house with what was left of their savings after paying for my father's operation. We began to drive to the lake every Friday. This caused tension between my father and uncle. Uncle Abe said if they closed Povich Floors every Saturday they might as well give away my grandfather's business.

On Fridays, as we drove across the bridge with the Allegheny River far below, my father's expression would change. Behind us sat Pittsburgh, shadowed by its sooty scrim. It was as if an unseen hand had lifted a curtain and revealed our new lives to us.

My parents would spend long hours painting the lake and its many moods. The previous owners left their furniture and their books for us. Nancy Drew continued to be my friend that summer. Nancy Drew lives with her father. Her mother has died, they never say how. Nancy Drew lives in a big house with their housekeeper Hannah who isn't as smart as Nancy and her father, but loves her as a mother would.

On one of my visits to my father in the hospital, he

told me that I was a girl with great courage. Nancy Drew has courage. She's not afraid to right a wrong. I wonder if her mother's dying words gave Nancy the courage she needs to face the evil in the world. It must be terribly sad to know that your mother won't see how you grow up. But that's not what Nancy Drew books are about.

Chapter 6

When I am thirteen my father becomes ill again. *"Just a little test,"* my mother tells me.

We are out back coaxing tomato plants from clay pots, planting and staking them. My hands smell of their potent scent. The seedlings have grown several inches in the past week and newly formed leaves uncurl in clusters. She hands me the watering can looking anxiously at the upstairs window. My father is in bed.

"Give them a good watering or they'll die of shock in this heat."

It's early May, the purple and green month. This year the interval spring is too brief to call a season. The entire week has been hot and humid. Cascading sweet-scented wisteria billows and sags, its jungle of vines clutching tenaciously at the tall poplar behind our fence. Sprays of lilac from the Kramers' yard hang over the wall. Wisteria blossoms last barely a week—the lilacs this year even less. Before my father's first operation the wisteria smelled sickly to me. Today it barely lingers in the air.

"You can finish for me, can't you? I want to try and get Daddy to eat something."

"But you promised me we'd plant flowers."

"Maybe tomorrow if Daddy is better."

She cuts a few more strips from a ball of twine then sets down the scissors. She leaves me alone to tie loops of cord around the new stalks. I knot a few more.

Our house has begun to whisper again. Its whispers hint at the irony of a complete cure—a different kind of cancer. No one can explain why.

This morning, Julie Kramer's mother asked me how my father was feeling. The sounds of his vomiting carry through the walls. I pick up my latest Nancy Drew, *The Hidden Staircase*, from the yard table and begin to read. It's an old edition and was my mother's. The drawings are printed from engravings. A face appears in a window of the old mansion. Nancy is suspicious and investigates. A picture on the yellowed page shows Nancy stepping from her roadster wearing a cloche hat and clutching her pocket book. Sturdy shoes manage to make her legs look long under a mid-calf dress that's gathered at the waist.

Three days later, my father faints at work. Tired blood, he tells my mother but then the results come back from the X-rays. When I come home from school, he is in bed again.

"I want to talk to you," he tells me.

I ignore him.

"Give me a hug." He pats the bedspread, and I reluctantly sit on the edge of the bed next to my mother. Tufts from the bedspread press into my bare thighs. I'm drawing. I draw when they draw. Now I create little worlds for myself—mostly secret places, verdant and green, with friendly woodlands and massive, looming stone structures that protect, envelope and isolate those who dwell within.

ひ◇ひ◇

In the fourth grade Miss Riley screamed at me for drawing. Today, her voice rings in my ears. "Can you hear me, Victory Povich? Should I call your mother?"

"I can hear you."

"I can hear you, *ma'am*. Why aren't you looking at the blackboard?"

She walked down the aisle to my desk, ruler in hand, buxom, straight gray gabardine skirt with white silk blouse ruffled at the neck. A regimental jacket hangs over the back of her chair. "I don't see how you can be listening. You're drawing. What were we doing just now, class?"

"Arithmetic, Miss Riley," the class chanted in unison. Miss Riley grabbed my notebook and held up the page for the class to see. Margin after margin was filled with my miniature landscapes— nothing like our yard on Sycamore Street or the dusty field across from my school. "Does this look like arithmetic, children?"

"No, Miss Riley!" Sniggers. Laughter.

"You must think drawing pictures is more important than school."

I don't answer.

"Well?"

"I can draw and listen."

She rapped the knuckles of my right hand with the edge of her ruler.

"She can draw and listen." More laughter. Furious, she ripped the pages into confetti. My secret places torqued and twirled before landing on the linoleum floor.

I tried to grab my notebook. "You'll ruin it."

"You little animal! I'll ruin it? You bet I'll ruin it!"

She pushed me down hard into the seat of my desk, scraping my vertebrae against its wooden back. "Now you stay there! You belong in a reformatory."

I looked down at my fingers where red welts form in a line across four knuckles.

இஇஇ

"Stop drawing so we can talk to you," my mother signs. I pretend I don't see her. She grabs my face between her hands and when she has my attention, she moves her right thumb from the fingers to the heel of her left hand—the sign for operation. *"Daddy is going to have an operation."*
"Why?"
"Because there's a growth." He points to his abdomen. "And the doctors think they can get it out."

An image of the operation rises in my mind. Outside, there are growths on the tree trunks, gnarled lumps of bark on the old elm growing through the fence in the corner of our yard. Then there are the weed trees—acrid smelling ailanthus—that keep pushing out of the cracks in the sidewalk, lifting entire pieces of cement until the pavement slopes at crooked angles. They become trees so quickly, yet they are not really trees. Ailanthus are invaders growing out of the past and pushing fiercely into the present—immortal.

"If you let them, they take over everything," my father has always told me. "You can see what they are doing to the sycamores."

Tall sycamore trees line both sides of our street. I like to gaze into the high canopy they form over the road—their cluster of leaves little vents to the sky. Their patchy trunks remind me of giraffes at the zoo. Curls of pasty bark constantly peel and drop to the pavement. The sycamore bark has a sweet smell. To save the sycamore trees, my father cuts into the ailanthus' roots with heavy

shears each summer and carts them, leaves and all, off to
the garbage.

"Will they have to cut you open?"

"Yep! And then they'll stitch me up like a turkey."

With my mother, I sign. With my father and mother,
I speak and sign. When I'm alone with my father, I speak.
Today, I refuse to sign.

"Why do you have to make jokes about everything?
I'm not two."

"That's why we're telling you about it. We think you
are old enough to be told about it."

"*Give Daddy a hug! Daddy needs hug.*" My mother
pushes me gently toward him.

As I shake my head, I catch my image in the dresser
mirror. The silver is peeling off behind the glass and it
makes my reflection dim. The same vague face of the little girl that appears in my fourth grade class photo. A little brown-haired girl, pigtails braided behind her ears,
who looks down and away from the camera while all the
other children gaze at it eagerly.

cɔcɔ

The second operation does not work. The surgeon,
Dr. Schon, opens him and closes him up right away. Doctor Frank explains to my uncle Abe and aunt Shirley. No
one explains this to my mother and father. My father expects to get better.

Chapter 7

I learn just how sick my father is from Lindy Glock who hears her parents' whispers and puts on her best dress to pay me a visit. My father had gone to the bank where Lindy's father works to ask for a loan to pay for his operation. I learned years later that his application was rejected.

I'm curled up in the living room with another Nancy Drew, and I hear her tap on the wooden frame of our screen door. There she stands in a starched blue-and-white-checked shirtwaist dress, a tortoise-shell diadem holding back her blond tresses. She's holding a fistful of posies from the trellis in her mother's little manicured garden. Lindy's eyes are a sea of ignorant blue wonder.

"Hi, Victory, I heard your father was sick again, so I came to invite you to dinner."

Lindy is not a friend I see a lot of, so the invitation is a surprise to me. Most of the kids live on my side of the street in doubles but Lindy lives directly across in a single. I could see into her bedroom from mine but her mother always makes her close the curtains. Lindy's baby nurse had deaf relatives and knew how to sign. She met my mother walking perambulators. I guess you could call Lindy my oldest friend. Mrs. Glock is very careful about Lindy's friends. When her daughter started signing, she saw to it that Lindy didn't spend a lot of time with me, according to my mother.

Mrs. Glock is also rather persnickety about Lindy's clothes. Once when we were eight, Lindy let me try on one of her organdy dresses to see how I would look in it. There I was, "Lindy," except for my brown hair and my face that somehow looked sallow swathed in pink and white. Mrs. Glock came into the room and asked Lindy to come out into the hall. "Don't let that girl try on your clothes," I heard her hiss at Lindy. "You will make her envious of you. She will never have the things you will have. Remember she's a public school girl and her mother is handicapped."

Lindy came back into the room. "I have to put my dress away now."

"Good! The starch made me itch anyway," I said.

I wanted to scratch her face and see tears and dirt run all over the scratches. A gingham and wicker bassinet sat in a corner filled with stuffed animals and dolls. It was Lindy's when she was a baby. She never played with the dolls. They were just there for show. I picked up a doll with blinking blue eyes and started to undress it. "Why don't we give it a bath and some food?"

She grabbed the doll and I held on to it by its arm. The arm tore from the doll's body. Lindy screamed for her mother who came running in.

"Gracious," she screamed at me, setting her cigarette on the edge of Lindy's dresser so that the ashes landed on Lindy's light blue rug. Lindy's mother took me back across the street to my mother. The doll had to go to the hospital, Lindy told me, and I was not allowed to play in Lindy's room anymore.

Lindy's schedule is very strict. She usually has dates planned far in advance with the girls from the private school she attends—little blond girls in pleated green and blue tartan uniform skirts driven everywhere by tall, pale mothers in wood-sided station wagons. Lindy could have stepped out of one of my Golden Books—a Walt Disney character come to life. Every little Jewish girl in our neighborhood wanted to look like Lindy Glock and the other private school girls. Sometimes I'd stand in front of the mirror and pull the skin of my nose back until it tilted up into a ski top like Lindy's.

"Why are you so dressed up?" I ask cautiously after she invites me for dinner.

"Gracious! We have respect in our family."

I watch her shift from one foot to the other. Her pocketbook matches her white patent Mary-Jane shoes. She is taking in my filthy white shorts and sleeveless shirt. Lindy manages never to get a spot on herself.

"So do we!" I retort.

She lowers her voice. "My mother says your father has the 'C' word. Gracious, it's much worse than polio, isn't it?"

Gracious is Lindy's only swearword and she uses it every other sentence, as if everything to do with my side of the street shocks her.

Now everybody I know talks about polio. In fact, my father read in the *Pittsburgh Post Gazette* that they were going to test Doctor Sabine's vaccine on the public school kids this year. Sabine's is better than that fellow Salk's, he opines. There are posters of kids with leg braces in every store and on television on the *March of Dimes* shows kids in iron lungs and asks everyone to contribute money. None of us were allowed to swim in August because that's polio season, and all of the parents were terrified their kids would come down with it. But the word "cancer" was never said out loud in our neighborhood. Christians and Jews alike knew that to utter the C-word was to allow death's angels into our midst. I wondered if Four and a Half had a special mark over the doorway— "C-word here." The Jews had God smite the first-born of the Egyptians and here was retribution. No one has ever mentioned death to me and it seems unfair that Lindy, with all of her advantages, should be the first.

"So we should all dress up and celebrate. That's pretty stupid, Lindy."

"I'm just inviting you to dinner. Ask your mother if it's okay."

If I say something to my mother, she might remember to send me to the drugstore or to Ben's Market. I go inside, say nothing to my mother, and come right back out to accept Lindy's invitation. Julie Kramer has come out to the porch to find out why Lindy is there. Lindy is more my friend. I mean, it's Julie and me, or it's Lindy and me, or Julie, Lindy, and me. Never Lindy and Julie.

Julie has a pretext. "I brought you something."

I don't want to let her think I'm interested.

"Here!" She clasps a satiny lump of elastic. "I don't need it any more. It's a triple-A. I'm now a double-A."

She hands it to me and I inspect the tiny bra. "She certainly doesn't look like a double A yet, does she Lindy?"

"I'd say it's just baby fat, Julie," Lindy tells her.

"That's not baby fat! You're both jealous."

"Why would we want to be jealous of you?"

Every day now, I check for breasts.

"Can I come in?" Julie asks.

I shake my head. "I'm going to Lindy's for dinner."

Julie looks at us with envy. "We could go to Lindy's woods before you have dinner?"

Lindy's woods is the space between Lindy's garage

and her yard. It's really just a thicket of honeysuckle sprays dense enough to hide in. It's fenced off from the grass part of Lindy's yard and you can reach it from the alley. Mrs. Glock has no idea kids are using it. Lindy never joins us there because she'd get dirty sitting on the ground. Julie and I used to go to Lindy's woods and stuff toilet paper in my mother's bras.

"No, there really isn't time. My mother wants us to wash up."

"Well, you look clean, Lindy, but I can't say the same thing for Victory," Julie snaps.

"That's because I'm standing here talking to you when I should be changing for dinner," I snap back. It occurs to me that Julie might be right about my uncleanliness. "I'll be over in a few minutes, Lindy."

I'm in a total dither about what to wear. My khaki skirt bags where my mother tucked it and my pink, oxford cloth shirt with the button-down collar smells like BO. The rest of my clothes I find in the hamper except for my blue shirtwaist and I don't want to seem to be imitating Lindy. I finally settle for my blue shirtwaist anyway. Hers has checks.

Lindy's house is filled with lovely things, draperies with matching ties and silk fringes. The carpet is soft and plush. We sit at the mahogany table in the Glock's Wedgewood blue dining room and eat creamed chipped beef over white toast points. The plates are filled in the kitchen and the table remains empty except for our two place settings on crisp, white linen mats, the silver candelabras, and a vase filled with red roses. Mrs. Glock brings her silver lighter and ashtray to the table in order to sit with us. There are little cut crystal jars for the cigarettes on the matching sideboard. The Glocks are very organized. The same little cigarette jars, ashtrays, and silver lighters can be found everywhere in the house.

I'm rather nervous when Mrs. Glock is near me. I'm not sure I'm holding my fork in the correct manner. The creaminess of the meal seems to emphasize the blueness of Lindy's eyes and her Goldilocks hair. I watch to see what Lindy does but Lindy hardly touches the food—so creamy, so white with the little flecks of beef floating in all that creamy sauce served with canned white asparagus. They're watery and stringy and taste like the metal can but somehow it all seems too wonderful. Mrs. Glock's white maid, Gloria, brings us very tall glasses of milk with the initials LBG etched into them and disappears. Gloria wears a gray uniform with a white apron. As Mrs. Glock sips her martini, she reminds us that Gloria goes home at six o'clock. She inhales smoke from her cigarette between these stylish sips and explains that she eats with Mr. Glock when he comes home from work. Lindy is by then usually ready for bed.

"We always have dinner at five-thirty when my father gets home from the store," I say as if my father is still going to work.

"Your father eats with you?" Lindy asks.

"Well, it depends."

"No offence, but you don't have a schedule?" Her eyes are wide.

"Not really!"

"Good gracious!" Lindy prattles on, looking at her mother. "The only time we don't have a schedule is on Sunday when Gloria doesn't come. Then we usually eat on trays in the living room."

I've seen the little folding trays stacked next to Lindy's living room sofa—each one painted with a different floral design.

"My father eats on a tray now that he's sick. We never use trays in our house except when someone is sick."

Mrs. Glock raises her eyebrows.

I remember my mother is making spaghetti and meatballs. "On summer nights, my mother leaves something out on the kitchen table if I'm outside with my friends."

"So, when do you have to get ready for bed?"

"It all depends. Sometimes we go for ice cream." I sense I have made Lindy jealous, even though I don't have a strict bedtime.

We've never had a sleepover but somehow, I divine Lindy's tidy and quiet bedtime. A subtle perfume I can't identify pervades all of Lindy's things and blends nicely with cigarette smoke. Her parents both smoke. The scent follows her under the lace canopy and plush comforter. It's there in the pretty powder room towels. Even the same old box of Kleenex smells different in Lindy's house.

In my own house noise and smells accompanied by Mrs. Kramer's bossy recommendations come right through from the other side of the wall. But we have our own sounds to compete with and are not bothered by theirs. Despite the fact that we sign rather than speak, our house is loud and chaotic. There's always a lot of pot banging, frying and sizzling. When we have dinner, my mother puts everything on the table at once. Food smells, on both side of our common wall, linger for days. I realize that Mrs. Glock's chipped beef in its milky sauce has no scent. This must definitely be part of some privileged olfactory plan, which begins in the trust funds created behind the heavy oak door of Mr. Glock's paneled office. Or that's how I imagine it.

Mr. Glock works at the bank, where he is sure to be promoted, Lindy says. Lindy's mother is a distant cousin of someone named Lynch. I act like I've heard of them. In fact, that's Lindy's middle name. Mrs. Glock has a trust, says Lindy and, when Mr. Glock's promotion comes through, they plan to move—this according to Lindy, too. I imagine they move to a dark brick house with ivy clinging to its walls, and a portico where Lindy's dates can park their sports cars. Nancy Drew would have a house like that, too. Only Lindy acts more like Nancy's friend Bess. I'm more Nancy-like, I think. I like to shock Lindy even though it makes her look down on me even more. Nancy's friend Bess was easy to shock and always reluctant to get involved in Nancy's adventures. I can't see dragging Lindy through a secret panel in someone's attic. Though I have to admit, she'd probably stay clean and free of cobwebs.

Lindy brings up the subject of Julie. "That was rather gauche! Giving you her dirty old bra. Gracious! Can you imagine, Mommy, Julie gave Victory this bra she'd already stretched out."

"Gracious! Those people have no couth," Mrs. Glock adds and lights another cigarette. "What does the father do? Do you know, Victory?"

"I think he's a kosher butcher." I wonder if owning a linoleum store is better than being a butcher. But it doesn't seem to matter to Mrs. Glock. She just draws deeply on her cigarette and looks at her wristwatch. She's blonde like Lindy and very tanned.

"Can I walk Victory back across the street after we eat?"

"If you promise to be back by seven."

I thank her as properly as I can for dinner.

Chapter 8

Julie comes over when we return from Lindy's house. Lindy and I are playing Jacks on my porch. We're too old to play but we like to anyway. "You want to walk up street for ice cream?" Julie means the commercial section of our neighborhood where my father and uncle have their store. The drugstore fountain sells Nancy Grey ice cream.

The creamy sauce and all the milk now rumbles around in my stomach and I don't think it could hold a scoop of ice cream. "I'm still kind of full," I say, "and Lindy has to be back at seven."

"You're just going to sit around and play baby games?"

I'm pretty sure I'm going to need the bathroom in a few seconds. "No, we want to stay right here, don't we Lindy."

Lindy agrees. She's on "foursies." I'm waiting to see if she gets to "fivesies" before I bolt. Nobody says anything. Pregnant pauses we call them. I guess Julie was thinking about pregnancy, too, because she blurts out. "Did you know the last time we went into your woods,

Victory and I found condoms, didn't we, Victory?"

I wasn't going to tell Lindy about the condoms. There were rumors going around that Mary Kruicick, one of the mill girls, got knocked up.

"We weren't really sure they were condoms, Lindy." I'm not sure if private school girls talk about things like that.

"Well, one of the girls in my school told me that some Jewish boys brought mill girls from Hazelwood into my woods and drank scotch."

"Jewish boys don't go out with girls from Hazelwood. And Jewish people don't drink scotch," Julie says.

"My uncle Abe drinks scotch," I report but add, "You shouldn't believe it, that stuff about Jewish boys. It was probably Bill Rile or someone like that."

Lindy looks dubious. "Billy wouldn't do that."

I think otherwise.

"Why don't we go to the woods and see if anybody left anything," Julie suggests.

"Not now, my mother's probably on the patio," Lindy says.

"Do you want to hear Johnny Mathis?" Julie asks.

We look at each other and shrug. Julie goes into her living room to put on some forty-fives and returns with "The Twelfth of Never" blaring out onto our adjoining porches.

"What did you eat for dinner?" she demands to know.

"Chipped beef."

"What's that?"

"You don't know?" I infer that she's not as sophisticated as I am. "It's like corned beef but it's cooked in milk."

Julie raises a nostril into a little sneer. "It's not Kosher then."

"Who said anything about Kosher?"

"It's not kosher to mix milk and meat," Julie maintains shrilly.

"Lindy's not Jewish," I say. My stomach is really gurgling now. "Shut up!" I say to my stomach, which is loudly rumbling.

"Was that you?" Julie asks.

"I drank milk."

"That happens to you when you drink milk?" Lindy asks. "I have to drink four glasses of milk every day."

"That's why your hair is blonde," I tell her.

"My father can't drink milk either," Julie announces. "That's why it's not kosher to mix milk and meat. God is punishing you, see?"

"I have milk with meat all the time." Lindy says in my defense.

"But you don't have a Jewish stomach like Victory," Julie says.

"Well, why did you drink milk?" Lindy demands.

"Well, I never know what's going to happen."

"Gracious!"

I'm mortified. I don't want to leave Julie alone with Lindy even for a few seconds, in case Mr. Kramer comes outside with his belly hanging out over his boxer shorts and his arms out of one of those sleeveless undershirts he always wears after work. Or worse Mrs. Kramer, who's always cleaning and dusting about in her rollers, her hips as wide as her housecoat, could put in an appearance. I wonder what the Glocks really must think about the people on our side of the street.

Everybody waves at everybody else in our neighborhood, but that doesn't mean you can tell what people are thinking. My mother might be deaf but she's rather pretty. I think Mrs. Glock would surely want to invite her to sips martinis, too, now that my father's sick but I'm stuck

here with Julie breathing down our necks. And then to
make everything worse, my mother helps my father into
the living room and makes him comfortable on the sofa.

"How's my girl?" he calls and waves at us. He's always unshaven and in his pajamas now.

Julie and Lindy stare at him.

Lindy is on "sixies" when Doctor Frank's black
Buick stops at our curb. Henry Frank, the doctor's son, is
sitting in the Buick with Howie Merlman. Henry and
Howie are one class ahead of me in school. They stare at
us and we wave. Dr. Frank mounts the stairs heavily,
holding his black bag. Lindy stops tossing the Jacks in
her hand and Julie just stares. They're thinking one word,
shots. Shots are now an everyday occurrence in our house
with my father in so much pain.

"Young lady!" Dr. Frank always calls me that and
says nothing else.

You'd think he'd at least say, young ladies plural,
since my friends are sitting there too. I get up and scurry
into the house ahead of Doctor Frank, and I can feel his
presence fill up our narrow entry. I'm angry with my father for being there in the living room. Why, I ask myself,
does Dr. Frank have to look at my father in front of the
whole neighborhood?

"*How are you Doctor,*" my mother asks. I translate.

"Excellent! Excellent!"

It's a condition of being excellent when others are
not. He has learned the art of saying nothing that will lead
into a conversation. Doctor Frank doesn't inquire about
my mother's health, although it's plain to see she is worn
out. He goes immediately to the end table and sets down
his black bag. I watch him remove the stethoscope and
put it to his ears. My stomach growls and gurgles. It must
be because it is furious at me for my little betrayal of my
Jewish parents.

I run upstairs and sit on the toilet just in time.

Lindy is on "tensies" and Henry Frank is sitting on the stairs with Howie Merlman, watching, when I return. Henry is the next smartest kid in his class, next to Howie who is a complete genius. Henry's grown taller over the year and his long shins hang out of his madras-plaid Bermudas. He still wears a brace and a thick shoe. Polio made his left leg shorter. He has nice brown eyes and he is going to be very tall like his father, despite his limp. Howie's a little chunky with hips that are broad for a man, probably from studying all the time but his face is cute. I like his face.

Henry always comes along in the car when his father makes house calls. He's never gotten out before so it must be because Lindy is here. Julie Kramer is getting impatient because Henry is focusing all of his attention on Lindy.

That's when Bill Rile rides up on his bike. Bill Rile lives in a huge, rather decrepit house across the street and way down the block. He and Lindy go to the same church. He's the only Episcopalian who goes to public school. I wish they'd send him to a private school, but maybe he isn't smart enough. He's in my class and has been mean to me ever since we were in third grade.

My father and mother brought me to school together the first day. Mothers, alone, brought the other children. Their fathers were long at work. Mrs. Levy greeted the children and told us to find a desk with a name card. Mothers in housecoats and rollers thronged the doorways. They chattered more than the children did and their voices echoed in the disinfectant smelling hallway and reverberated back into our classroom. My parents were the last to leave. Mrs. Levy noticed them through thick, pink-tinted glasses that magnified the size of her eyes. Her hair was pulled into a mousy gray bun. She addressed herself to my mother. "Will Victory be going home for lunch?"

"She has a lunchbox," my father quickly answered, "and if she needs anything special for class, could you please write it on a piece of paper for my wife."

My father would never say my wife is deaf, but left people wondering why he was her spokesman. It was perhaps his misguided way of protecting her from their curiosity.

Mrs. Levy stared at my mother and my mother smiled at me and asked me with her hands if I was all right.

"*Yes!*" I signed.

"*I will miss you all day!*"

"*I will miss you.*" I both speak and sign when others are present unless I don't want them to know what my mother and I are saying.

"Bye, Victory!" my father called.

"Are those secret signals?" Bill Rile asks.

When he was younger, he had golden freckles on puffy pale skin and he was fat with tidies the kids used to pinch. Now he's very tall and he's lost the fat but not the meanness.

"That's how my mother talks."

"C'mon!"

All the kids turned to look.

"I saw her mother in the store. She's loony, right?" he says, imitating sign and making his own sign for nut case.

"My mother doesn't care what you say. She can't hear you!"

"Class! Class!" Mrs. Levy turns the lights off and on. "We will now pledge allegiance to the flag."

Milk and corn flakes soured on my tongue as I sat in the attached chair of my hardwood school desk surrounded by fresh-faced children—my toes barely touching the floor. All the desks had the sloped tops that lifted up and a hole for an inkwell.

"Please put everything away in your desks." Mrs. Levy tells us.

Under the lid of my desk, I kept my pencils, my notebook, and my lunchbox. As we stood to pledge allegiance, the principal Mr. Tierney entered the room. That's when Bill Rile poked me with his pencil and looked up at the ceiling. When I got called to the blackboard in arithmetic, he stuck his foot out and sent me sprawling on the floor. I picked myself up and he was still looking at the ceiling. But when he said they should lock my mother up at Western Psyche, I slugged him with my loose leaf and sent my own papers flying all over the room. I had to sit in Mrs. Levy's wastebasket for the rest of the morning. She called her wastebasket an upside-down dunce cap that was ready for anybody who wanted to misbehave. For me, it was like sitting on a toilet in front of the entire class with my skirt flowing over it and my rear end sinking in. I was so small my bottom sank down on all the garbage. I could smell rotting banana peels, milk souring in cartons, and old baloney sandwiches. When the bell rang, I couldn't budge and Mrs. Levy had to pull me out of the wastebasket. That was third grade, and Bill Rile hasn't changed.

I'm glad Howie and Henry are here, even though they came over with Henry's father. They're a year ahead of us in school, and I want Bill Rile to know there are some boys who might like me—older boys. He gets off his bike and stands on the sidewalk with his tongue folded over his bottom teeth. You can always tell when Bill Rile is going to do something mean by the shape of his tongue in his mouth.

Lindy says that Bill Rile has a swimming pool in his back yard but it has cracks and they don't use it. There is a pool table in his basement. He lives with his mother and father in his grandmother's house. His grandmother is supposed to be very rich but she doesn't seem to take very good care of their property. The house has dark green shutters, hanging on loose hinges, and the peeling paint drops into all the dead leaves left over from last fall. Mr. Rile ought to get Billy to rake up those leaves. It's too much to expect an elderly person to do.

A huge tree hides the Rile house from the street and keeps the sun from hitting the ground so there's no lawn to speak of, just clumps of grass and dirt. If they don't cut back that tree, the branches are going to grow right through the windows.

"Hey, Lindy!" he sniggers. He's got something under his arm.

"Hi, Billy!"

"Can I come up?"

"It's up to Victory," Lindy tells him.

I'm thinking about how Billy's father caught him a few months ago and gave him a licking. That day on the other side of Sycamore Street, the peace was shattered by screaming loud enough to bring Lindy and Mrs. Glock out on their porch and Julie and Mrs. Kramer out on theirs. I heard Mrs. Glock say over the commotion, "Whatever has that Rile boy done now?"

The screaming of two women drowned out her next sentence. My feet were bare as usual, as I walked down Sycamore Street and waited opposite the Rile house. Heavy damask draperies were parted enough for me to see a large man careening down a curved staircase. Billy Rile emerged from the bushes that separate the back of the yard from the front. The neighbor's stucco wall stops at the corner of the house where bushes line the side yard. Billy waited with terror in front of the wall. The front door opened. Mr. Riles's heavy steps made the wood creak. His face was flushed with spider veins. He saw me standing there across the street. "Have you seen Billy?"

I shook my head. Ridgely Rile searched the yard, an angry snarl on his sotted face. I noticed Bill Rile crouching in a spray of hollyhock but quickly lowered my eyes.

Drunk as Ridgely was, he was able to follow my eyes and stomped out on the veranda. He descended the stairs and surveyed the square but ample front yard. A broken mower, a shovel. A once formal garden needed pruning and weeding. Not a happy house with its dark green shutter. Since that day, dark green has struck me as an angry color—the color of malaise—overgrowth in a dark place—murky color. Why did they paint with that color in the first place? Was it once a shiny welcoming green?

Was Mr. Rile once a happy man?

Billy crawled along the bottom of the wall toward their next-door neighbor's front walk. Mr. Rile stepped out onto the sidewalk and surveyed Sycamore Street. The wind wafted his acetone-reeking breath across Sycamore Street. "What are you looking at, Victory Povich? Your dad never gave you a walloping in your life, I bet. Just lets you run wild all over the block like some urchin. C'mon, Billy, be a man. You're going to have to own up sooner or later."

He drew himself up to his full height. Then seeing what he has missed, pounced. He had Billy by the back of his shirt and was dragging him, kicking and screaming, across the Sedgewick's lawn to the sidewalk. Billy's mother followed by grandmother Rile—two dowagers in flowered housecoats were now on the front porch. Mr. Rile pulled Billy up the veranda stairs and the women tried to grab the squirming boy.

"Leave him alone, Ridgely, please."

"Stay outta my way."

"Please, Ridgely."

"Please, Ridgely," he mocked. Then pushed his son into the arms of his mother and grandmother. "Do you know what, Billy, you sissy? You think these women are going to protect you, think again?" Ridgely slapped his wife across the face. His mother covered her mouth. He staggered on into the house and slammed the door. The lock clicked. Vera Rile tried to hold back the tears. Mrs. Rile senior tried to open the front door.

"We'll go in through the basement," said Vera Rile.

"I'm not going back in there, ever," said Billy.

"He'll sleep it off and forget about it."

"One day I'm going to kill him."

"Don't talk that way, Billy." Then the three of them noticed me.

"And what are you staring at?" Vera Rile suddenly assumed an aristocratic tone.

"What did Billy do?"

"Mind your own business, Victory."

"In other words," said Billy. "Mind your own beeswax."

I burst into tears and walked away.

Billy leans on his bike with a pleading look. I can't very well say no, you can't join us on my porch. I say yes, thinking maybe it will make up for his embarrassment.

Bill Rile takes the steps two at a time and sits down with us. The thing under his arm is a magazine.

"I didn't know you knew each other so well," he says to Lindy.

"Gracious! We've been friends since we were babies," I say.

I can see Bill Rile finds that hard to believe.

"You guys want to go to Lindy's woods?" he asks Henry and Howie. He opens the magazine and lets the centerfold fall out—a brunette with a negative suntan for a bikini and breasts the size of watermelons.

"Bill Rile!" Lindy admonishes him.

I can tell she's enjoying it all.

"C'mon, guys!" Bill insists.

Howie's about to follow Bill and I'd like to see the inside of that magazine. But Henry doesn't want to. "No, my dad won't be that long. I'm supposed to sit in the car, anyway. We were driving Howie here home."

"Oops! Gracious! It's almost seven o'clock." Lindy realizes it was time to go home so we all walk Lindy back across the street and up the driveway. Her mother's reclining in a chaise on the patio and sipping another martini. Mr. Glock, she says, is upstairs getting into a pair of Bermuda shorts. Mrs. Glock asks us to sit down and Howie plunks himself on a chaise next to Lindy leaving Julie, Henry and I the chairs. Mrs. Glock makes room for Bill Rile on her own chaise. We sit there a few moments and nobody seems to have anything to say. It's not quite dusk but the fireflies are already blinking and circling like tiny planes. A weird scent gets on your hands when you catch fireflies, but that doesn't seem like something I ought to mention.

Howie Merlman looks closely at Lindy's nose. "Can I?" he asks. Howie Merlman was born with a mouthpiece. He says anything he wants and everybody listens—even adults. He's smarter than the teachers.

"Can you what?"

"Wiggle your nose."

"Good gracious!" Lindy laughs, tilting her little ski-top nose into the air and crossing her blue eyes to watch it. I divine a flash of something rodent-like in Lindy's perfect face—a white Easter bunny.

"You don't mind, do you, Mrs. Glock?" Howie asks.

"Go ahead wiggle my nose." Lindy's laughing at him and offering him her face.

He wiggles her nose ceremoniously. "You know, in one more generation you probably won't have a bone in your nose."

"What are you talking about?" Mrs. Glock is looking a bit uncomfortable.

"Do you know what phrenology is, Mrs. Glock?" Howie looks at her very seriously and she looks away.

"A very important science," adds Henry. "Where is your caliper, Merlman? Here is your opportunity to do some measuring on non-Jews."

"By measuring the skull and the bones of the face, it is possible to tell where a person has been and the horrors that person has seen. Joseph Conrad writes about it in *The Heart of Darkness*—great book, They used to measure the white Europeans returning from Africa—changed!"

"He's just shooting the bull, Mrs. Glock," says Bill.

"Gracious," say Lindy and Mrs. Glock together.

"No he's not." I'm beginning to enjoy what started out a very uncomfortable encounter. I'm no longer worried what the Glocks will think.

"It's healthier to mix the gene pool," Howie says very seriously.

"Good gracious!" Mrs. Glock pulls smoke into her lungs with annoyance.

"Your noses," Howie continues seriously, "are an example of inbreeding. If Lindy marries someone who looks like Rile here, you'll both have kids with no-bone noses."

"He's right," Henry Frank adds doing his best to keep a straight face. "It's healthy to mix up the gene pool. You should consider intermarriage."

"I don't think so!" Mrs. Glock takes some more smoke into her lungs and a sip of her drink. "It's not that we're prejudiced against anybody. We think it's just better for the kids not to marry out of their faith."

How can there be so many religions and only one God? The milk in my stomach begins to gurgle again as if it's trying to prove Mrs. Glock's point. I'm sure Mrs. Glock can hear it. If I married a Christian boy, I'd probably have to drink milk with meat all the time.

Mr. Glock comes out to the patio in his Bermuda's and a short-sleeved shirt. He carries a cocktail shaker in one hand and a martini glass in the other. "Can I freshen you up?" he asks his wife. He's referring to her martini. He strains the liquid into her glass and then into his own.

"We're going to need another chair out here," he observes but Henry is polite and thinks to get up.

When Mr. Glock sits down and has taken a few sips, he takes a cigarette out of a pack in his shirt pocket. "Light me up!" he tells his wife and she lights the end for him from her own.

Then he asks the typical father questions. "Where do you go to school? What grade are you in? What do you want to be?"

Both Howie and Henry say doctors and I say I might want to be one, too. I'm learning a lot about medical things I tell them. "I could probably put an IV in someone's arm right now if they needed fluids and nourishment. My dad has to be hooked up to one and I've seen how it's done."

"That's very interesting." He turns to Lindy. "Well, young lady," I'm sure you have things to do. And Rile, I have some papers for your father so stick around." There's a pause and we all get up to leave, except Bill Rile.

I can see what Howie means by the bone in Lindy's nose. Mr. and Mrs. Glock have exactly the same kind of noses and they gave it to Lindy.

Howie extends his hand to the Glocks. "It was nice to meet you, Mr. and Mrs. Glock, see you around Lindy."

"Well, it was fun," Lindy says.

Mrs. Glock lets Mr. Glock take over. "Nice to meet you, boys. Oh, Bill, why don't you come into the study with me?"

Henry, Howie, Julie, and I hold our breath all the way down the driveway.

"'I'm going to bust my kishkes laughing!" Howie screams when we're across the street.

"You know why you said that stuff, Merlman?" Henry says to Howie.

Howie's still laughing, "No?"

"It was your deep-seeded inferiority complex talking, schnozie!"

"Aw, come on. You don't really believe all that Freud stuff."

"It wasn't really funny, you know," Julie tells them.

"Sure it was," I tell her.

"You might have hurt Lindy's feelings!"

"The Glocks remind me of Belgium endive," I say but don't explain. Howie and Henry give me a queer look. "I read about how hard it is to grow. It's called blanching and it takes place at a very tender age. You deprive the endives of sun. It's like binding feet in China."

A little while later, Bill Rile's in the middle of the street cruising in circles on his bicycle. Howie and Henry sit on the hood of Doctor Frank's car and Julie and I sit on the steps. A moaning sound comes from my house. None of us speak.

"My father's a good doctor," Henry tells me after a long pause.

"Yeah, he's really good," Howie chimes in.

I run up the steps with their eyes and Julie following me. She tells them, she'll be right back but I know she just wants to listen through her living room wall. She and her older sister listen through their parents' bedroom wall with a glass. I've tried it too.

I hear the voices of Doctor Frank and my father and the pauses where he signs to my mother. "Keep your chin up, Morris. Next week is your last radiation treatment and then we'll take an X-ray."

"I don't know if I can stand the pain of this. Please can't you give me a little more morphine?"

"And turn you into an addict?"

"Would it matter?"

"You shouldn't talk that way."

Chapter 9

My father was not doing very well the week my school sent home the forms for the polio vaccine. The pain has traveled to his feet and, if someone accidentally touches them, he screams. He can't get out of bed now. Each new pain means a little test. A new machine on which to contemplate the meaning of life or news of miracle cures. The doctors seem to know less and less. Neighbors and friends seem to know more.

I'm in the eighth grade but I should be in the ninth. I attend a school that goes from grades seven to twelve—a big school sitting high on a hill. To get there, I have to take a streetcar and then a bus. All the eighth grade girls wear girdles and say they are too fat. You can't be considered dressed without one. I weigh ninety-five pounds and still look eight so the last thing I need is a girdle. We no longer stay in the same class all day but there is a homeroom period where you can study after the pledge of allegiance and the principal Doctor Waldrop's announcements over the loud speaker. On Tuesdays, we have assembly and the polio vaccine people came to talk to us about Polio last week. A man from the health department told us how we are contributing to one of the greatest medical discoveries in human history. All of the kids in my class have signed up to be guinea pigs for Doctor Sabine.

I don't bring home the mimeographed form for my mother to sign. I can't explain why. When I didn't return the form, the principal's office called for permission. I answered the phone. 'Yes, this is Victory Povich's mother. The polio vaccine? No, I don't think we'll take that one. Some other time.'

e/se/s

My uncle Abe has ordered a hospital bed and it's been set up for my father in the dining room. My father will never see the upstairs of our house again. He can't eat but my mother cooks and cooks. She wages a food war from the kitchen. My father is being eaten and he has to eat, she explains to me. New foods enter our family lexicon. Foods of many colors—deep greens, scalding vermilion. "*B 12 is good for triggering the immune system. Calf's liver.*" She's become knowledgeable. The Lipmans down the street know a lot about vitamins we never knew existed. My mother reads Adele Davis and begins to think that maybe we have been eating wrong all these years.

The scent of oil paint has dried up in our house. My father no longer has strength to paint. My mother has no time. We haven't been to the lake in months. The steel mills belch acrid soot into the air but no one wants to complain—jobs are too important. This morning, I woke up at nine a.m. and thought it was night. There was a black scrim of soot hovering over our entire neighborhood, making it difficult for my father to breathe. The scent of illness mingles with the scent of mothballs from the closets and the acrid air carries a chill only he can feel. My mother takes out winter clothes to warm a man shivering even in hot weather. We ordered oxygen but the truck never arrived. Too many people are sick from this smog.

September passes into October. I trot to the store each time there is information on how to cure death. Everyone has heard of a miracle cure and we are eager to try it. You can't bribe cancer but you can threaten it the way you threaten the class bully and it still does no good, I think, as my mother stirs and pounds, pulverizes—trying to be a conjurer.

"What's for supper?" My father asks. He tries to participate in his staying alive. He eats bits and specks.

"*Kale*," she signs. "*Victory's going to go to the store*," she tells him and turns to me. "*Run now!*" She hands me her change purse and ushers me out of the door. I'm wearing a thin cotton blouse and my breasts have begun to bud. Last week I found a lump in one of them and was afraid to tell my mother about it, but she noticed that I was hunching over. I was so relieved it wasn't cancer. I love my mother.

"*Take a sweater.*"

"*It's not cold out.*"

"*You need a wrap.*" My mother takes her own woolen cape off the hook in the hall and wraps me into it like a miniature princess. The fringe tickles the back of my bare legs. "*Now go before it gets too dark!*"

It's Howdy Doody time and I hear kids laughing in front of their television sets while their mothers stir heavy pots filled with stews and soups. Hearty food! The air fills with the deep smell of onions roasting in the juices of meat and chicken—and there's a *for sale* sign on the Glock's front lawn. Lindy's father must have gotten a promotion. My own father is dying, I think. It's a

Wednesday but somehow it feels like a Tuesday. Tuesday's child is full of woe, echoes the old adage. I believe in omens. I wonder as daylight fades in the opaque autumn sky if I was born on a Tuesday. The sun has found its refuge behind the brick facades and a sliver moon sits on my horizon. An inky haze drifts past it and ascends into the night.

Ben's market is three long blocks away—a neighborhood store surrounded by residences. Ben's has a rough wood floor darkened with foot traffic and smelling of disinfectant. Ben carries everything in tiny-sized packages. His baldhead is barely level with the top of his spanking clean meat counter and this gives customers the impression he's hiding.

My thoughts have slowed me down and it's fully dark when I get there. The door is open and Ben is chatting with someone. The voice has changed over the summer, deeper, hoarser but familiar. The wind carries the name outward. "Mr. Rile, you sure these are for your mother?"

Bill Rile in a prep school jacket pays Ben for his mother's cigarettes and leaves with a smirk on his face. Just now, I enter. I haven't seen him since the day I had supper at Lindy's. I'm surprised he's wearing a uniform and ask him if he changed schools. He smiles at me with his half-smirk smile and says that he's at St. Andrews. It's the brother school to Lindy's school. The St. Andrews boys attend Lindy's school dances.

"Hi, Victory, isn't it a little late for you to be shopping?" asks Ben Krupsky, the Ben of Ben's Market, wiping his hands on the skirt of his white apron. Something he does as a matter of habit between customers.

"My mother needs some kale."

"Well, I'm not sure we have any. But you never know," he tells me with the aplomb of a magician about to pull a rabbit out of a hat. He goes to the back of the store and leaves me alone with the extensive assortment of penny candies that clutter the area next to the cash register. I'm hoping there will be some change. I'd do anything for a grape sour right now.

Ben finds a can of kale in the rear of the store. It's rusty and the label is ripping. "Lucky I had some. People don't usually ask for it."

I nod shyly and open my mother's purse. Ben puts his hand into a jar of miniature Tootsie Rolls and presses three into my hand along with the change. "You're getting to be very pretty, Victory."

I blush and leave with the brown paper bag, clutching the tootsie rolls and still feeling the pressure of Ben's hand. Broken glass embedded into the asphalt glitters like myriad jewels under the street lamps. Down the block, Bill Rile is tossing a cobblestone the size of a sheep's heart. A cigarette dangles from his lips. He seems to be waiting for me. This time his smirk turns to a real smile like a friend.

"Your dad any better?" he asks in imitation of a concerned adult.

It occurs to me he might want to be friends. Woman inchoate, budding breasts under my mother's shawl. I'm no longer ugly. Maybe there's a space for us to be friends. The public school girls all want to go out with the St. Andrew guys in the navy jackets and gray pants— preppies in shirts and ties, sons of future bank presidents. Bill Rile must be growing up, too.

"Maybe a little." I've never smiled at Bill Rile before. It seems easier suddenly just to be friendly.

Bill Rile puffs himself up a bit. He's still tossing the cobblestone sort of oblivious. "Well, you take care now."

"Thanks, Billy." I turn to go and carefully thank God in my mind.

My prayer's like an amulet I always remember to say to myself to bring my father luck. I'm some ten yards beyond Bill. A leaf falls from a tree and gets caught in my hair. I stop to pull it out. The noise of an object striking my vertebrae hits first and then the pain, square in the middle of my back and diffusing though my body. Bill Rile's cobblestone at my feet—iridescent in the evening light.

"Sucker! I had sex with your mother. She's one hot, deaf-mute!" He's blowing smoke rings that curl into feathers in the dusk and he wiggles his crotch at me.

It occurs to me that the real hurt is that somebody wants to hurt me. I cry. No one has ever wanted to hurt me like Bill Rile wanted to hurt me. When other kids have wanted to hurt me, they've done it with words that cut sharp into each and every neuron—coursing, flowing, ebbing. Pain comes first in waves and then turns dry at certain times like the lake when the water's down. I'm somehow to blame but can't find where and how. All at once, I realize I'm the reason people want to hurt me. They all say I can't avoid being a spectacle. The price of a certain freedom of the spirit. Crazy girl. Crazy deaf mother is what they don't say. Only Bill Rile says it.

Chapter 10

They brought the new polio vaccine to school today. Lindy moved away without saying goodbye. The Glocks left the curtains and the carpet for the next owner and there are dark blotches on the carpet where Lindy's sofa and chairs covered it. Bill Rile is back in public school. There are rumors that St. Andrews kicked him out. My father seemed better for a while but now he's very bad. Why isn't there a vaccine for the C-word?

I was in gym class when a doctor drove up in a station wagon with coolers of vaccine. We could see the doctor and a nurse unloading white coolers and carrying them into a side door.

"Did you get your permission slip in?" Julie asks me.

"My mother put it into her apron and washed it," I tell her.

"Why does she always do things like that?"

I shrug.

Only God knows how much I hate gym. I have Miss Alshouse this year. The girls call her "outhouse" behind her back. Karen Fishman started it. You can be excused from gym if you have your period so I always tell her I have cramps so she'll think I'm getting one. Now I'm sorry I haven't signed up for the vaccine trials. Outhouse is staring at us with those beady eyes. Her hair is brown mixed with a lot of gray, cropped short, and pulled severe and flat behind her ears so it's out of her way. "I've got twenty/twenty vision, so what does that mean, girls?" Her eyes wrinkle downward into a squint. No one answers. She'd fall over if someone actually answered. "It means if you get out of line, I'm going to see you."

Outhouse wears a blue uniform, too, only it's longer than ours—a culottes skirt, matching blouse and the same white Keds everyone wears. She carries a stick to point at particular kids and keeps her trigger finger on a stopwatch. "Line up! Line up, girls!"

We're lined up—thirty-four girls in our little blue prison toilet cleaning uniforms. She divides us into groups. Twenty in lines for the broad jump and the rest of us, Outhouse says, will go get on the chin bars and hang by our arms. We're supposed to do chin-ups for girls—meaning you raise your legs up and down 100 times. That's supposed to make your arms stronger? But first she does a girdle check.

We're not allowed to wear girdles in gym. She walks up and down our lines and, when she spots a girdle, twang! Twang! Most of the girls just stand up straight but Julie Kramer stands there covering her legs so it's obvious she's got on a girdle.

"Kramer!" Outhouse screams and points toward the dressing room. The other kids are laughing. Julie's got on this girdle that goes down her fat thighs. "Go to the dressing room and remove that girdle!" Then she turns to the class. "Kramer gets three demerits, anybody else?"

Honey Sachs and Judy Greenfield leave the line. The two of them follow Julie. If those girls get into trouble, they don't get embarrassed, they just sass Outhouse along so it goes worse for the other girls.

"You girls don't believe me when I say no girdles."

I wish she had told me to do broad jump. At least you spend a lot of time waiting around. I'm still hanging from the chin bar after twenty minutes and I feel like I have to pee from lifting my legs up and down so much. I stop and just hang. There is no escaping her twenty/twenty. "Povich, you'll never get strong if you just hang there!"

Fortunately, the principal Doctor Waldrop came in. Outhouse didn't see him but I did. "Povich, what is it? Is it your stomach again? Each and every class you have some sort of excuse." She still doesn't see Doctor Waldrop but those hawk eyes see me looking at the door and all the kids are laughing but then there is silence because Doctor Waldrop says, "I need the girls who signed up for the Salk Vaccine trial."

"Sabine" some kids correct him.

Outhouse is a bit put out but she has to obey Doctor Waldrop, "Doctor Salk's kids can go downstairs with Doctor Waldrop." No one moves an inch. "Girdles, I mean girls,"

Laughter.

"No one here signed up?

Silence.

"Line up! Line up and follow Doctor Waldrop!"

The other kids were saved from Outhouse by the polio vaccine.

When the kids are gone, I'm the only one left. And I'm still hanging from the chin bar. My hands are getting blisters, "Can I get down now?

"Not volunteering, Povich?"

God, my hands are aching but I know she's going to play with me. "No, ma'am!" How polite I sound.

"Rather get polio?

"No, ma'am!"

I got a gym warning and my mother had to come to school so now they know she can't hear. They always start on my mother in school and this school is no different. "Your mother didn't understand."

"No, ma'am! I mean yes, ma'am, she understood but she didn't want me to take it."

"Well, you can work on your push-ups then. Go on! Get a mat!"

Oh god, my arms are numb by now and I can't manage a push-up.

"You are very sickly, aren't you Povich?"

"No, ma'am!

"Don't 'No, ma'am!' me! You need to put on some weight, Povich."

I don't answer and she's staring at me when there's a crash in the girl's locker room.

"Whoever you are, come out of there right now!"

We can hear the latch open on the toilet stall.

"On the count of three!"

Julie Kramer comes out of the locker room. "I forgot today was gym."

"So?"

"So I don't have underwear," she tells Outhouse in a barely audible voice.

Outhouse is furious. "Kramer, aren't you one of Doctor Salk's kids.

"Yes,"

"Well?"

Julie's frozen to her spot. Beads of sweat form on her lip and forehead. I'm starting to hate her, and I'm so glad she's in trouble, I could jump around the gym. "I'm afraid of shots," she sobs.

"Two cowards!" Outhouse roars at us. "How ridiculous! Kramer, you get yourself downstairs and take your turn. It's your duty! How are they going to find a cure for polio if you don't volunteer?"

The rest of the period, Outhouse makes me run around the gym while she works on her grade book. Outhouse will never let kids do regular schoolwork if they're not taking gym. At ten till, she tells me to go to my locker and get dressed.

"Gym is the most important subject taught in any school!" she tells me as I rush toward the locker room.

I dress quickly. I don't like undressing when I am the only one there.

૬✧૭✧૭

Downstairs, kids are lined up the entire length of the hallway to have their blood drawn. From the nurse's office, big kids are screaming for their mothers. And the office is crowded with kids waiting to be stuck by the doctor. They leave holding gauze to their arms. I'm thirsty from all the running and get in a line for the water fountain—two lines for two water fountains. When it's finally my turn, I hear a snigger.

"Why didn't you get a shot, Victory?" Maryanne Wilkins asks. She is standing in line with Bill Rile.

"She's already got the pox, don't you, Victory?" he tells her. "Watch out! Don't drink from that water fountain, Maryanne!"

The entire line of kids moves over to the other water fountain and Maryanne keeps screaming, "She drank from that water fountain and you can get the Victory Pox."

I don't know what to say to any of them. More kids join Bill and Maryanne and everybody is screaming, "You're going to get the pox." And then they run away.

I blow on them and they scatter like pigeons on a plaza. Even Julie joins in. "Here, Victory, get me!"

But Maryanne turns to Julie. "Oh! You've got the pox, too, Julie Kramer!" she says coldly.

Julie stops in her tracks—her face burning bright scarlet. But I chase the kids. I don't understand why, but I do. Whenever someone new tries to see what's happening, Bill Rile, and Maryanne scream, "Pox! She's going to give you the pox!" And finally a teacher blows her whistle.

"What a mell of a hess!" That's Mrs. Baum's favorite expression. Outhouse and Mrs. Crowley have followed her to see what the commotion is about.

Outhouse sees that I'm involved, "Did you hear Mrs. Baum, Victory Povich? Some name for a loser." She laughs.

"They—" I start to explain.

"I don't want to hear about them. Oh, and your friend Julie Kramer had to mix into it, too. The two of you can stay after school."

"Chasing boys around is very unladylike," says Mrs. Baum.

Bill Rile and Maryanne just stand there and snigger.

୧୬୧୬

At three o'clock, the bell rings and kids pour out of the building. Julie and I sit in the principal's office until four o'clock. I refuse to talk to her. When the secretary tells us that it's four o'clock, I let Julie go ahead of me.

I see her walking to the bus stop. When the bus comes, she acts like it's too crowded and doesn't get on. I ignore her while we wait for a second bus.

"You want to go to Ben's when we get home?"

"I have homework." I continue to ignore her.

"I'm sorry I did that!"

"You did what?" I ask.

"The pox thing. With the other kids. I'll buy you a grape sour."

"Why, because none of the other kids are around, Julie?"

"I didn't mean to," she pleads.

"Then why did you do it? You're supposed to be my friend."

When the bus comes, I don't get on. I walk the entire way. It's late when I finally get home. My mother is standing at the door and waving a prescription. Dr. Frank has come and gone.

"*Where were you?*"

I shrug.

"*You were just hanging around with some kids, weren't you? You're very selfish. I need you to run to the drugstore. Your father is in terrible pain.*"

The drugstore is in the same little block as Ben's market and I stop there and buy a grape sour. Ben says it's a pleasure to see me and presses it into my hand. He won't take money for it. I walk home pressing the paper bag tightly around the prescription bottle. The grape sour raises bumps on my tongue.

Chapter 11

When I return, my father is asleep and I can hear my mother running the shower. I leave the medicine on the kitchen table and go out to the backyard.

Our backyard has room for two green metal chairs. There's a round enameled metal table missing an umbrella. When I was little, high winds carried it off and dropped it mangled back down in the yard. Little tufts of grass and dandelions sprout between crooked flagstones. My mother has managed to grow roses in this small plot. It's too late in the year for blossoms and thorny stems now lean with the weight of plump, crowned rose hips. The bushes need to be pruned back for winter but we've forgotten this year.

The front doorbell is ringing and all the house lights are flickering which means Aunt Shirley and Uncle Abe have let themselves into the house. I don't know why they bother to ring. My father always complains about it. I don't bother to greet them.

Little ants crawl into and out of one of the stones. Someone has left out the small hand shovel and I take it and lift up the flagstone. Where it has left its shallow imprint, a myriad of dark-loving creatures clamber in and out of the dank soil. When I was very small, I made funerals for birds and hamsters in this spot. Then we paved over the yard.

I'm familiar now with the slow particulars of death–the somber processions of cars following a hearse up the winding hill toward the cemetery. All the children say if a hearse passes you on the road, you get bad luck. I count the times the hearses have passed me—Tuesday's child is full of woe. The ants find the flesh of my hand and swarm over it and through the dirt.

Aunt Shirley appears in the back doorway. "What are you doing, Victory?" she asks and descends the stairs to the garden. The wood creaks under her weight. "Oh, Victory! You'll get bitten. Go to the hose and wash." Aunt Shirley shakes her head and her *bisungas*—my father's word for them—bounce in the "V" of her dress. Only her hair stays in place, It's wound round and round her head, the shape of a hive of bees and the color of honey, stiff and sticky-full. She has spent the morning under a beehive-shaped dryer at the hairdresser.

"It's okay! I'm not two years old."

"Why do you want to look at ugly things?"

"It's just nature."

"Come in at once. Your parents don't need you to bring them more trouble than God has wished on them already."

"God didn't wish my father to be sick!"

"It's just a figure of speech, Victory."

I pat the earth around the stone and follow my uncle's wife into the house.

Everyone surrounds my father's bed. He's awake now and seems to sag into himself. I'm almost afraid to hug him. I wonder if he knows how he looks with the white bed sheet clinging to his broomstick legs. My mother bought him extra pairs of tan pajamas last week. He never dresses now and my mother has to bring him a white bottle to pee in. It sits in a bedpan under the dining room table. Nobody seems to notice, but I wish they would put up some curtains up on the arch to block off the room. When people come to the front door, they can see right in. My mother says the sick need to see out.

The linen-covered diary my father gave me on my last birthday lies on the end table next to his bed. He's been reading it, I think.

He sees I'm angry. "How's my girl?" he asks.

Aunt Shirley sees the book too. "What a pretty book."

"It's Victory's diary."

"You keep a diary?"

"She's always writing in that diary. Someday she'll turn it all into a book about us." He seems a bit more animated suddenly. It frightens me. My father and I listened to "La Traviata" on the radio last Saturday. I remember how the soprano rallies before she dies.

I take the diary and cover it.

"I don't know if I want to be in a book. What is it you are writing about?" Aunt Shirley demands. "Is it secret?"

I jet her a hostile glance. "No, private!"

"Isn't that the same thing?"

"Well, not exactly." I am as condescending as I know how to be. "If I keep a secret, it doesn't have to be secret forever. But if something is private, it means it is part of me that I don't have to share."

Shirley doesn't know how to answer. "I hope, if you write about us, you say flattering things."

My mother notices Aunt Shirley's displeasure and signs to me. *"Are you being nasty again?"*

"No, honest!"

"Well is 'honest' nasty?"

"You are always saying things about her and her melon ball husband." My mother and I call him Melon Ball because his paunch is the size of a watermelon.

"Victory!" Weak as my father is, he manages to look sternly at my mother. "Esther!"

Aunt Shirley is flustered and keeps chattering. "Well, I wasn't going to ask you to share it with me. I was just making some conversation with you because you are my niece and I care about how you turn out."

It's hard to picture our family's conversations because while she is making her little speech to me, my mother and I continue to sign. I scream at my aunt. That's a figure of speech like aunt Shirley's figures of speech since I'm not screaming with my voice and she can't understand what I'm saying. *"I wouldn't fit into one of your Shirley doll molds."*

And my mother screams at me in sign. *"Victory, stop talking!"*

"Fine!" I tell her.

She brings chairs to my father's bedside. My uncle Abe sits in one and leans on my father's bed. He has a manila folder in his pudgy hands. "Well anyway, I brought everything, Morris. It would be best to sell the lake property."

My father nods wanly.

"What is he saying?" my mother asks.

"We should sell the lake house, Esther, to free some cash in case we need it."

"No." She's adamant and tears brim in her eyes. *"You know how I feel about that. Don't let them talk you into it. They don't understand. There is a piece of us there and I don't want to lose it."*

My father turns weakly to my uncle. "She's very much against it."

"What good is it to a deaf woman who doesn't drive a car? She can't get there."

My mother signs and I translate. "She says I will drive in two years."

"Don't let them sell it out of desperation," my father says. "Loan them against it from the business, if they need something."

"And put their future in jeopardy?" my uncle asks.

My father's gasping for air, "The lake house has to be Esther's decision!" When he regains his breath, he looks at me. "How's my girl?"

"Get Victory out of here," my uncle roars.

Aunt Shirley picks up the tin of buttery yellow cookies she has brought—the kind with red candied cherries at the center. "Come, darling, you'll show me where mother keeps the instant. I'm sure Uncle Abe will have some. I'll get your father some ginger ale and maybe some tea would be good for him, too. Uncle Abe has papers for your father to sign. It won't take too long.

"*I want to stay here,*" I plead with my mother.

"*Just give us a few minutes, sweetheart.*"

"*I'm old enough to be here!*"

"*Don't make trouble, your father is too ill.*"

"*I won't be trouble. The way things are I need to learn about business things.*"

"*Please go with your aunt and don't make my life difficult!*"

I follow Aunt Shirley into the kitchen. She turns the cold faucet on the stack of dishes in the sink. "We'll just let it run a while." She's chatting for both of us, "Where is the tea kettle," she says, indicating our stove. Dirty pots sit on four burners.

"Oh, we just use any pot," I tell her indifferently and

find a beaten-up saucepan from inside the oven.

"I guess it's as good as anything." Aunt Shirley sighs as she fills the pot with water from the tap and sets it on a burner. Then she turns the hot faucet on and begins to fill the basin of dishes with sudsy water. "Is there's an apron? I might as well wash these up."

I get her one of my mother's soiled aprons off a hook in the hall and Shirley puts it on. It seems doll-sized on my buxom aunt. My mother and I have secretly named her "The Milk Factory." She's always trying to get me to drink milk even though she knows what it does to me.

"Now, second question: Is there a sponge?"

"We'll have to use a wash cloth, the sponge fell into the garbage accidentally."

"It's not sanitary to use items from the bathroom in the kitchen, darling. I'll tell you what. We'll just use the dishtowel. And if you don't have a clean one for drying then they can drip dry. I like to swish my cup with boiling water anyway. It's much more sanitary. Especially with illness in the house."

"You can't catch a tumor."

"No one knows for sure. Sit, darling!"

We're seated at our tiny kitchen table with tubular steel legs. The marbleized plastic seat covers match the Formica tabletop.

I continue the thought. "That's not what Dr. Frank says."

Aunt Shirley ignores me. I'm sure she's thinking about her immaculate kitchen with its stainless steel counters and well-stocked closets, everything with a place.

"Let's relax for your father's sake, Victory. Not so many questions."

Her neck and arms issue a powdery scent.

"Okay."

"Can I pour you a glass of milk, Victory?"

I mumble something indistinct, thinking how it will curdle in my stomach.

"Did I hear you say yes?"

"Uh, uh!" I mutter again.

"Don't the deaf expect niceties?"

"Uh huh."

"In the hearing world you have to make yourself heard, young lady. Someday, you'll go out with gentlemen to fancy restaurants and order fancy dishes. And then you'll have to make yourself heard in a polite way, like a lady. Then you're more likely to get what you want."

My mother once told me how she used to sign with her friends when the teacher wasn't looking. The children at the oral deaf school were forbidden to sign. Their teacher was hearing and never knew what her pupils said behind her back—at least the children who could sign. The other children were "souls lost to language" my mother says.

"I'll just pour a half glass. You need to grow, Victory."

Aunt Shirley takes a bottle of milk from the refrigerator and shakes it.

"You don't have to shake the milk. It's homogenized," I say.

"That's a big word. Maybe we could get your father to try one of the cookies. Wouldn't that be great?" she tells me as she pours cold milk into blue metallic glass and hands it to me.

I take a sip and set the glass onto the table. Homogenize, intermingle, coalesce, combine, all the things missing from my life right now. With my finger, I draw a face in the condensation. Nancy Drew would have succeeded in getting a sick man to eat.

"How do you sign 'please help yourself'? I want to make your mother laugh."

I show her and Aunt Shirley makes an awkward attempt to imitate me. Maybe she means well.

"Was that right?"

I sign yes and Aunt Shirley laughs.

I haven't touched the cookies. "Eat, darling!" she proffers.

Hannah proffered baked goods to Nancy—there are always biscuits, warm rolls, and a hearty meal of ham, fried chicken, mashed potatoes, and gravy waiting for her when she returns from an adventure. It's a wonder Nancy stays so slender.

I take a cookie and bite into it to be polite. It leaves a sweet, grainy sludge on my tongue. I like the centers and pick the jellied cherry from two more cookies. They are thick skinned and moist.

"What's wrong with the cookies?" Aunt Shirley demands.

"They're good."

"Then why are you only eating the cherries?"

I shrug. A garish new ring flashes on Aunt Shirley's finger. "Do you like it? Uncle Abe bought it for my birthday. Or I'll let you in on a little secret. I picked it out and had it sent to myself from him, wrapped up and everything."

I think I'm supposed to laugh at the foibles of her marriage and bond to her the way I've heard other women do at the beauty parlor. Aunt Shirley sits under the dryer at *Monsieur Jason's Salon* every week to have her hair done in the beehive hairdo that she has to keep under a scarf for the rest of the week. I only stare and Aunt Shirley reflexively wipes crumbs from the table.

I can see my mother in the dining room mirror. She flounders between my father and Abe with watchful eyes.

My father translates what Uncle Abe is saying. *"The insurance is not enough. You'd do well to put the house in Victory's name so no one can touch it."* My name suddenly takes on a different meaning. It never occurred to me that it had another purpose.

"Morris?" I see my mother's alarm.

"Let Abe handle it, Esther!"

"I appreciate Abe but let me handle it, too!" My mother is adamant.

When she's angry, her red hair grows more profuse and fiery. Faced with Uncle Abe, her gestures seem like a helpless butterfly caught in a jar.

"Your daughter's sitting there in the kitchen! Don't you care about her?" says Uncle Abe.

"If the lawyers and doctors won't talk to me, how can I have a choice? You have always been lazy about these things, Morris."

"You are blessed to have Abe. What would we do, Esther?" My father takes his brother's side. He is too weak to argue—weaker still to sign. *"He will need to be able to make decisions about the business on your behalf in case I become too ill to continue."*

"You are *too ill to continue,"* she retorts sharply.

I think maybe this is the first time they both acknowledge he's dying.

Aunt Shirley doesn't bear long silences too well. "Doesn't look as good today. I don't know how she does it, poor woman, with such a handicap."

"My mother's not handicapped!"

"So, are you helping your mother?"

"Yes." I let my aunt talk.

"I'm going to try to find a colored girl to help your mother out. My Janie will know somebody."

"Why do you call Janie a girl?"

Janie is older than Shirley is and walks with a limp

because a bus hit once hit her when she was on the way
to work for Shirley.

"It's just the way it is, Victory. I don't have anything
against the colored. Your uncle Abe employs three colored boys and they're very grateful to have the work, unlike some other colored you see. I once had an Irish girl
but she stole my mother's silver when her husband lost
his job and I had to let her go. You know the Irish have
some of the same problems as the colored. Now I'm not
saying all Irish. Some are very respectable like the Kennedys. Only, I don't think anyone would elect them to be
president."

What power places Aunt Shirley in judgment over
the deaf, colored, and Irish?

I lower my eyes toward the cover of my Nancy Drew
book. *The Secret of the old Clock.* It, too, was my mother's. It has a library card pocket. Perhaps she loved it so
much she never returned it. Nancy has an innate disdain
for people with new money. She'd probably dislike the
Kennedys and their brash ways.

"When you're not writing, you're reading. What are
you reading, darling?"

I push the book toward her.

"Another one?

"Uh, huh!"

"I read Nancy Drew when I was a little girl. Oh let
me think—what's that one called. *The Secret in the
Parchment.* I don't remember that one but, you know,
Victory, they have new writers. They call it writing by
committee."

Where would Shirley fit into the Nancy Drew
scheme of things, I wonder. Nancy knew how to handle
helpless matrons. They came to rely on her, admire her.

"I want to go back to the dining room."

"The big people need to talk. You keep me company here."

There is an unwritten understanding that the business is more Uncle Abe's now. That heralds from the weekends at the lake when my dad stopped working on Saturdays. Their age disparity plays into the arrangement. Uncle Abe's paternalism controls the dialogue now that my father is so ill. However, the truth is that my father has never wanted to be bothered about work and worldly things. That's why I have always been included in what transpires until now. I'm always at my parents' center, nodding and understanding like Nancy Drew. I sign better than my father, who flickers the electric switch to get my mother's attention.

"*I won't let you put your signature to those papers,*" my mother insists.

I watch from the doorway. I am as suspicious as Nancy, but I haven't the gumption to interfere. Nancy would have already been in trouble. If Nancy Drew had learned sign language, she could have sent secret signals with it.

Uncle Abe assesses his sister-in-law and jets a pleading look at his brother. "You don't trust me, Esther?" Abe's heavy paunch heaves with indignity. "We're family, Morris. Maybe she never saw us as family because of the communication thing."

"Abe, we're all getting overworked about this thing." My father is racked with pain.

"*We need time to think, Morris. Before we sign such a thing,*" Esther pleads. "*Tell him to go.*"

"*You don't just tell somebody to go, Esther.*"

My mother is never plagued by the need for the hearing world's niceties. She's other and uses it to her own advantage.

No one in the hearing world trifles with her. Only a

few, like my father, have ever bothered to become more than a mere acquaintance.

"She's really stubborn," I hear Uncle Abe tell Aunt Shirley in a hushed whisper.

"And the child gets stranger the older she gets." Aunt Shirley gets up to follow him out of the door.

I'm afraid it's the end. Our house is hushed in anguish. My father makes my mother give him more pills than Doctor Frank has prescribed. He's sleeping now.

Chapter 12

After Shirley and Abe drove away in their green Chrysler, I noticed that there were lights on in the Glock's old house. A realtor took down the "for sale" sign and then we heard rumors that a famous scientist had bought it. A tall man comes out of the house and walks around the driveway to the back. Maybe he's the scientist, but he seems interested in the gutters and the roof and he's looking up at them with displeasure the way my father always did. Minutes later a moving van rumbles onto our block and the driver carefully positions the back doors to the bottom of the driveway. Three burly men jump out of the truck with dollies and rope.

A house is never so wide open as on a moving day. You get to know its occupants first by their possessions, the ones that can't fit into boxes, or the ones that nobody has time to properly pack. The first thing the movers set out on the sidewalk is a mirrored coat stand that looks as if it could hold the army jacket and boots of a Prussian general. The lyre sticks and pedals of a piano come next but not the piano. That truck is like a magician's false-bottomed trunk. Even after three hours, more and more treasures come out of it. A mover stacks box after box labeled 'books and journals' on a dolly and pushes them up the driveway and into the side door. You have to climb a flight of steps to reach the front door of Lindy's house so it is better for the movers to use the side. I sit on our steps with Nancy Drew but I'm really watching the move the way some people watch the test pattern when there's nothing to watch on television. The drapes are open and I can see the tall man pointing to various corners as the strong men toil with the big furniture.

Then I catch my first glimpse of the new girl. A Ford sedan, driven by a woman, moves slowly down the block. The girl is sitting in the passenger seat. I'm wondering how old she is and whether to welcome them when my mother comes out to the porch.

"It's the new people! There's a girl," I sign.

"Your father's pain medication is wearing off. Please call Doctor Frank, Victory."

"He's going to be angry that you gave him so much."

"I don't care. You've got to call him for me."

My father is screaming in agony. I pray twice. Once for my father and once that the new girl cannot hear what is happening in my house.

Doctor Frank comes very quickly this time and gives my father a shot. "This is what happens when you exceed the medication, Morris." He talks to him like he is a small child. He expects me to translate for my mother but I don't say it exactly as he wants me to. I know that my father will die from the pain without enough of the medicine. "Please give them enough," I plead.

"Young lady! I can't kill my patient."

I want to say, "But your patient is dying," but I can't say it in front of my father and when the medicine begins to work I follow Doctor Frank outside to his car. He pats me on the shoulder. "The shot will make him sleep well.

You take care of your mother. You're a grown girl now."

"Yes, but..." What I have to say doesn't come. I want to say something about my mother, and how she takes such good care of all of us. "I'm too young to take care of my mother."

"Chin up!" he says and gives my shoulder a special little squeeze.

My mother is the only one of all of us who has kept her chin up, I think.

When he drives off, the new girl comes out of her house. She's very tall and blonde. I guess she's been watching for me from the window. I wave and she crosses the street to where I'm standing. I guess blonde girls somehow go with that house. I begin to sense immediately that this blonde girl has a darker layer underneath.

"Hi, I'm Lisanne Glick. I'm just moving in—I mean, I guess that's obvious."

We both laugh.

"I'm Victory."

"Victory, that's an interesting name. Are you British?

"My last name is Povich."

"That's not very British."

I'm almost afraid to say it. "We're Jewish. It's a Russian name, shortened from something or other."

"Well, mine was shortened from Glickstein or changed or something. I'm half Jewish. But we don't do anything religious, that is."

We laugh together.

"You know your name almost sounds like the previous owners. Did you know their name was Glock. But I can tell you for certain that it was never changed from anything." I grin at her. "Just think you'll only have to change one letter on your new mailbox.

"Is your father a doctor? I saw the man with the black bag drive off."

"No, my father is sick."

"What's wrong with him?"

"He had a tumor operated on."

"That's too bad. Is he going to be all right?"

"Of course," I lie. "Where did you move from?"

"Oak Ridge, Tennessee. My father's a doctor, but in physics."

I'm not sure what to say about that and let her continue.

"A PhD's a doctor. Only he kills people."

"So are you trying to shock me?" I ask in a kind of admiration. I'm incredulous that this blonde with straight teeth and blue eyes is so glib. You'd never have gotten something like that out of Lindy. "So how exactly does your father kill people?"

She laughs. "He helped to build the bomb. And, no, you shouldn't have had to guess that. A lot of people just know that. He's listed in *Who's Who*. But don't worry, you'll get to meet my father and my mother who just might be a bigger killer." She nods toward her new house. "And there she is now!"

Ilse Glick steps out onto her porch. "Lisanne!" she calls in a clipped German accent. Her blonde hair is graying and she's piled it up in a neat bun. She's still wearing the steel-gray walking suit with the fur collar she has traveled in. "Lisanne!" she calls again and then she sees us.

Her black pumps crack briskly on the pavement as she crosses to us.

"Are your parents strict?" Lisanne whispers.

I think about Lindy and her schedule and shrug. "Not really."

"Mine are. You'll see. They meddle into everything I

do. I am under strict control, like an atomic secret!" she whispers.

"Are you going to blow up the world some day?"

"Let's hope so! Do you smoke?"

"No, I tried it and I gagged."

I sense she's discovered some defect in me. "I learned last year. You get used to it. It does incredible things for you when you're down. It's worth getting over that."

"Do you know about your woods?"

"No!"

"It's back behind your garage! A lot of kids go there."

She smiles. "Oh! Really? And what do they do?"

Her mother now joins us before I can describe the escapades rumored to take place in Lindy's woods, now Lisanne's woods.

"Mama, this is Victory," says the sweet, compliant Lisanne.

Unlike Lindy, who put forward one face to the world, I sense this girl has a personality for each day of the week. I find myself looking forward to the others. I pray that maybe she hates school as much as I do.

"How nice to meet you," says Mrs. Glick. Even Mrs. Glock would have had to work at it to sound this formal. There is something about her German accent that begs formality, I think, as I offer my hand. She holds it limply for a second and looks from one of us to the other. I would have expected a firmer handshake to go with such a taut face.

"You are about the same age, aren't you? Lisanne is tall for her age." It sounds like a clinical assessment of two subjects.

"I'm almost fifteen," I tell her.

"So am I!" Lisanne says.

"Well, tomorrow will be your first day in the new school," Ilse adds. "Do you go to the public school, Victory?"

"Yes."

"Are you in the advanced placement?" Lisanne asks.

"No, you can't be in the advanced placement until ninth grade." I try to avoid saying that I was held back.

Lisanne looks disappointed. "Oh, so you're in eighth?"

"My birthday's December."

"Mine is March but I was skipped."

Mrs. Glick became impatient. "Well, you girls will have lots of time to talk. So, Lisanne, come inside now and get your things ready." She turned back to me. "It was nice to meet you, Victory."

"How do you get to school?" Lisanne asks. "Maybe we could go together."

"The first day, your father and I will take you, Lisanne."

"We could ride home together," I offer. "I take the bus then the street car."

"We will see how much homework Lisanne has. Come, now we must have supper and you need to organize for bed." Ilse Glick turns to cross the street and Lisanne follows.

That house is going to be back on a schedule, I'm thinking, when she turns to me and whispers, "Sometimes bombs go off by accident!"

I watch until they are inside and Mrs. Glick has closed all of Mrs. Glock's curtains then I go inside myself. My mother is on the staircase with a pile of blankets and linens. *"Can you help me with a mattress. I can't sleep another night on that sofa. My back is aching."*

That's when we hear my father ask if I was there. Because he spoke, it was a question my mother could not answer. I went over to the foot of his bed and smiled. "Do you want something, Daddy?"

"Is it Sunday?" His words were barely audible, and he was making gulping noises.

"No, Daddy, it's Monday. I went to school today, remember."

"Oh, Who brought you?"

"I went myself!"

That seemed to disturb him. "I'll take you tomorrow."

"I'd love that, Daddy."

My mother went over to him and signed something. He just stared blankly. At first, we thought it was the morphine. *"Talk to me!"* She began to cry. *"Talk to me, please!"*

"Daddy, sign for Mommy."

"I'm not idle," was all he said.

ℰↃℰↃ

Tuesday, I sleep on the sofa in the living room, my mother on a mattress. In the morning, the sun sends a fan of light through the front window where the curtains part. My father seems a little better. He looks around the room. At first, I think he is seeing the pictures he painted at the lake. But I sense he is looking at something we aren't able to see.

"I don't want to go to school," I tell my mother.

"You can't stay home from school but you can go late, Victory."

Chapter 13

I missed homeroom. In science class, the kids were already gathered around the big table listening to Mr. Lane. Mr. Lane is very strict and he's not too happy that I have come in late. "Today, guys…" His voice trails off when he sees me. *Guys? You'd think we were in third grade.* The girls are wearing girdles and gobs of make-up and are crazy for boys half their size—crazy for the cute faces of eighth grade boys. I wonder what Lisanne Glick will think of these kids and whether she is already in her class. Julie makes room for me, but I squeeze in between Eliot Goldstein and Tom Rogers across the table from her.

Most of the junior high science teachers just wear regular clothes. Mr. Lane wears a white coat for special effect. His blond flat top is clipped like a dense hedge and sprinkled with just the right amount of gray. His posture is strictly military. But he wears English Leather, his eyes are very blue, and his skin is deeply tanned. Every weekend he takes some of the boys with him on science expeditions. They bring back specimens—once someone found a fossil of a rodent jaw, and they've come back with fresh water crabs, water samples from the Ohio River, and even arrowheads. Some of the girls think he's very cute but he's never taken any of the girls on his trips. I guess they'd wear their girdles and wouldn't be able to bend down. Aunt Shirley never goes anywhere without a girdle. She has to ask everyone to bend down and pick things up for her. Uncle Abe says she keeps him young.

"Well, well! Our ten-o'clock scholar!"

"Pox!" I hear and, of course, the usual sniggering.

Eighth grade science is basically what my father used to call kitchen chemistry.

"Today, guys, we are we are going to make a cabbage indicator."

"Fart food!" whispers Bill Rile. He's changed places with Tom. Now Bill's next to me and I inch toward Eliot.

Mr. Lane gives me a cold and piercing stare. "Is there something the matter?"

His blue eyes don't blink once and I lower mine. "No, sir!"

I'm thinking about how my father's eyes appeared not to see me last night and I shiver a bit. I'd like to ask Mr. Lane if he can explain it to me. There must be a reason in science for everything we think, feel, and see.

"Don't act silly, *anyone!*" Mr. Lane continues. "This will be on your test next week, so pay close attention. The girls can cut up the cabbage and put it in the jar. I will boil distilled water. Do you know why we might want to use distilled water?"

I raise my hand, thinking to right my previous wrong, but Mr. Lane ignores me. He turns to Tom Rogers instead. Tom hasn't raised his hand.

"Tom, can you tell us why we want to use distilled water?"

"It tastes better than Pittsburgh water."

Everyone laughs.

I'm still laughing when the rest of the class has qui-
eted down. The laughing wants to come out of me like
my father's shallow breaths. My mother thinks the water
gave my father the C-word. Doctor Frank finds the idea
preposterous. I haven't taken a drink of Pittsburgh water
since the water fountain incident, drinking soda pop instead. When I was small, we used to make frozen orange
juice with our tap water, and it ended up tasting like mill
soot. On some days, the taste is worse than on others. In
Pittsburgh, there are three rivers to carry the flavor of the
black and stinking smoke from the mills into our homes.
Unholy water bathes away the scent of our own body fluids. Some days it's thick enough to cover even the odor
of the deaths it causes. Most of the kids prefer to drink
pop, I think, because we can't drink the water. Mr. and
Mrs. Glock were smart to drink martinis. My mother
likes beer. My father has to take his fluids through plastic
tubing.

"We are not experimenting with our taste buds today," Mr. Lane continues as if no one said anything terribly stupid. I keep my hand in the air, still hoping he will
call on me. But he doesn't. "There will be some interesting experiments about taste later in the semester. So, nobody seems to have any idea why we would not just turn
on the tap and fill up our jar?"

"It would ruin the experiment, if the water were too
acid or base," I blurt out.

"Victory, I don't accept answers spoken out of turn
whether they are right or wrong."

My face feels hot and flushed. "But I was right!"

"Are you arguing with me?"

"No, I'm sorry. My mother puts eggshells in the water when she waters the plants. She says."

"Eggshells! Were we discussing eggshells, class?"

When the laughter subsides, he continues. "Boys and girls, I will tell you the answer. The hot distilled water is PH neutral. It dissolves the colored chemicals in the cabbage. We will be working later with those chemicals but first I want to remind you that the science fair entries are due next week. Guys, if you want to be considered for the AP science classes next year, you should be finalizing your exhibits. Rile, what are you going to do?"

"I'm building a model airplane." His tongue is folded over in his mouth again. The kids laugh at him.

"There's no need to laugh, class."

"Yeah!" Bill Rile tells them.

"There are many things you can demonstrate with a model airplane. For example—" says Mr. Lane, as he walks over to the black board.

"I'm going to fly in a vaccine for the pox," Bill Rile tells me.

"Shut up!"

"Ooooh! You told me to shut up? I'm going to get you."

Mr. Lane is drawing an airplane wing on the board, and Bill Rile is smiling appreciatively at him when I feel a sharp jab in my thigh. He points under the table to the point of the compass he's holding in his hand. "I inoculated you from yourself!" he whispers.

"He poked me," I scream.

"I can't have you in my class, Miss Povich, please go down to Doctor Waldrop's office for the rest of this period. Tell Doctor Waldrop that I am giving you detention. You'll have to do it in the principal's office because I have a meeting, and please have your uncle come to see me. I think you should be considering the vocational curriculum."

All the mill girls take the vocational curriculum. Everyone knows they drop out by sixteen anyway. In my neighborhood, the mere mention of "vocational" is humiliation itself. The kids in my neighborhood are expected to go to college even if their parents haven't. No one holds it against a parent if he or she was in the war or went to work. But no one would dare drop out of high school. Sometimes the college-bound girls take vocational subjects like shorthand and typing in the summer. When you get to college, you're expected to type papers for the boys so it's acceptable to take vocational subjects in the summer.

Tears are streaming down my face.

"Why are you crying?"

I don't answer.

"I have a 'no crying' rule in this classroom."

"He poked me with his compass," I tell Mr. Lane again.

"I don't care what he did. First, you come in late and then you disrupt my class. Some of these guys are serious science students, and I have to prepare them for the AP exams." Mr. Lane folds his arms and watches as I gather my things. The class watches silently for a sign from him. "This project is a major component where if you're college-bound, guys, you can demonstrate scientific ability," he continues as I leave the classroom.

My thigh is throbbing. It's ten-forty five and the hallway is empty. Tuesday is meatloaf day in the cafeteria. The odor wafting through the school makes me nauseous. I think I'm going to be sick and lower my head to vomit. *I could just leave school here and now*, I think, and that's when the throbbing stops and a great warmth begins to rise through me. First, my feet feel warm as if they have been placed in someone's warm and comforting hands. From my feet, the warmth spreads through me. The hallway floor and the long avenue of green lockers seemed to warp and wave and then everything becomes still and bathed in a warm, yellow haze. The yellow warmth passes through all my vessels and pores. I am its conduit to a certain space where it can encircle me—keep me. I want to escape and embrace it at the same time—but it dissipates before I can react. So powerful was its pull on me that I need to sit down. I wiggle my toes and fingers. Once I am sure I can move, I stand up and everything is like it was before.

Twice in my life, I've been able to lift myself on air. I don't believe it was something I dreamed. I remember being in my back yard and finding a certain level in the air where I could lay down. It was a pleasant, floating feeling that lasted for a brief time. When I tried it again, the space eluded me. It happened one other time. I cannot place this sensation in time. I might have been three or I might have been ten. But that I have been able to lie down in air is part of my reality.

I wonder what my mother will say if I come home. The principal has no way of knowing that I was on my way down. I stop in the girl's bathroom to think about what to do. Curls of smoke come out of the stall next to the window. The window is open but the wind blows the smoke inside the room. I go into a stall and lift my skirt. Where Bill Rile poked me, a big purple blotch has formed. Like the blotches on my father's arms from all the needles. *Is this how he feels each and every time his body is invaded? Do the doctors feel like Bill Rile when they stab instruments into their patients,* I wonder? A scab had already formed in the center where the needle penetrated. I pee, flush, and leave the stall. The smoker is gone and the air has mostly cleared. I tried to wash my thigh at the sink but the truant officer, a heavy-set woman named Mrs. Clem, comes into the girls' room.

"You're not smoking in here are you?" She places her hands on her hips and glares through thick eyeglasses.

Usually she sits at a desk in another corridor and asks for your passes. Today she's taking a stroll. I wonder if she does the boy's bathrooms, too.

"No, ma'am!"

"Are you cutting class?

"No, ma'am!"

"I smell smoke. Where's your pass?"

"I wasn't smoking. I was on my way to the principal's office."

She finds a package of cigarettes and some matches taped under the toilet bowl in the stall next to the window.

"I'll say you're on your way to the principal's office. I'm going to give you an escort."

I was in enough trouble to be suspended for two weeks. It's exactly what I have prayed for, but no one answered at my house so the principal decided to keep me in school for the afternoon and then for detention. I sit through lunch and four more periods on one of the oak chairs in the outer office—in front of the counter so the secretary Miss Newman can see me. I pretend to read whenever she looks at me but I'm not taking in a word. I sit there all day, acting like I'm engrossed in this book I took out of the library last week. I can't even remember the title and keep closing the book to look at the cover, in case someone asks what I'm reading.

Every time some kid or teacher comes into the office, I get those looks, like *What did you do to deserve to be here?* My question precisely. At three o'clock, the bell rings and I begin to gather my things. My leg is so stiff I can barely stand on it and I think hard about the yellow warmth I had experienced.

Mrs. Newman jets a piercing look at me. "And where do you think you are going?"

"My mother needs me to go to the drugstore."

"The drug store will be open when you get home. So I don't think so."

"But I always get my father's medicine. He can't wait for it."

"What kind of a cockamamie excuse is that? I was told to keep you here until Four o'clock."

I sit down to serve my detention—watching Mrs. Newman run off notes on the mimeograph, thinking these are notes of the kind I would no doubt forget to bring home. I think about getting up and leaving but I'm not so heroic as my name might indicate. I weigh all the options in my own narrow balance. If I bolt, Mrs. Newman will most probably scream, and the principal or the vice principal, or maybe Outhouse, or Mr. Lane, will chase me all the way home. There's another problem. My coat is in my locker and it's cold outside. That's when the haziness comes to me again first through my feet—warm yellow.

The counter and Mrs. Newman behind it begin to sway. She places a stack of mimeographed pages onto the flat paper cutter and raises the blade. This time I laugh at the yellow warmth. I laugh at the thought of all of those notes getting sent home to all the parents but mine. Mrs. Newman looks up at me. I wonder if Mrs. Newman can tell that something is happening to me. "Wipe that silly grin off of your face, Victory Povich. I'm sure you have something better to do for the next hour."

"You'll scare it off!"

"I'll scare what off?" She peers at me over her reading glasses. "Are you in your right mind?"

The yellow warmth has now left as it did before. It has left the school and gone somewhere. I am back in my right mind and so I cry.

I need to go and find it, I think.

That's when Lisanne's mother comes into the principal's office followed by Lisanne. Mrs. Newman beams at them. "And how was your first day in our school, Lis-anne?"

Lisanne mumbles something that sounds like fine, or fine if I have to say something.

"Lisanne!" her mother demands.

"It was fine. I really enjoyed it."

Ilse Glick looks at her watch. "I was wondering if I could speak with the principal. My husband wanted to make sure that you give Lisanne extra mathematics to do. She was in a more advanced level back in Oak Ridge. I'll only take a minute of his time."

Lisanne rolls her eyes and smiles at me. I avert my head so she won't see my face is swollen from crying.

"Are you all right, Victory?"

Mrs. Newman is surprised we know each other. "So, you know Victory Povich?"

"She is our new neighbor." Mrs. Glick explains in her stiff fashion. Lisanne smiles at me.

Mrs. Newman jets me a chastising look. "I hope you won't be a bad influence on our new student, Victory."

Mrs. Glick looks me up and down as if she is seeing something she never saw before about someone she has known a long, long time. "My daughter has no time to be influenced by anyone."

"Some of our girls just don't know how to act like ladies."

Mrs. Glick scrutinizes me even closer. "Oh!" is all she can say. She spits out disdain as if it were an insect flown into her mouth. Lisanne rolls her eyeballs but at her mother. I roll my eyeballs, too.

Mrs. Newman goes to the inner office.

I've already made a stunning debut and, for sure, Mrs. Glick will keep Lisanne too busy to have anything to do with me or the kids on our side of the street. Now is the perfect chance to run, I think, but still I don't go. Lisanne and I are exchanging surreptitious glances when Mrs. Newman returns with a beaming smile on her stupid face. "Dr. Waldrop will be glad to see you, Mrs. Glick."

"Lisanne, why don't you take one of the chairs and start your homework? When you get home you have to practice the piano." Lisanne rolls her eyes again and takes a seat. That girl can really exercise her eyes.

"Go on! Open your notebook! You, too, Victory! I don't want Lisanne distracted."

"No!" I say to her. "I'm going to be leaving now."

And that's how I ran. No one followed me out of the door. I have no idea what the secretary said to Dr. Waldrop. Or when Mrs. Glick closed her gaping mouth.

Sometimes bombs go off by accident.

Chapter 14

I don't wait for the bus, in case someone decides to haul me back into that fortress of a school and lock me up in the gym. I walk a mile to the streetcar connection. I have to pass the linoleum store but there's a "be right back" sign hanging on the front door. I cross the street to avoid the delicatessen, in case my uncle is sitting there having a cup of coffee. When I get to the pharmacy, no prescription had been called in that afternoon. I run home, angry that someone has forgotten to call the pharmacist. Doctor Frank's Cadillac and Uncle Abe's Chrysler are double-parked in front of my house. I know it's too late when I enter our house. The large figure of the doctor and my uncle screen me from my father's bed. My mother comes forward tearfully. I push past her and scream for my father.

"He's no longer in pain, Victory," Doctor Frank tells me.

And my uncle says it's better this way. Only my mother holds me while the tears flow out of me. For a brief second, I feel the yellow warmth between us. I look at my father, so still in that bed that became too large for him over the course of several weeks.

ℰↃℰↃ

My mother takes a scissors and tears into the sleeve of the blouse she is wearing. I'm frightened at first by her behavior but neither Doctor Frank or my uncle seem to notice. She realizes she has frightened me and she explains it is an ancient custom that helps vent the anger she is feeling. She hands me the scissors and I make a deliberate cut into the ends of the sweater I am wearing. Julie knows a girl who cuts into herself in some misguided way. I wonder if this, too, relieves her anger. I can hear someone practice on the piano. I've never heard music from the house across the street before. Lisanne must be at home. Her mother said she had to practice. She's playing a passage from something familiar. I don't know the name of it. But I've heard it on the radio after *Lowell Thomas* and *The Lone Ranger*. Lisanne can play very well it seems to me. The music causes emotion to well up in me again.

Men in black suits come with a black hearse and my mother takes me upstairs. Tomorrow will be a funeral at a Jewish Chapel. The rabbi comes to speak with Uncle Abe.

Chapter 15

I sit with my mother, Uncle Abe, and Aunt Shirley in a little room off to the side while the chapel fills with people.

"A funeral helps those who grieve to accept the death," Aunt Shirley tells me. "Poor orphan!" she tells her friend from the beauty parlor then nods at me and at my father's casket.

A black ribbon has been pinned to the collar of my dress. My mother, aunt, and uncle wear them, too.

My father's casket is closed. I wish I could be where nobody would look at me, too, where they'd only see a box or a shell. But I'm on display today in this hive of a chapel. People file past in a line to tell us how sorry they are and then find seats for themselves. I've never met most of the people who take my hand, plant wet kisses on my forehead, and shake their heads at me. *People are bees*, I think angrily—*they buzz like bees. Women with beehive hairdos like Aunt Shirley and men with paunches from too little activity—drones.*

Then the rabbi comes forward and the buzzing and kissing stop. My mother and father's friends from the deaf club fill up several of the pews close to the front. Nobody translates what the rabbi says—for them or for my mother.

I've never met this rabbi but he seems to know us. He tells us how Morris Povich was the son of Emanuel and Sarah Povich and what a loving son, brother, husband, and father he was. "We give back a jewel," he tells the sea of serious faces.

And I hear Aunt Shirley praise god that neither Emanuel nor Sarah had to outlive a child. I never knew my grandparents. But the rabbi never mentions what my father gave to us. How my father painted the lake, or how he learned to sign because he loved my mother, or why he thought of me as his victory. While the rabbi talks, I feel an urge to laugh as strong as my urge to cry.

I try so hard not to laugh that my right eyelid begins to pulse. Thwong, thwong. It won't be controlled. I squeeze my eyelid in a tight blink but it doesn't help. Aunt Shirley is seated at my right and places a hand on my hand. A hat and a veil cover my mother's face, but mine is plain for everyone to see. I bury my face in her arm and shake and shake. Aunt Shirley then puts her arms around both of us and tries to free me from my mother, but I cling fiercely and pray for the rabbi to stop talking. When the pallbearers lift the casket, I am able to cry again.

A long ride to the cemetery on a hill follows the service. Most of the people go home after the chapel, and we, who remain, ride behind the hearse—a small procession of cars waving funeral flags. We drive a winding road through an old neighborhood. The wooden houses and a dilapidated tavern sit right on the road. The road becomes more countrified as it winds slowly uphill. We pass tiny houses with huge yards. Some are filled with rusty machinery. We find the cemetery smack on top of someone's back yard. Two tow-headed children, playing on a wooden swing set, stare at us and return to their play—indifferent. Over "The Lord gave and the Lord has taken away," I hear their mother call them in for lunch. The coffin is lowered.

"May he come to his place in peace."

My mother takes a folded paper from her pocket and throws it onto the casket. It is her drawing of the winged victory, she tells me. We throw token handfuls of dirt into my father's grave and return home. The grave diggers, local men who smoke behind a stone shed, will push the mounds of dirt back into the grave when we have left.

Chapter 16

The door to our house is open and people come in and out. If we're put on this earth to eat, then eat we must, and Jews eat for seven days and seven nights when someone dies. When the black hearse signaled to the neighborhood that my father had passed away, the neighborhood women must have held a great can-opening and Ben must have run out of Ritz crackers. Everyone has brought us casseroles topped with crumbs in glass Pyrex bowls.

We peek under the aluminum foil covers. There's green bean casserole made from frozen green beans and cream of mushroom soup, macaroni, and Velveeta cheese. Tuna-noodle casserole. Aunt Shirley outdid herself with her ginger ale Jell-O mold, and she's installed herself in our kitchen to make sure the casseroles get to the table. There are fruit baskets filled with waxy, tasteless, oversized apples and navel oranges bedded down in cellophane grass along with tiny jars of exotic jellies. A man in a soiled white apron delivers a platter of smoked fishes wrapped up in red cellophane.

Aunt Shirley and the neighborhood women keep

making more space on the counters in the kitchen and on the dining room table.

The hospital bed was taken away while we were at the funeral and the urinal and the bedpan are gone with it. The dining room table is spread with a white, linen table-cloth. Paper hot cups are stacked next to my mother's china. The china she painted when she worked at the factory. My father bought it for her as "seconds" at a factory store on one of our drives to the lake house. Schnapps, coffee, and soda sit on the sideboard. Food just sits there for hours at a time. People visit, eat, shake their heads, and go. More people come and do the same. The other children in our neighborhood visit on their way home from school. Cars are parked up and down our street. Sometimes, it almost feels like we're celebrating, but when I think about my father, I start to cry. No one minds if I cry now. The "no crying" rule has been lifted.

At sundown Uncle Abe's friends from Rhoda's Deli-catessen come to pray for my father. They don't have the ten men needed to pray. How silly not to use women when there were so many around anyway. I walk outside and sit on the steps.

Lisanne's father has come home from work, and he climbs the double staircase leading to their front porch. There are oak benches out on the porch now, but it's too cold and no one sits on them. The empty plant pots are waiting for spring.

He sets his briefcase down on a bench and taps on the living room window. The curtains part and I see Lis-anne's face bathed in light from a porcelain table lamp. She runs at once to the door and opens it. I wave. She waves back. "I've practiced, can I go across the street?"

"It's up to your mother."

"She says she's having flowers sent."

He thinks for a second and then I hear him say. "It

will be nice to visit. For a few minutes, we'll pay our respects."

Lisanne almost flew across the street and hugged me like a long-lost friend.

I brought them inside and introduced them to my mother. My Aunt Shirley made sure Dr. Glick tasted her Jell-O mold. As usual, I think she thought my mother needed help to do what everyone expected.

The first thing Uncle Abe asked was whether Dr. Glick was a Jew. He said he was not a religious one, but Uncle Abe handed him a prayer book anyway.

"Once a Jew, always a Jew. Even those who don't practice are obligated in the Mitzvos!" my uncle tells him.

I guess that means you can work on Saturday, something Mr. Kramer doesn't do. Mr. Kramer came over from next door wearing a dark suit and Mrs. Kramer in a dress instead of her housecoat but fitting the same way. They had their quorum and now could pray for my father. My mother and her friends from the deaf club said the mourner's prayer in sign. I am allowed to pray for my father in sign but not in spoken language.

Dr. Glick knew about five sign-language words—not quite ASL, our sign language. He told a story about a famous spy who knew how to sign and showed Lisanne. My mother and I showed Lisanne some signs and then show her how to finger spell. Then Mrs. Glick came over with the yellow chrysanthemum plant she had planned to bring over in the morning. At one point, she took Dr. Glick aside. "Why didn't you tell me where you were going? With a dinner sitting on the table, I have to guess?"

"It's okay, Ilse. It's okay. We just visited for a while."

"Your daughter has homework," she warns her husband. "Lisanne, in five minutes we will take you home."

At this point, Lisanne has learned about twenty-one words in ASL from my mother's friends, and she signs to Mrs. Glick. *"Not go home!"*

Her mother simply repeats herself.

My mother teaches Lisanne to sign, *"You should do your homework. You are always welcome in my house,"* which I translate for Mrs. Glick. Mrs. Glick does not say that I will be welcome in their house but Dr. Glick suggests that when our period of mourning is finished, we should study at the Carnegie Library after school some day, and he will drive us home. I say that it would be great and I'm looking forward to it, all the while I'm wondering why my eyes are now dry and if I will cry again. The crying and the desperate feeling of sadness that makes the crying happen has dried up in me. I look over to see my mother smiling, too and wonder if it is normal to have these wet and dry periods when someone has died.

I don't have to wait long to answer my own question. By nine-thirty the left-over casseroles and Jell-O molds are bedded down in Tupperware containers in the fridge. I think about my father bedded down in a wooden casket out in the frigid cold cemetery, and I'm able to cry again. This time the feeling is welcome, like the first clap of thunder on an oppressively humid day. My mother and I are completely alone for the first time in either of our lives. The sign for being lonely is to slide your left index finger down from your mouth to your chin with your thumb folded over the rest of your fingers in a kind of fist.

"Yes," she says and holds me.

There is no light in Lisanne's bedroom when I get ready for bed. I'm wondering how long she has been asleep when my mother comes into the room. My feet are on top of the covers. I've forgotten about the puncture mark on my thigh and my mother sees it before I can hide it.

"Pick up your nightgown again!"

"It's okay."

"It's not okay. Let me see that."

I show her the wound.

"How did you do that?"

"I don't know," I lie.

"What do you mean you don't know? That's a bad mark. Did someone do that to you?"

"No, Ma."

"Did you do that to yourself?"

"Of course not!"

"I'm worried about you."

Maybe Mrs. Kramer has told her the story about the girl who cuts herself. She'd have to write it out. But maybe she did. Sometimes she writes my mother notes about things.

"I'm all right," I insist.

"You need to put something on that. You might even need a tetanus shot." She finger-spells T-E-T-A-N-U-S. *"I bet you never put anything on that."*

I admit she's right.

She leaves the room, returns with iodine, and washes it over the wound. *"Tomorrow I want you to show it to Dr. Frank."*

"No, Ma! I'll be fine."

She sighs and takes a small box from her bathrobe pocket. *"Daddy wanted you to have his ring."*

It's his gold twist wedding band. Both my parents wore bands with braids. I take it from her.

"We'll buy you a gold chain for it when Shivah is over."

Then we both notice the light in Lisanne's bedroom. She's sitting at her window watching us hug, cry, embrace, and she signs to us and finger spells, "*Peace*."

"*I think she will be a nice friend,*" my mother tells me. "*Not like that other one.*"

Chapter 17

My father used to sing a song he'd translate from the Yiddish for us into sign. It always made my mother laugh.

I cannot be a rabbi because I am ignorant.
I cannot be a merchant because I have no merchandise.
Surely not a ritual slaughterer, because I have no knife;
Nor a teacher because
I do not know the Hebrew alphabet.
I cannot be a cobbler, a baker, or a smith.
And I cannot be an innkeeper because my wife is sloppy.

What can a wife without a husband be? And what of the daughter? A candle burns the seven days. Shiva is a cycle—a time suspended between times. A genesis, a gestation of seven days, defined unlike the question of life—when does it begin? When does it end? I walk around in my thin white socks, always against the rules but not now. The very moments when everything seems so normal are the moments that divide the grieving from the other. I look at the toaster and think of all the toast he burned and claimed he liked his toast burnt, or I look at the peeling paint in the bathroom.

"*Open the window just a crack to let out the steam,*" he'd always remind us.

I can see him on a ladder, the shower curtain pushed to the wall, sanding and scrapping little flaky patches above the showerhead. There are the moments when I find myself so steeped in the sadness that I want to tear at my chest—open it. But we suspend all aspects of our lives in this week—even anger.

In the museum, when the curators remove a painting from the wall, it is replaced with a cardboard notice: *This exhibit has been temporarily removed.* I, too, am temporarily removed. I am protected from Mr. Lang, Bill Rile, and that Fischman girl. The scab on my leg has disappeared and left a tiny patch of shiny white skin the size of a nail head. The angry bruise is gone. I remember it as a yellowish cloud without a sky.

My mother sleeps—naps she calls it—during the day when people come and go. I am left to deliver their condolences. At night, wraith-like in her nightgown, she wanders through the house. Walls cannot contain a grief bigger than the rooms of a house. At five in the morning, she sits beside me and rakes my hair with her fingers. "*Before you were born, your father and I had a bet you would have red hair like me because my brother has red hair.*"

My uncle, whom I've only met once, is expected this afternoon. He is coming alone, without his wife and two children, the cousins I've never met. "We'll have to get together," he will say.

The years have passed without our getting together. He calls each year, long distance from California on my mother's birthday. My father would convey his news. "*He never signed,*" she explains. "*He was eleven when I was born.*" The deaf still have no phone of their own.

Grief has its mundane aspects, too. I get up to take my cereal bowl to the sink. I've been eating puffed wheat and heavy cream left for a strawberry shortcake that someone made us—that no one bothered to whip. It sits better in my stomach than milk and I keep refilling the bowl until the pint of cream is gone.

We're not supposed to do anything for ourselves during Shiva, I think. Aunt Shirley's Janie scrubbed the house again yesterday. It's never been so clean. Aunt Shirley brings a bag of bagels and several cans of Maxwell House into the house. Coffee, sitting in the big urn since seven o'clock no longer smells fresh and aromatic.

"I'll make fresh," Aunt Shirley tells no one in particular but glances proprietarily at the men.

Ten men all heavily dressed for business, the quorum. They sway and mumble prayers in a corner of the dining room. It seems so disorderly, for a practice handed down by the generations since time itself began.

I hope Aunt Shirley won't launch into her "I'm glad I'm not a man" speech in which she explains how women are exempted from all obligations except those of caring and nurturing. The men pray they are glad not to be a woman but Aunt Shirley's thanking God she isn't a man. She makes it sound as if caring and nurturing are not work at all—God's gift to mothers and daughters. That's why caring and nurturing continue even on the Sabbath.

"Men can only work on the Sabbath in emergencies," she explains. "How lucky to have been born with a male organ. For whom can a girl pray, if the poor unworthy boy must pray before the King of Kings for children, wealth, and life insurance?"

Aunt Shirley sees to it that things get done—the things we've never gotten around to doing and, in all probability, we'd never do. Shirley, looking for a space

on the dining room table, sees the mum pot and smiles
with satisfaction. "Mums like cold weather, I'll put Mrs.
Glick's mum plant on the front porch. Mrs. Kramer's
bringing noodle kugel." Aunt Shirley is also keeping ac-
counts and she manages to identify each offering with its
donor. There will be thank you cards to write.

"She'll think we don't like the mums," I protest.

"No, she'll think we like her mums so much we want
to show them of. Of course, you know, Victory, Jews
don't send flowers!"

"Even to Christians?"

"Well, I suppose when in Rome…"

"The Glicks are Jewish."

Aunt Shirley shrugs. "There are degrees of everything, even being Jewish, I suppose."

"Why can't you just say they meant well," I snap at
her.

The yellow mums have encouraged me to hope for a
return visit. I jump when the doorbell rings and the house
lights flicker to announce someone has arrived. I would
like to go across the street and say thank you for those
mums. Show superior Mrs. Glick that I have manners,
have an excuse to exchange a few more words with the
pretty, blonde girl who studies and practices. Let her
acknowledge me, the mourner, once again. I crave this
friendship. I imagine us Nancy, Bess, and George. Of
course, only Nancy has a boyfriend, Ned. What a wonderful name, Ned. Which one am I?

*We ride in a green roadster up the winding drive to
the portico of an old mansion—haunted, they say, but we
know better—brave girls, suspicious girls. Save a kidnapped scientist. Not one who dropped the bomb. This
man looks like Dr. Salk.*

But a Shiva isn't something you go out and issue in-
vitations to. I must wait until Lisanne finishes whatever is

required of her and can only hope she will come to see me on her own.

A yellow cab stops in front of our house. A tall man with graying red hair pays the driver. The driver carries his valise to the porch. Aunt Shirley answers the door. "Barry. I would have known you anywhere—a few grays. Victory, do you remember your Uncle Barry?"

I am unsure what to say. He sends us a family picture and newsletter every year. He comments how grown up I look. He's lived away so long his accent is no longer Pittsburgh—a bit of Texas and a bit of California, but I'm not sure since I've never been too far from Pittsburgh.

"Victory, put your uncle's valise in the guest room."

"I have a reservation at the Sheraton. I'm flying out to Boston tomorrow. Where is Esther?"

"I'll get her," I say and fly up the stairs with relief. *"Ma, it's your brother Barry."* I fingerspell his name. She goes to check her appearance in the mirror, but it is covered with a sheet for Shiva. We descend the stairs together. My mother takes her brother's hand and gives him a hug.

"I'm sorry, Esther." I translate for him. "You were always adamant about the sign thing."

"Yes, that is our language at home," I tell him.

She shakes her index finger. *"It's better for Deaf to sign."*

"She never liked to read lips," he says. "Your father signed. Rest his soul."

Chapter 18

On the fourth day, Howie Merlman comes with his father Cy to help my uncle pray for my father.

"Have you met the new neighbor?" Cy asks Abe.

Across the street, Dr. Glick returns from work with his locked leather case. Or at least Lisanne has told the kids at school that her father's briefcase has to be locked and opened in private.

"Atomic secrets!" Howie chortles.

That's what we call Dr. Glick from then on.

"We should not have dropped the bomb," Howie says.

"Hindsight is the best sight," Cy tells him. "Remember Pearl Harbor."

"What if we hadn't dropped the bomb? Wash your mouth out and bite your tongue," my uncle tells Howie. "You don't mind if I set your kid straight? Well, anyway, Ha'ard—" That's how Abe pronounced Howard in basic adenoidal Pittsburghese. "—thousands of our boys got killed over there."

"Your politics isn't everyone's politics, Tut," Cy says to Howie.

"They shoulda dropped the bomb on that animal Hirohito," Abe tells Howie.

"The emperor's palace wasn't strategic enough," Howie retorts. "We were about power. The power of the bomb. We wanted to be recognized by the world, so we dropped the bomb on Hiroshima. On innocent people."

"Ha'ard, smarty pants, if you was going to drop the bomb, where'ud you drop it?"

"I wouldn't have dropped it."

"There were no innocent Japs, Ha'ard," my uncle says. "Cy, what are you teaching your boy?"

"Tut, this isn't the time or place for this discussion."

"You're right, Pop."

Julie's cat crouches on the back fence. He's gray with white socks, a stretching sphinx, about to pounce on a squirrel. But the squirrel hops onto the branch of an elm and skitters out to where the smaller branches, precariously thin, extend. *Smart squirrel*, I think. The branch bobs with its weight. The cat settles back and licks its belly.

"*The cat knows better*," my mother signs, unaware of the discussion.

"*What is Hiroshima?*" I finger spell the name.

"*A city in Japan that was bombed. The world could have caught fire. But we had to end the war.*" Her eyes darken to the color of cobalt. "*Your father thought there was another way to end it.*"

"*Did Dr. Glick make the bomb?*

"*Not alone. I doubt he was so important.*"

"*Cy Merlman asked Uncle Abe to ask Dr. Glick to meet Howie.*"

"*That's funny. Well, that's how the world works—at least for some people.*"

∽∾∽

"That kid's mishugana!" Abe says when they have gone. "Better play his cards right. He's gotta mouth on him. Cy lets him say whatever he wants."

It's been four days since the funeral. Julie comes every day after school to tell me what I'm missing. I still haven't told her about my stay in the principal's office. It occurs to me that someone from the school might visit. And I have a recurring daydream about how I will translate to my own advantage—right in front of Howie and Henry if they happen to be here, too.

"You didn't hand in your report on Madame Curie?" Julie says. "It was due before *it*." She doesn't say it. "Mr. Lane won't let you hand it in. He told everyone no exceptions."

I would rather die than let Howie and Henry find out that I haven't turned in my paper. They are both in Lisanne's class—the smart kids who skipped.

"You need a B-minus to get into Penn State," Julie says. "You can go to Kent State with a C. We're all going to get married, anyhow."

Not me, I think. I find it hard to say anything, except when I'm angry. *I'm considered dumb*, I think, *all these people coming and going and I don't know what to say to anyone.*

Chapter 19

We begin the game of guessing what would please and what would displease my father, mostly according to others.

"Your father would have been so proud to see how you and your mother have handled everything."

"Your father knew how much you loved him."

"Your father was a lamed vov, a special man who took on special burdens."

"Your father, may he rest in peace, should have, would have, didn't get, etc…"

Platitudes in abundance, meant as salve. Perplexing in that, in every wish for our welfare is the nagging idea that my mother and I are my father's creations—that we have no stake or claim in this tragic debacle of our lives. Everything we do from now on is what my father would have wanted.

Everything that happens is what would have saddened my father to see. We are coaxable, malleable, and suggestible to those little words. "Your father would have wanted…"

I decide not to do what my father would have wanted. We hear the reasons why he got sick, too. So maybe he wasn't so smart after all.

"Your grandma painted luminescent dials in the watch factory before she met your grandfather."

"A tumor grew on her neck when your father was a baby. No one knew."

"Madame Curie died of exposure to her new element that was supposed to cure people."

After his radiation treatments, my father returned with purple blotches, sicker. He couldn't swallow. In the shoe store, you can wiggle your feet in the X-ray machine and watch your foot bones dance.

"In Israel, they used to treat kids from the concentration camps for ringworm with X-rays," Uncle Abe says. "It saved having to shave their heads."

Mark Gruder, the kid with raspberry knots clinging all over his face, gets X-ray treatments for his acne. He comes back to school with his face looking like a faded plum. But he's cured.

What cures us, kills us.

Dr. Glick helped make the bomb they dropped over Hiroshima, and Dr. Salk's vaccine works, they're saying now. Most of Hitler's people don't look too different from the people I see each and every day. But no one trusts the people with slanted eyes called Japs. "Jap mother," I've heard Julie's older sister Barbara scream at Mrs. Kramer. The boys have started coming to call. Nice Jewish boys. Barbara's a senior, the prettiest Kramer. She sits on the front porch with all of her friends, and Julie sits on the stairs, watching.

In the morning, Mrs. Glick backs the car out of the driveway and into the street to where Dr. Glick waits with his briefcase. He gets into the passenger seat and they wait. I can see Dr. Glick open his newspaper. Mrs. Glick honks the horn impatiently. In a while, Lisanne comes out of the front door with her arms wrapped around heavy textbooks. I raise my window to try and hear what they say.

"You'll make your father late," Mrs. Glick scolds.

I see Lisanne climb into the back seat of the Ford wagon. Her mother looks like a fixture in this car, dressed in another one of her gray wool suits, nipped at the waist over a straight calf-length skirt, her hair in a neat bun. Mrs. Bomb-maker. Curiously, she returns in an hour with a brown bag of groceries and goes into her house.

When Mrs. Kramer gives Julie and me a ride, as she sometimes does when Mr. Kramer leaves her the car, she wears a housecoat and has her hair in rollers. I wonder if Mrs. Glick stays dressed in her suit all day but I don't see her come out again until a quarter of three when she drives Lisanne home from school—still dressed in her suit. Piano practice begins ten minutes after Lisanne returns, every afternoon. Are there cookies with milk set out and waiting?

The lights flicker off and on. My mother is calling from upstairs. Impatient. I run upstairs to see what she wants. There is Aunt Shirley with Janie. My father's closet door stands open, his clothing sorted in neat categories along the rack. Jackets, pants, shirts. The shoe rack is tidy, with shoes lined up like a small choir on risers.

Shirley's had Janie empty bits and pieces of paper from the pockets. *"Tell her she has no right!"* my mother signs vehemently.

"Tell your mother I had Janie tidy the closet," Aunt Shirley says. "It will be easier to get things ready for the thrift shop."

I translate.

"I don't want to send his things to the thrift shop."

"Maybe it's early," I tell Shirley.

"That bitch! You tell her to mind her own business."

My mother's pulling empty pockets inside and out. "*I wanted to go through those things. Victory, ask her where the garbage was put?*"

"She thinks there were things in his pockets she wants to see."

"Only some scraps of old paper."

"They mean something to her."

"Please, with everything to deal with, she has to go on about old gum wrappers. Tell her she's being very childish. Next week she'll be overwhelmed."

This I translate as: "*She says she's sorry and that she'll get everything out of the garbage.*"

My mother smiles and gives Shirley an apologetic hug.

I go out to the garbage. In a bag of dust and lint carefully swept by Janie, I find bits of paper; tickets to a college ball game, a bus timetable, a gas receipt, a dry cleaning ticket, Beamen's Gum wrappers—he loved to chew Beamen's Pepsin.

Clues, clues in the closet! Nancy Drew steers the green roadster out on the highway past quiet tidy farms. Pretty! She comments to herself. Oh, why can't all people be nice like this scenery and not make trouble?

I walk through the kitchen where Aunt Shirley is telling Mrs. Kramer how to make brisket with Coca Cola. Shirley sighs when she sees what's in my hands. She hands me a paper bag for the scraps.

Chapter 20

Shiva has ended. On Wednesday, I come downstairs early to find my mother dressed in her gray gabardine suit, hair done up in a bun—on her feet are black pumps. She is sipping from a cup of coffee and the remnants of a soft-boiled egg protrude from an eggcup. She is standing so I know she is in a hurry.

"Why are you dressed like that?" This suit is usually reserved for rare visits to a lawyer's office or to visit a bank.

"I am going to work."

"At the factory?"

"No, in the store. Abe says he'll pick me up." She consults the Bulova watch with the Roman numerals that was my fathers. It's heavy for a woman but she says she likes to feel it on her wrist now. *"You can have a ride to school."*

"It's too early. I don't want to be there so early." It's my first day back. *"I don't want to go."*

"You have to go. You missed so much."

"When are you coming home?"

"At five o'clock when uncle Abe closes the store. Do

you think you can make something for dinner for us when you get back from school? She points to some bills on the counter. *You can go to the Giant Eagle on your way home. Maybe a chicken? You could put it in the oven at three-hundred-fifty degrees."*

"Why do you have to work?"

"We need money. Can you get yourself breakfast?"

"I'll make a soft-boiled egg, too."

"You can squeeze color into the margarine." She indicates the clear plastic packet of white fat with a yellow dot in the center. *"I used the other one up. I need to go outside to wait. He should be here now. Kiss, hug?"*

I turn my cheek.

"Why didn't you tell me you were going to work?"

"It was decided before Daddy died."

"Can I work? I'd rather work than go to school."

"You need to go to school. Not a lot of money for everyone in linoleum store. I'm thinking of making tiles and selling them from the store."

"Tiles?"

"For floors, walls. I can paint them just like I used to do china in the factory. Okay, I better go outside in case. He says he'll honk."

I look glum.

"That's a joke."

"I get it."

"I'll see you this evening."

Alone in this house, I'm left with a feeling of stark emptiness. It's somehow too clean—uncluttered and bleak. My mother now wants to keep it that way.

I walk around, taking in the new arrangement of furniture. The folding chairs loaned to us during Shiva have not been picked up and remain in a circle, flanking our shabby sofa. The leather bound prayer books are in a stack on the side table. I think they came on loan from the synagogue. Some of the men who prayed came in with their own prayer books, prayer shawls, and yarmulkes. The sofa, for me, now carries memories of illness. My father spent his days on it until he was unable to get out of bed.

"*I think it should go to the Goodwill,*" I keep telling her.

But, for her, it keeps a little bit of him for a little bit longer. But I won't sit on it.

A gentle rap on the front door; interrupts these thoughts, and I see Lisanne peering around through our window. I open the door for her. She's humming "A diller, a dollar, a ten o'clock scholar."

"My mother had to take my father to the airport for an early flight," she says. "I'm supposed to take the streetcar so I thought I'd go with you. Where is your mother?"

"She went to work at the store with my uncle."

"And left you to your own devices?"

"And now we would miss homeroom, if we left right now."

"That's exactly what I intended." We both giggle. "Hmmm, that begs some possibilities," she says. "When does your mother come home from work?"

"Five o'clock. I was thinking the school probably still thinks I'm in mourning."

"You have a good excuse."

"And my mother would never know."

"My mother said she'd pick me up at school. That might present a problem."

"Not if you show up at the right time."

"And run smack into the principal. Let me think this through. How about I leave my mother a note to pick me up at the newsstand. I need a notebook. Do you have something to write on? She'll be back by nine-thirty."

I grab a few pieces of paper and a drawing pencil. Lisanne scrawls out a note instructing her mother to pick her up at the newsstand instead of in front of the school. She runs across the street to leave the note on the kitchen table and comes back quickly.

"You might want to close the Venetians. I don't want my mother to see me over here."

I go to the front window and close the slats. "Would you like some coffee?" I ask her.

"You know how to make it?"

"I think so."

"I always like the smell and taste of it."

"My mother won't let me have it. She's worried it will stunt my growth."

"Old wives tales!"

I take the Pyrex perk from the stove and empty the coffee grounds from the basket into the garbage. Then I wash and reassemble the pot, fill it with water, coffee grounds from a can of Maxwell house and set it on the flame.

"My mother uses Eight O'clock coffee," Lisanne says. "She says that's the best you can get in this country. For someone who went through the war deprived, she sure is snobby when it comes to things European. When we go to Vienna to visit her brother, we always have Viennese coffee with chocolate and whipped cream. So let's plan our day. I got my period so she let me sleep in—until seven-thirty. Did you get yours yet?"

"No!"

"Did your mother give you a book yet?"

"My mother already told me about it."

"Really! How does your mother explain things like that to you?"

I look blank. "What do you mean?"

"I mean if she can't talk."

"My mother talks. There's a sign for menstruation." I tap my fist on the side of my chin.

"How do you say, 'how do you say?'"

I sign.

"When I first got mine," says Lisanne, "my mother thought I didn't know but I looked in a medical book they have. Do you want me to show it to you?"

I sign, "*Yes.*"

"I'll bring it over, only it's hush, okay? There are a lot of things in it they don't want me to know about yet."

I translate what she says into sign.

"Are you really saying that?"

Coffee aromas fill our kitchen. I set out cups and saucers, sugar and cream. We leisurely drink our coffee at the kitchen table, butter some toast, and spread it with jam. We keep our voices low in case Mrs. Kramer suspects I haven't gone to school but her soap operas are blaring as usual. I didn't hear them during Shiva.

I ask Lisanne. "Who could watch that drivel?"

We hear a car and peek through the slats in the Venetian blinds. Ilse Glick has returned from the airport and she carries a bag of groceries into the house.

"So what does she do all day?" I ask Lisanne.

"She types my father's papers, manages his schedule. In Germany, her official title would be Frau Doktor—Woman married to doctor, basking in his reflections, with a child to promote her status, too."

"Do you ever go to the library?"

"I could have to go to the library."

"I like the library. We could go to the stacks. There are some books in the library a lot of people don't know are there," I say.

"Do you ever cut school?"

"Yes," I lie but it's not far from the truth. "It would be nice to spend the day in the stacks. The stacks have glass-brick flooring and you can look up and see a myopic view of whoever passes on the floor above."

"It's not very, hard is it?"

"I have to translate for my mother so they can't call her."

"That is an incredible advantage."

"*I know*," I sign with a smug look on my face.

"My parents are worried because they think you have difficulties in school. My mother says it's because your mother is—"

"So go on and say it."

She shrugs. "My mother says my father never sets limits. Makes her the bad guy. They never let me have friends. You should hear my mother: 'It must be a difficult life that child has,'" she says imitating her mother. "My mother asks questions but she always has her own answers anyway." She parodies her mother. "Lisanne! Lisanne! Are you out here? Oh, here you are. How are you, Victory? Come, it's time for you to practice, Lisanne."

"Always time for something."

With Lisanne for company, the day passes quickly. I open a can of tuna fish. We chop onions and celery and mix it with mayonnaise into the tuna. We heap our concoction onto toasted rye bread left from our Shiva. We make another pot of coffee and dip some Ruglach left out to stale into our cups. At two-thirty, we sneak out of my back door and stealthily run to the alley in order to meet her mother near the newsstand. "It was one of the best days of my life," Lisanne tells me.

Chapter 21

I'm almost asleep when a light phenomenon swirls over my ceiling and walls. Figures dance in kaleidoscopic patterns. At first, I am fearful that spirits are trying to contact me from another world then I realize the lights are making the sign for "*Hello, girl! Wake up!*"

I go to the window and find that Lisanne, across the street, is causing this phenomena. Lisanne perched on a stool in her window with a mirror and a flashlight, signing.

"*Hello, girl!*" I sign back.

She fingerspells "*LINDY WOODS.*"

"*Now?*" I ask.

"*Meet me at one a.m.*"

"*Are you crazy?*"

"*Yes! That's when my father goes to sleep.*"

❧❧❧

My mother doesn't sleep too well these days. Light is also on in the Kramers' living room, and I'm careful to duck low as I descend our porch stairs. I cross Sycamore

Street and walk around to the alley behind Lisanne's house. A dog barks. The ground is cold—two girls in bathrobes, shivering.

"How do you sign? I thought my father would never go to sleep,"

I show her and ask in sign and voice, "*How did you make that light?* How did you make that light?"

She catches on very fast and fingerspells her response.

"*It's physics.*" Then she says, "That's how a movie projector works."

I show her how I would sign it and then tell her in sign and speaking simultaneously so that the words in sign are clear, "*You could have woken my mother instead of me.*"

She looks flummoxed. "*At least it would be better than waking up my mother, but she takes a pill so there's no chance of that,*" she says, trying to fill in some sign words.

We hear low voices and a scurrying around in the bushes. Sounds of whimpering,

"*Someone is in the woods,*" I sign.

The whimpering becomes a terrified pleading. We crouch and practically crawl in the direction of the sound. Through the bushes, we can see a man and a woman. He has her pinned to the ground and his hands pull at her clothes. He puts his hand over her mouth to keep her from screaming. "Bitch, you asked for it," he hisses.

"I think it's Bill Rile with a girl," I whisper.

"*Who do you think the girl is?*" Lisanne signs. "*What do we do?*"

"*I don't know. We could scream for the cops.*"

The girl stops struggling. The man unzips his fly and hovers over her. Her eyes are crazy with fear light the dark. "You did this to me, you little cock-tease, so now you're going to let me fuck you." He pushes himself between her legs.

It is Bill Rile. I sign. *He's going to kill her.*

But it's over before either of us can react. Spent Bill zips his pants and runs out of Lindy's woods. We hesitate and then go to the girl when we are sure he isn't lurking around.

"Are you all right," Lisanne asks.

I repeat it. "Can't we help you?"

She begins to gather her torn clothing around herself. "Leave me alone."

"*I think she's a mill girl*," I whisper and sign to Lisanne.

"Can we help you get home?"

"You'll get me into trouble."

I shake my head. Oh, I don't think I ever want to be alone with a boy.

Chapter 22

In the morning, I go to school. Our school sits back on a hill and I mount the stairs, to the front entrance, hoping to avoid the office. Mrs. Clem, the truant officer, is sitting at a table in the front hall. I lower my eyes and head into the staircase foyer hoping to mingle with the crowd of kids heading up to their homerooms. Mrs. Newman is coming downstairs in the opposite direction with a stack of papers.

"Oh, Victory Povich, there you are. I'm so sorry for your loss. Please convey this to your uncle."

"Thank you." I lower my eyes again. Does she realize that my father was dying as she held me hostage in the office and that I wasn't there for him at the very end.

"Mr. Barnes wants to see you in the counselor's office," she says, abruptly changing the subject.

We call Mr. Barnes "Boom, Boom." When the marching band goes out to the field, it passes the counseling office. The drummer always salutes Mr. Barnes and hits his mallet extra hard on the drum. This always annoys Mr. Barnes when he is counseling some student, so the kids have dubbed him "Boom, Boom." I wonder why

Boom, Boom would want to see me. Maybe it's also to say that he is sorry about my father. But he doesn't seem to know anything about this.

"Come in, come in, Victory." His voice is rather cheery for someone about to say words of condolence. *Maybe someone got into Harvard,* I think. If you get into a really great school, Boom, Boom puts your picture up on his wall. Boom, Boom is in awe of the smart kids— who don't think he's very smart, according to Howie. In the spring when all the college acceptances are in, Boom, Boom posts them on a bulletin board in the entryway. The kids mill around and grouse, usually about the unfairness of the whole procedure. The students have to tell him where they want to apply and he decides if there are too many applications to that school, then someone can't apply and the parents come hollering and screaming at Boom, Boom.

Boom, Boom squints at me. "Victory, sit down."

I sit on the edge of the chair in front of his desk, hoping the marching band will pass by for its morning rehearsal.

"I've been in conference with your teachers," he continues, "and they think that you might be more appropriately placed in the vocational section of our school."

Only the "mill" girls matriculate in the vocational program in our school. Their fathers toil in the extreme heat of the steel mills, pushing fiery ingots in and out of huge ovens. We can see the flames from the chimney stacks on the distant horizon. Mills line the rivers of Pittsburgh. I only take gym with the mill girls. I'm terrified of field hockey. These are big, strapping girls, and aggressive with their hockey sticks. They don't like the Jewish girls—all college bound. I cannot imagine sitting through a day of classes in the midst of the mill girls.

I'm horrified and it probably shows on my face.

"You will learn skills for life—typing, shorthand. Just think, you could someday be a secretary."

"I don't want to be a secretary."

"Now look, Victory, your grades are not going to get you into a college. You need a C+ average for Kent State."

A school snobby, Boom, Boom would probably look down on. It hasn't become famous as the scene of a war protest yet. It's just a good old fall back school for the Julies of this world who can't afford a finishing school.

"Everybody's time is wasted by having you matriculate in the college bound program, and, between you and me, there's no real difference for our girls anyway."

"So, do I have a choice?"

"My job is to make suggestions."

"I'm not interested in learning how to type or to take shorthand."

"Then I am afraid you will just keep sliding farther and farther behind. I worry you will drop out at sixteen without any preparation for the world."

"I'm late for my homeroom. Can I go?"

"Yes, yes of course. I'll give you a pass so the teacher knows you were seeing me."

"Aren't you forgetting to say something?" I stare at him and he looks away.

As I exit, I hear him mutter to himself, "Strange one, that."

Chapter 23

Esther's crouched over the bottom drawer of the old green metal file trying to stuff the "Ws" into the right folder. Wishnick, Weinstein, Wunderlich. Everything is out of order—her dead husband's mess. She's so intent on fixing the folder that she doesn't see Abe standing in the doorway wiping sweat from his brow. He begins a dialogue, "If you could hear, you would understand. I always wondered why my brother would give up so much opportunity to be married to a woman who couldn't talk."

Esther's hair is now streaked with gray, but it's thick and flows simply from a pony clasp down her curving back. Even in a sweater and skirt, she's beautiful.

"You wouldn't understand what life with Shirley can be like," he continues. "She's slept with drain pipes on her head for the last thirty years. Can you imagine having to make love to a piece of metal? 'Who're you dressing like this for?' I ask. She can hardly turn over. She once had an ass, you know. Last week she buys a leather suit. Green leather. It takes the whole cow to cover her. 'Tomorrow, Abie, tomorrow!' Always tomorrow! May God forgive me, you are beautiful, Esther."

He rushes toward her. Esther smiles nervously and back away.

"I think you might look good if you loosen your hair." He mimes undoing a ponytail clasp.

Esther shrugs, not understanding what he wants.

"Let me," he says.

She shakes her head and points to her ear to remind him that she can't hear, just in case he's forgotten in the excitement of whatever he is trying to say. "You poor beautiful thing."

She stares at him blankly.

He beckons and gestures toward the door, indicating that he wants her to go with him. "I want to show you something. Follow me."

She closes the drawer warily. It jams. Abe rushes to her aid. "You're so provocative. Don't you know that? Look! look!" He grabs her hand and makes her feel his swollen crotch. "Can't we?"

Esther pushes him away roughly.

"My god! You're strong, too. Like an ox. Esther, I'll pay you more than you're worth."

Esther now has no doubt about what he wants, and it disgusts her. How could he? She shakes her head, frightened, and tries to leave. He places his hand across her mouth. Her eyes dart wildly, seeking escape but finding none, and, finally decides changing tactics is her only hope. She takes her hand and turns it toward his, as if she is about to offer him caresses.

He hurriedly unzips his gabardine trousers. "Oh, you could make me so happy," he moans, letting them drop. His fat belly protrudes over his swollen organ. "Come, wild one. You need it, too. Too long! It's not good for you either." He gets down on the floor. She takes his pants from him and then his under drawers.

"Lock the door!"

She sees his lips move but doesn't care what he's saying.

"I'll be good to you," he moans.

Esther smiles benignly and, with the pants and undershorts folded over her arm, she exits and locks the door behind her. Being deaf, she can only feel the vibrations from his pounding on the door.

ϲ϶ϲ϶

I'm surprised to see my mother home at three p.m. *"Mommy, Mommy. You're home early! Don't you know what happened?"*

She acts surprised. *"No! I didn't feel so well and told Abe I needed to go home early."*

"Oh my God, Mommy! Uncle Abe got robbed after you left. Aunt Shirley called. They made him take of his pants and they locked him in the back room."

"Really? Clever thieves."

I never learned the truth of this until after Uncle Abe's funeral many years later.

Chapter 24

Early on the morning of my fifteenth birthday, my mother came into my room glowing with excitement. *"We have to go to the lake and check on the house."*

It's a wintry day and still dark. I groan and put the pillow back over my head. She grabs it from me.

"Ma!" I protest. *"It's Saturday. I want to sleep until noon or maybe three o'clock. As long as I want on my own birthday."*

She fans me with a pink paper. It has the watermarks of an official document. *"You have a lesson,"* she signs vehemently.

I grab the paper out of her hand. *"What's this, Ma?"*

"A permit."

"A permit?"

"A permit to drive."

"To drive?"

"Why not?"

"Why not? I'm only fifteen. That's why not."

"Read it."

I look at it closely. *"It says I'm sixteen. I'm fifteen."*

"Your father's car is in the garage."

"You can drive, Ma."

She's adamant. *"They never let me. Now it's too late."*

"Why?" I ask. *"Annette drives."*

"Annette will show you how."

Annette is my mother's friend from the deaf club—a big woman with tawny skin. She and my mother worked together in the china factory before I was born. Annette still does. Sometimes she brings my mother pretty plates and trinkets from the factory kiln. My mother says they're defective. Sometimes they're slightly warped but only an astute eye could tell. Today Annette has had someone call in sick for her and she has come to teach me how to drive.

"What if someone finds out?"

My mother doesn't seem to care. She wants to go to the lake and, once she's there, she likes the solitude. *"I don't want to have a guest every time I go there,"* she tells me.

That's why she's never asked Abe or Shirley to drive her there. She lives in her world of silent seasons—of ripples on the water—a world of hands and gestures.

"Hurry up and get dressed."

"What if the neighbors see?" I wonder how best to disguise myself.

The three of us are in the alley—my mother, Annette, and me. Along the back alley, there are garages of every size and shape. Ours is a rickety wood and stucco structure that holds only my father's car. I'm wearing my disguise—a babushka covered with a hat and sunglasses. The collar of my coat is pulled up over my chin, and I look like a spy. My mother is carrying a picnic basket, and it's too cold to have a picnic.

"Why are you bringing a picnic basket?"

"*Just in case, you are hungry.*"

My stomach is doing flip-flops. I just had breakfast.

My mother unlocks the padlock on the narrow garage. It's dank and cobwebs have formed. A spider has hung a web over the back fender of the ford. "Okay, Victory," now Annette says. "You get into the driver's seat and there's a lever to bring it forward." The stucco walls are close and we can open the car doors only wide enough to get into the car. My father used to pull the car out and bring it around to the front, but today it is better that no one sees what is going on.

I sink down into the driver's seat. I've gotten much taller this year, but I seem to be growing in my legs and not in the length of my back. I can barely see over the steering wheel. My mother always has a solution for everything. She takes off her own coat, rolls it up and tucks it under me. The buttons press hard into my buttocks but I can see the stucco wall and old garden gear out of the front window and don't complain. Now I want to try to drive.

"*This is the clutch.*" Annette finger-spells this word.

I move the gearshift as I am shown and the car rolls forward into the wall and smashes an oil can.

"*She doesn't know the brake!*" my mother signs furiously.

She and Annette are not aware that someone might have heard the loud crash.

"*There's no damage. It's a rusty old can,*" my mother continues as if nothing has happened. "*Show her the brake and how to reverse.*"

"*Ma, I'm not sure I want to do this.*"

"*If you get scared, you'll never do it.*"

"*Is that what happened to you?*"

"*Yes, my father never trusted me, so I had an accident.*" She's never told me about this. She shakes her head. *"It wasn't bad but everybody thought it would be for the best if I didn't drive."*

Annette winks at my mother. *"This is about freedom."*

I restart the motor. The ignition squawks in protest.

"Just relax. You didn't turn it far enough." Annette has a soothing manner. *"Nothing's wrong. You're just learning to drive and no one is going to make any kind of fuss about it at all. The brake's here, and that's the shift and clutch. Don't step too hard now. On farms, kids drive when they're eight."*

She shows me how to let the car roll out into the alley far enough to turn the wheel. Once in the alley, I roll down the street then the boulevard. I follow the route to the highway over the bridge. I don't drive the car off the bridge and into the river—this has been my greatest fear since I have turned on the motor. I'm only wishing for a year to pass so I can hold my head high and be the first sixteen-year-old to have a license. It's like the world is opening up for me.

That's what it feels like to drive, that is until Annette tells me to make a right turn onto a highway ramp. I panic, and pull onto the gravel shoulder, wheels spinning.

My mother has fury in her eyes. *"You are doing so well. Why are you stopping?"*

I'm defiant. *"I don't think I want to go onto the highway. I'm just learning."*

I'm more trusting of Annette. "Just listen, Victory," she says in her speaking voice so I don't have to look at her. "I'll talk you through it. It's not so different from the other streets."

She guides me back onto the asphalt and I cautiously follow the turns in the ramp. "Now whatever you do, don't stop. You want to have speed when you get onto the highway. There's enough space. Just go."

I don't quite believe her. I hesitate and see a truck in the rearview mirror. It is gaining steadily, and now the driver's angry face in the windshield fills up my mirror and the sound of his horn fills my ears. Neither Annette, nor my mother has heard the honking. It feels like the truck is sitting on top of us. Annette turns around and looks.

"Don't let him bother you."

"I can't!" But I don't dare to sign with my hands on the wheel or look at Annette.

"There's lots of room. Just step on the gas," Annette screeches.

Unlike my mother, Annette was not born deaf. Her deafness was caused by meningitis she contracted as a small child.

"He won't let me." I pull over again to let the truck pass.

The truck driver stops, too, right beside me, leans far over to the right, and through his open window screams, "Woman driver! Go home and scrub your floors!" Then he screeches off to Annette giving him the finger.

"Don't let anyone pressure you, ever! You can do anything you want to do. Do you understand me, Victory? Did he bother you or did he bother himself?"

From now on, I am not bothered. My driving lesson at fifteen started the era of "Victory not bothered." I know I should not let my eyes stray from the road ahead but I have a sudden impulse to check my attire. With one hand grasping the wheel tightly, I glance quickly down at my disguise. I am emboldened by a vision of Nancy Drew's roadster with its lengthy nose sporting headlamps and vertical grill, with barely enough space for Bess and George in its cockpit. But there is a rumble seat not covered by the convertible top. That's where I'd put Lindy should I ever have to transport her. She'd be exposed to the elements while Lisanne and I stayed warm and secure. I'd put Julie Kramer into the rumble seat too.

The shiny body of Nancy's roadster is camouflage green. Considering that Nancy always takes it on her adventures into the dark and murky countryside, green is a far better color for getting stuck in the mud or having to move a downed tree in a thunder storm. *This is what driving a roadster feels like*, I tell myself as I yank off my headgear and toss it behind the seat.

I catch my mother's surprised look in the rearview mirror. Maybe Nancy learned to drive at fifteen, too. Isn't that something an over-indulgent father would see to? Maybe the roadster was her mother's. Today I'm driving my father's roadster off for unknown adventures. We haven't been to the lake in months and maybe evil lurks there that my mother and Annette won't be able to hear. I am called to ferret it out. Of course, I will have to bring along admiring friends to help with my adventures.

"Now you're driving too fast!" My mother is leaning over the seat. Both she and Annette are astonished by my sudden transformation. I partially release the accelerator and the passing countryside once again fills my peripheral vision.

Relieved, Annette and my mother forget me for the next hour. They chat and sign, and I fix my eyes to the road. I am not bothered until I have to pee and pray we get to the lake house. I don't want strangers at some diner to wonder at the new driver. To my relief, the highway begins to narrow into a local highway and an old abandoned gas station looms in the distance. The last machine anyone serviced there, an old Ford truck, stands rusting at the pump. It stands on its axles with tires leaning against its door. The windows of the gas station have been boarded up forever. If anyone ever tears it down, we will have no way to finding the lake road.

"Okay. Now you have to clock five miles. It's five from the gas station," she reminds me.

"I remember, Ma. I started already."

"So, now you are a driver." Annette beams proudly and smiles at my mother.

Our property is dotted with small boulders. Mature trees rise out of the ground on thick trailing roots—evidence that once the lake encroached farther into the shoreline. We find the remnants of a heavy snowstorm we have missed. Originally a cabin, the house has been added onto, in a haphazard way, by my father and mother. It has been boarded up for the past six months and seems smaller. The property is darker than I remember it. I drive on to the gravel bed and park. The plumbing is turned off and my mother tells us to pee out by the shed. There we are, three women lifting our skirts and steam-peeing into the frozen ground. Annette is wearing a girdle and has to struggle to get it down far enough. First, we're laughing and then the three of us begin to cry.

My mother walks ahead while Annette pulls up her girdle again. We find her by the front entrance, searching over the doorjamb for the key.

Across the lake, I see the clapboard, screened-in structure that serves as our community house. It, too, is now boarded up. It contains a television set, a bar from which Rolling Rock and Iron City beer flows, and stacks of folding chairs.

We hearing members are always expected to translate the sports events for the deaf. My father will be missed. He and I were the main translators.

My thoughts return to the house. Everything is musty and moldy. It was closed up in the summertime with the humidity from the lake, and now that it is cold, dankness pervades the glum interior. My father's paintings are still stacked against a windowless wall.

ɛ↗ɔɛ↗ɔ

"*Is it difficult for you?*" Annette asks me.

I nod.

"*What will she do with all of those pictures? They deserve to be in a museum.*"

I never thought of my father as a dead artist before. I can see the *Winged Victory* room, not marbleized and gray but spiked with deep colors and bold shapes the way my father painted them.

I wonder what my mother is expecting as she opens the door. I am familiar with the sounds of our house—the rattling door because the latch doesn't hold, the airy buzz through the pipes when the cold water runs, the swish and tread of rubber soles. I try to remember the last time we visited. I want so desperately to bring back all of these sensations—to bring back a little bit of my father. Maybe the warm feeling will come again now that we are here.

My father created my room out of an attic crawl space. I helped him hammer the nails into the panel board. My window rises from the floor and I can't stand anywhere but under the a-frame of the roof. There was no choice for my bed but the middle—like a princess with a slanted rooftop under a canopy of trees. I lie down on the white, tufted spread and feel it press into my face. Once I pressed my face into it so long and hard my mother thought I'd caught the measles.

The lights flicker. My mother is calling for me, and I come back down my ladder stairs. The boarded windows give the house a sense of intense closeness.

"*It's too bad you can't really see it,*" my mother tells Annette.

"*Oh, but the lake must be so very beautiful in the summer. Are you going to come back here this summer?*"

"*I'm thinking to. But I suppose it will depend on*

what Abe will pay me and when I will be free."

"You didn't tell me that, Ma. Are we poor?"

"Well, we will have to pay for food, clothes, and our house mortgage. We can always rent this if we need to."

"I don't want to rent it."

"Just for part of every summer. It brings in good money."

The reality of making plans without my father has been an abstraction until now. It's settling slowly into my fifteen-year-old psyche that someone will have to bring in money for us to survive. Like the story, my mother and father once told me about their marriage—the *Winged Victory* might have wings but it doesn't have a head. Every day chisels away at some other part of me. My father has, after all, left the mess to our own devices. Our car seemed so big out on the highway today. It seemed to rock like the rowboats that pitch about on waves coming into the dock before a storm. When the water gets rough, a boat can be tossed good and hard.

A stack of canvasses sits in one corner. His painting span was so short, I know my mother will never part with them. I'm angry, however, and say for spite in a tone that rings practical, *"Maybe someone will buy one of Daddy's painting. You can't leave them here."*

"Never!"

"You're going to just leave them here to rot?"

"I'm going to take them back to Pittsburgh but not today. They will be fine for the winter. We will come up every weekend and make sure everything is fine."

"I don't want to come up every weekend if we're just going to rent it to some old stranger."

Annette puts her arm around my shoulders. *"Victory, you have to help your mother now. You have to help each other."*

I want to nest there in the crux of Annette's arm but I resist and turn away.

My mother taps me on the shoulder and I wipe her hand away. "*Victory, go to the car and get the picnic.*"

I stomp out, leaving the front door wide open. From the car, I can see into the house.

"*She'll get over it,*" my mother tells Annette. "*I'll go see if there are some Rolling Rocks in the fridge and a Coke for Victory.*"

Our fridge is a Frigidaire—the old kind with rounder curves and a handle that locks.

We eat and then my mother and Annette begin to hatch their plans.

"*A kiln?*" I ask.

"*Have to bake tiles.*"

"*You need to put it at least twenty feet from the house and build a shed around it.*" Annette begins to walk an area, counting the feet by the size of hers.

They fingerspell words like "*thermo conductivity, high fire, low fire, immeasurable degrees of temperature*" and how to reach them. They are so immersed in their plans that they startle when I leave the shore edge where I've been skipping flat stones over the water to join them.

"*So you are interested. Can be business for you, too, someday.*"

Annette nods. "*Your mother is smart lady. Soon no need for store. She gets all the orders she can handle.*"

Mother sighs. "*I wish I had done this when Morris was alive. He wouldn't have needed linoleum store.*"

Chapter 25

Lisanne now knows enough sign to carry on a conversation with my mother, and my mother loves her for learning. We are sitting on my porch, eating freshly-baked oatmeal cookies. My mother's are so caramelly, just enough stick to the teeth. We're drinking lemonade, fresh squeezed with squeezed lemon halves floating in the pitcher. Ilse Glick is madly waving and pointing to her wristwatch.

"I'm deaf," Lisanne signs across the street to her mother. Then she turns to me. *"What was it like?"*

"What was what like?"

"You know. I saw you drive your car."

"It wasn't me. It was my cousin."

"Well, it sure looked like you."

"I don't have my license yet.

"Do you swear to tell me the truth?"

"It wasn't me!"

"No, it was. Fess up!*"* she all but screams at me.

"Okay, her friend taught me how. My mother needs to go to our house at the lake. She can't drive."

Ilsa Glick now crosses the street. Lisanne's father

loads two suitcases into the trunk of the Ford Wagon sitting in their driveway. "Lisanne, our plane leaves in an hour. Mrs. Schmidt is making your supper."

She signs that her parents are going to New York for a convention.

Ilse is now more impatient than ever. "I need to leave."

"You can go," Lisanne says in the sweetest voice ever.

"You need to practice Czerny. Mrs. Josephs will be here tomorrow for your piano lesson. She says you need to work on your left hand."

"Don't worry. I can get everything done."

"Can you stop that for a minute, Lisanne?" Ilse says testily. "Come with me for a minute." She pulls Lisanne aside but not so far that I can't hear what she tells her.

"You never let me have friends!" Lisanne says.

"That's not true. I want you to be selective in your friends. I think that's a reasonable thing to expect from one's daughter. It doesn't mean we can't have sympathy for those less fortunate than us. Lisanne, you will always have more than that girl will. Is that a sound basis for a friendship? No!"

"Why ask questions when you always have your own answers, anyway? Mom, you're a Nazi!"

She slaps Lisanne hard. "My family defied the Nazis and your father came from one of the best Jewish families. Do you think we didn't suffer in that war, too! You are making us late for our plane. You have five minutes and then you go inside."

Lisanne returns, rubbing her cheek. "The bomb makers are getting together."

Ilse nods to me. "Homework for you, too. Victory."

"We might do a project together," Lisanne says.

Ilse looks doubtful and turns to leave. Lisanne points

to the livery statue that heralds the front walk of her house.

"When they're gone, I have plans to paint the face and hands white. They have them all over Oakridge but this is the north."

"They're all over Pittsburgh, too. Boy ones and girl ones. Aunt Shirley calls adult colored people boys and girls."

"What do they call kids?"

"Colored boys and girls. Just think if everyone woke up with white boys and girls?"

"Now that's a project I could sink my teeth into."

We both laugh hysterically.

"But what if we get caught walking around with a can of paint."

"Say it's pancake batter."

"I'll drive us." It suddenly occurs to me as Ilse and Konrad wave, pulling out of the driveway, that I have a new-found freedom.

"Well, what are we waiting for, let's get some paint."

"Don't you have to do your homework?"

"Ilse and Kon are gone for two days."

"I don't have any money."

"I can get some," Lisanne says. "C'mon."

Mrs. Schmidt is fixated on the soap opera *Love of Life* and hardly looks up.

"No homework?" she asks Lisanne in a thick German accent.

"I have a science project, and I need to buy some things."

"You want I drive."

"Not necessary."

Mrs. Schmidt looks relieved as she opens a drawer in her nightstand and retrieves a wad of bills. She hands several bills to Lisanne. "Your mother left this for us."

Out on the street Lisanne grins. "So now you've seen Dingle-pooper. You know my mother doesn't want me to speak German to her because she has the accent of a butcher."

I think about that. Julie's father is a butcher and he has a very thick Pittsburgh accent.

"Now what about your mother?" Lisanne asks.

"She and Annette are always busy painting tiles these days. It's my mother's new business. She intends to sell them out of Povich Floors."

We go inside. Esther has the dining room table covered with tiles. In the basement, twenty-five-pound packages of white clay are stacked next to a dusty table. She feeds moist clay, that comes out looking like thick lasagna noodles, into an extruder. She then cuts them into squares and various shapes.

"She hates linoleum and working for Uncle Abe. All he lets her do is file the invoices. She's starting a tile business. She can talk to a customer as well as the next person, she says. She's building a kiln up at our lake house."

Annette sits at the dining room table painting a lily on a three-inch bisque square tile. My mother has lined up broken tile samples.

"She can make replicas and replace broken tile," I tell Lisanne. "She's always mixing glazes. Right now, she does the bisque in a garbage can out back and the neighbors are wondering why she burns so much garbage. That's how you have to do tiles, you can't paint them until they are bisqued. I'm going to learn how to do this, too."

We make a fuss over the tiles.

"*Going to be successful,*" Annette signs to Lisanne and me.

"*We have to get some supplies for Mrs. Schmidt,*" I

tell my mother. *"We're walking so don't ask me to get anything."*

"Annette and I are taking these to the store." Mother indicates a box of glazed and fired tiles. *"She can give you ride."*

"No, we want to walk."

"Well, you can have ride back."

"No, thank you," Lisanne signs.

Chapter 26

Esther sits in the rear of the store at her dead husband's scarred desk, juggling between the linoleum invoices and her own orders to fill.

Abe is in the front when a plump middle-aged woman with a mane of unruly gray hair enters. "Can I help you, Madame," he asks.

"I don't know. The plumber left a mess on my bathroom floor," she wails. "I need hexagonal dark green and white tiles and they don't make the same kind anymore. The plumber told me to come here."

"I sell linoleum, madame. Why go to the expense of tile? Let me show you."

"But I want to see that tile woman."

Noticing the broken tile the woman is waving and sensing the inquiry might be for her, Esther comes forward, her pad and pencil at the ready. Exasperated, Abe throws up his hands.

Esther writes: *What are the measurements?*

The woman takes another tile out of her pocket book, this time an unbroken one, and hands it to Esther. The glaze is a green from another era, cracked and chipped. *I can make!* Esther writes. *How many do you need?* The woman writes a number on the paper Esther hands her, and Esther writes up an order. The woman leaves, pleased.

Abe scrawls furiously: *I sell Linoleum.*

She scrawls: *Why not tiles?*

He scrawls: *It's another business.*

She scrawls: *It covers floors. It can even cover walls. Who puts linoleum on walls?*

He scrawls: *I won't let you do this here.*

She scrawls: *Then you buy me out.*

Abe: *That's outrageous.*

Esther: *No, it was my husband's business, too and I can't live on what you pay me.*

Abe: *I took you under my wing. Where would you be?*

Another woman enters holding tiles.

"I'll be at Rhoda's getting a cup of coffee." He stomps out.

Chapter 27

Mr. Berger of Berger's hardware is a harried little man with a thick Eastern European accent. Berger serves customers from behind a counter over which hang a myriad of gadgets and tools. The kids all know to look at his wrists. He has numbers tattooed there from the concentration camp. He won't answer questions about the tattoos. The wall behind Berger is lined with drawers crammed with nails, screws bolts, and sundry items of attachment. Lisanne and I wait for our turn.

For Berger, we seem to be a breath of fresh air after all the demanding workmen. "Ladies, so nice of you to stop by. What can I do for you?"

"We need paint for our science project?"

"Any particular color."

"Oh, white, it has to be white," we both say in unison.

"It so happens, I have to see if I have white paint in stock." Berger laughs as our faces drop in disappointment. "Don't be so worried, ladies. I always have white paint in stock."

We purchase two cans and some brushes. "Give my regards to your uncle, Abe," he says as we exit, giggling, onto the sidewalk.

Then we notice Uncle Abe having coffee in a booth near the window with Cy Merlman and Howie at Rhoda's delicatessen next door. It is no use trying to sneak by. They notice us too. Howie waves to us.

As we enter Rhoda's Delicatessen, I hear Uncle Abe's interpretation of his day with my mother. "My brother, may he rest in peace! Well, anyhow, I don't want to go back in there. It's so hard having that woman around. I'm writing notes all day long. It was bad enough when my brother was alive, but now it's impossible."

I see Cy put his hand on Abe's and Abe turns around.

"Hey, Victory and Lisanne," he calls out.

Cy pats Abe on the shoulder. "So who's the little shikse with your niece, Abie?"

"The little shikse is Jewish—at least half. And you should know she's the daughter of Konrad Glick. He's nuclear physicist with Oppenheimer and the crowd that made the bomb." Uncle Abe has that dyspeptic look he gets when he's in Rhoda's with his male friends. He's not too happy to see me and is surprised that Howie has invited us in.

"Yeah, Howie told me about him. Didn't you, Tut? Tell the girls to join us, my treat."

This pleases Howie and he beams. "Really?"

"Girl shy?" his father asks and Howie conveys annoyance. "So bring them on over," his father continues.

Howie is up out of his seat. We are invited to eat with them. "I'm eating the most humongous pastrami sandwich you ever saw," he says

"*I guess I should tell my mother I'm here,*" I sign to Lisanne.

"Are you faking?" Howie asks.

"No," says Lisanne.

"She's telling you the truth. My mother and I are teaching her." I sign as I say this.

"Are you girls going to cheat on tests?"

"Well, that has never occurred to us," Lisanne says. "But the possibilities are endless."

As we make our way to their table, we pass the deli case to watch Frankie the owner pull a huge, red fatty corned beef brisket out of its hot brine. He cuts slices on a butcher block and slaps them onto rye bread. The waitress Loretta stands in front of the case waiting for her order. "An institution in an institution," my father used to say.

She's as wide as she is tall. Five feet square. "Ladies, you joining those fellows back there?" she asks.

"They are!" says Howie. "Cy's treating!"

"Ess mayn kind. He's a rich man." She looks us up and down, probably thinking we could both stand to put some weight on.

Cy takes advantage of Howie's absence to ask Abe about the lake property. "So tell me something, Abe."

"Shoot!"

"Isn't that your brother's property up in Lakeville?"

"Yup, that's another story."

"Is she going to keep it now he's passed away?"

"She says so or rather she signs. Well, anyway—"

"Well, here's something to think on."

"I'm listening," says Abe.

"If she ever wants to sell, the group I'm invested with might want to take it off her hands."

"It's not much of anything. The land is nice but the house is a privy if you know what I mean."

Over hearing this, I'm conscious of how we talk in Pittsburgh. Sluggish, loggy, Schwah. The pollution has gotten into our sinus cavities, and the scrim hangs over Pittsburgh speech, too. Lisanne's speech is bright and perky.

"Anyhow, now that it looks like Ike'll bring the highway through, Murray Schwartz is fixing up that hotel up there, the one I've been sitting on," Cy says. "I invest with Schwartz. You know Schwartz. He married a Stark from the restaurant Starks. I'm sure we'd be interested in the land."

Abe nods. "Maybe I'll feel Esther out again."

"No, don't if it's too soon for her. Wait a bit. You might be interested in going in with us yourself. These fellows have a lot of experience."

"Tell me more."

We have just about reached their table. "Later! I've got guests." Cy raps his fingers impatiently on the table. "My matzoh ball soup is getting cold."

Lisanne and I sit and quickly put the bags with the paint under the table before anyone can see what is inside.

When we came in, I was surprised to see Uncle Abe with Howie Merlman's dad, although I've heard him drop Cy's name ever since the day Howie showed up with Henry Frank.

I reluctantly give my uncle a hug. Cy signals Loretta. "Loretta, get over here! These girls are starving."

The coffee pot dangles off her wrist. "What'll it be, ladies?"

We open the huge menu. Three pages of Pastrami and chopped liver combinations, herring, soups, egg salad, lox and eggs, coffee, Sanka, cheese cake.

Lisanne and I shrug and look at each other. "How 'bout corned beef?" Cy says. "On rye. Pickles."

"I can't eat all that," says Lisanne.

"No protesting!"

We giggle. Loretta writes on her pad. "Two corned beef on rye. Coleslaw. Gentlemen, kin I git yinz sumpin' else?"

"No for me but maybe for your boyfriend here." Abe means Cy but Loretta says. "Which one? Junior or senior."

"You lay off him, Loretta," says Cy.

"He knows uhm kiddin. How about you, son? Coffee?"

"He don't drink coffee," says Cy. "I'll take more of that drain opener you got there and don't you dare give none to Howie, and that's final, Tut."

"Dad, I always drink coffee," Howie says and shoves his cup over to Loretta.

She pours a cup for him.

"Since when?" asks Cy. Their eyes lock.

Howie takes the sugar dispenser and holds it upside down over the cup. The granules swirl in the brew like new galaxies.

"I'll have coffee," I say.

"So will I," says Lisanne.

"Well, I'll have to talk to your mother about that," says Uncle Abe.

"Girls are different," Cy tells him. "They grow up faster."

The pot in Loretta's hand is almost empty. "I'll git yinz fresh."

As Loretta waddles off, Cy turns to Lisanne. "They tell me you're almost as smart as Howie. He's going to Pitt for some math this year."

"She already knows that, Dad."

"Okay, Tut! They don't have any courses left for him to take in high school."

"Dad!"

"I think it's great!" says Lisanne.

"See? Listen to her. Let me have my pleasures, Tut. If Abe and I had gone to college, who knows?"

"Anyhow, who knows?" says Abe. "Your father's a smart man. You got your brains off him."

"Thanks, Abe."

"High school is pretty useless if you ask me," says Lisanne.

Cy laughs.

"My niece doesn't need any more negative influences," Abe says,

"She's an under achiever," Lisanne says in my defense.

"Well, I have to say, I never saw anyone read as much," says Abe. "Now explain that to me."

"I don't need anyone to explain me, Uncle Abe."

"Well, pardon me for living." He turns to Howie. "Well anyhow! What do you want to be, son?"

"He could do physics like Lisanne here's father," Cy answers. "Maybe Lisanne here will talk to her father about you, Howie?"

"Dad!"

"Men of talent are always interested in other men of talent."

"You can come over and meet my father anytime," Lisanne tells Howie.

"*See?* Was I right? You've got to be a little more aggressive Tut. Her father worked with the bomb crowd."

She's not proud of that, I think but she doesn't say this to Cy. Instead, she turns to Howie. "It's complicated. Maybe you don't want to blow up the world."

"Then how's about medicine?" asks Abe.

"Medicine, never," Cy roars, "Doctors aren't so smart. What are they? Glorified plumbers? Howie's going to do a PhD."

"If you say so." Howie shrugs and we laugh.

"I say so, Tut," says Cy.

"Just call me by my name. You gave it to me. Why don't you ever use it. Tut? I'm not two anymore."

Loretta returns with a tray and puts huge corned beef sandwiches in front of me and Lisanne. She slaps down a bowl of coleslaw and a huge bowl of sour and half-sour pickles, the half-sours are my favorites. She takes the coffee pot and pours sloppily. The coffee brims over into our saucers. Uncle Abe picks his cup up to take a sip and it dribbles onto his tie. Loretta takes some extra napkins out of her apron pocket and sets them on Abe's saucer to sop up the spill.

"Abie, you need a bib. No mustard, girls?" Cy proffers the glass mustard jar toward us. Mustard has dried on the glass spreader.

Abe turns to Loretta. "Loretta, anybody ever tell you, you got style?"

"Sure, every day someone is imitating me. How are you, Victory? How's your mama?"

"She's good."

"I knew her family. They're from East End. She had a brother who went to Peabody. Handsome guy. He played football. But your mother they sent away to some school so I never saw much of her."

Loretta had been in Cy Merlman's high school class. They both grew up on the Hill. The Hill used to be Jewish before it was "colored." Or as Uncle Abe says: "The Schwartzies moved in."

It seems to me, no matter what my family calls people, it's wrong. The Jewish people have moved into houses with little lantern boys to light the way. *Well, Pittsburgh is in for a big surprise*, I think. *Lisanne and I are going to light a new way.* I take a huge bite of my sandwich, a swig of coffee, then a bite of pickle. In that order, I continue to polish off the first half of my sandwich. Now I'm staring the other half down.

Loretta refills my coffee cup and then Lisanne's. She slops some coffee onto the linoleum, stoops with her tochas in the air to clean it up.

"I didn't know you could touch your toes, Loretta," says Abe.

"Always been limber. You surprised?"

Abe looks over to the owner Frankie, behind the counter. "Loretta, you should tell Frankie he needs a new floor. You're gonna slip, especially upside down like that."

"Yeah, Franky!" says Loretta.

"Don't you know a scheister when you see a scheister, Loretta. He sold me the crap that's down there now."

"That was thirty years ago," says Abe.

"For what I paid, the floor should of lasted fifty," says Frankie.

"For what you paid? He actually remembers what he paid?"

"Of course I do. Two dollars a yard. That was a lot of money for linoleum back then."

"See? He don't care if I slip," Loretta explains. "He's got all the insurance in the world. Don't he, Cy? You sell it to him. I got my life insurance. Don't I, Cy? So I'm double insured. I'm worth a hell of a lot more dead than alive."

Cy winks at us. "She's complaining about the tips again. Don't I treat you nice, Loretta?"

"Yeah, you're the only one who worries about me."

"This is very nice of you to treat us," says Lisanne.

"My pleasure," Cy says. "You both have to come to the house." He peeks under the table. "So what's in the bags, ladies?"

"We're doing a science project," Lisanne says.

Howie gives us a knowing look.

Then she signs, "*They don't believe us.*"

"*I'm sure Uncle Abe knows that you and I aren't in the same science classes. He probably suspects some other mischief.*"

"*Won't everyone be surprised when we go to bed at eight p.m.?*"

"Are you really signing?" Howie asks.

"Of course."

"Well, I'll be," says Uncle Abe.

And I'm thinking, *Yeah, 'you'll be' when Lisanne and I ride out tonight—our mission to paint out bigotry and hatred.*

The idea of a prank has now risen to the level of a mission in my mind. I feel a frisson of excitement and look over at Lisanne who is also lost in thought momentarily.

"A penny for your thoughts, ladies," Cy says. "Or is this a privileged cogitation?"

Chapter 28

S treetlights, shining through the canopy of sycamore branches, cast macabre shadows onto the sidewalk. Lisanne appears from the back corner of her house and waves. It is eleven p.m. and my mother has gone to sleep. I wait in the shadows of our porch wall while Lisanne crosses the street. We've already stowed the paint in the car—no chance of it being found there. When she reaches me, I can feel a surge of adrenalin.

"Let the white avengers ride," she whispers loudly and we hold our hands over our mouths to suppress more giggling.

We stay in the shadows of the sidewall of our house—the one not attached to Julie Kramer's half. In the backyard, we half crawl to avoid being seen. The gate to the alley shrieks as we open it.

"It's a good thing my mother can't hear." I open the garage doors, hoping no neighbors see or, worse, think someone is stealing our car. I've grown a little bit and no longer need to sit on a high cushion. Lisanne gets into the passenger side of the Plymouth. The paint and brushes are at her feet.

I put the key into the ignition and, after a cough and sputter, the car starts.

"Number one is Lindy's house." Lisanne has found out that Lindy moved to Ridge Way. I've told Lisanne all about her predecessor, and she hates her about as much as I do. We cruise slowly. The streets are empty. Lindy's new house is not too different from the one I imagined. It has a portico and you can see through it to a triple bay garage in the rear. The walk curves and is semi-lit by the lantern on the little statue's arm. We're out of the car, brushes in hand, and quickly paint the black face white—we also paint the gloved hands. The more white the merrier. The little guy is now as white as the pants of his livery uniform. We are afraid to take time to admire our handiwork and rush back to the car.

There was no way to make an advance list so now we just drive around and when we see a little statue, we quickly paint him white. White faces now glow in the moonlight. We've just finished one high on Beechwood Boulevard when a police car appears in my rear mirror.

"Cop!" I say.

"Just act nonchalant. He probably won't stop."

"And if he does? Do I pull over again?"

"Just drive slowly away. And keep going."

The police car suddenly blazes with light and loud sirens but he passes us by.

"That was close."

"I don't think it had anything to do with the statues."

We manage to paint at least fifty more statues. It is now close to three a.m., and my mother rises at five. Time to call it a night or, rather, a morning.

We are painting Lisanne's little statue when the porch lights suddenly blaze—Ilse Glick stands there.

"You stay away from my daughter." She takes the can of paint from my hand and the brushes from Lisanne.

With the brush, she makes a grand stroke across Lisanne's face. "Do you like that?"

Lisanne and I spend the rest of the night frantically signing back and forth, she in her bedroom window and I in mine. Mrs. Glick called from New York City to check up on things and Mrs. Schmidt answered the phone inebriated. Mrs. Glick hopped the next plane back from New York. She will probably tell my mother or, worse, Uncle Abe. Somehow, I fall asleep for a few hours and wake to my mother flickering the lights.

"Come downstairs. I made scrambled eggs for your breakfast."

On the kitchen table, today's *Post Gazette*: *VANDALS PAINT THE TOWN WHITE.*

At school, everybody is discussing our prank only they don't know it was us. Ilse Glick, it seems, has chosen to keep silent and protect her daughter's reputation.

"The paint and brushes have been carefully disposed of," Lisanne says as she passes me in the hall. "My mother threw a bucket of ice water on Mrs. Schmidt."

The police are quick in making an arrest. I hear the story from Howie Merlman, who knows a college student at Pitt involved in a work project in a poor neighborhood. The kids paint houses, black kids and white kids involved in salvaging neighborhoods. The leaders of the project are white college students, along with black clergy. They organize the residents—mostly colored.

"Do-gooders," says my uncle Abe.

I imagine them working side by side to paint a sagging wooden house. The cops hover around, swinging their nightsticks and making crude remarks. The story we hear—two colored teenagers Jimmy Johnson and Aaron White are getting out of a VW bus with cans of paint. One of the cops hollers, "Hey, boys! Where yinz goan with that paint?"

Aaron and Jimmy freeze. One of the college students comes over and explains to the cop that this is a work project. "We're painting houses."

"Somebody did a lot of that kind of work last night over in Squirrel Hill."

"What's that got to do with us?" asks Jimmy Johnson—the son of Dr. Johnson, one of the community pillars.

The cop leans in close. "Uppity are you?"

Then the college students confront the two cops, but the cops push the college students away.

"Get outta my way, college boy. I'm going to talk to these here boys." He turns to Aaron and Jimmy. "Where were yinz last night?"

"Sleeping, what's it to you?"

"You paint all those little lawn niggers white last night?"

"With gray paint?" Jimmy asks sardonically. "Are you accusing us of something?"

The cops look at each other. "I'd say we got our boys."

"Where's your evidence?" Aaron asks.

"You don't have to talk to them," says the college student but the cop shoves him.

"I oughtta arrest yinz, too. Let's see your IDs boys."

"You don't have to show them anything. They have no cause to stop you," says the college student, gaining his feet only to be pushed down again.

"It's okay, will a driver's license do?" Jimmy asks.

Chapter 29

My mother has placed a serving of scrambled eggs before me. She's dressed and ready for work. The *Post Gazette* lays open on the table. *NABBED: WHITE PAINT VIGILANTES.*

My reaction is swift. Mortification flows through my veins. It was just a funny prank and I have caused someone harm. I imagine the black—as I refer to them now—boys beaten to a pulp. I've read *To Kill a Mocking Bird.* I've heard they are making it into a movie. We all have. The new social justice now divides many of us from our parents—as if our parents could have never divined right from wrong. The parents of my generation seem to want to protect us for all the wrong reasons. I've never known colored folks in a personal way.

Nabbed in twenty-four hours and handed up to the proper citizens of our city. Two colored youths.

The paper talks the way Uncle Abe talks. Good kids, too—one the son of a doctor, the other kid's father is an architect. Pillars of their community. Outrage all around. It never occurred to me that they would catch someone, or that someone would be found with such proper qualifications and charged with the mischief created singly in my own mind.

I go upstairs to use the bathroom. My bowels have begun to churn. I see the light from Lisanne's mirror flashing on the walls—our signal for *Radio Free Sycamore Street.* I think about the black teenagers in jail.

"We have to say something."

"My mother won't do anything. She prefers to blame you."

"Does she know I drove the getaway car?"

"No, that she doesn't know about. She says I'm influenced by left wing kids and their misguided parents in school. She blames the Quakers. Kids are going to their meetings. She thinks they make my father look like a criminal for working on the bomb."

"A gallon of white paint used up on one little black face?"

I see the door to her bedroom open and she scurries away from the window. Mrs. Glick gesticulates. Lisanne gesticulates back and reluctantly follows her mother through the door. I see her get into the car with Ilse.

Not knowing what to do, I come downstairs again.

"You're not eating your eggs," my mother signs.

How can I think about food. *"I just want coffee."*

"Not healthy." She glances over at the newspaper. *"They caught the gang."*

"Not a gang. Two kids."

She opens her compact to powder her nose *"We can all feel safe now."*

"Why should you feel safe now, Ma?"

"You make me late."

"Paint isn't going to kill anyone. If I did it, you'd think it was funny."

"You wouldn't do that. You're not colored."

"I Deaf because I your daughter."

"*Not same thing.*"

"*I notice no one painted the white faces black again.*"

"*Scared. You go with me?*"

"*No. I need the bathroom.*"

"*I can't wait this morning.*"

"*Ma, what if I did something really wrong?*"

"*Is there something the matter?*"

"*What if you think you've done something good and it hurts someone?*"

"*Then how can it be good?*"

"*Because maybe, in some way, it is a good thing, you have done.*"

"*But if you hurt somebody, you have to make it right.*"

∾∾

Outside the high school, a demonstration of solidarity with the black youths is in progress. The "smart" kids seem to lead it, brandishing megaphones—Howie, the leader among them. They refuse to come into the school. The principal watches from a distance, not daring to inflame the incipient anger further. Howie offers me a pamphlet. "It's massive," he says. "No classes at Pitt, Carnegie. We stand in solidarity."

Henry stands on another part of the staircase. "Don't go in there." He points to the massive front door and challenges his fellow students. "No one go to classes. Stand in solidarity. At noon, we make a human chain around the courthouse. There will be busses to take you downtown."

"Victory, can you take a stack of pamphlets over to the bus stop so people get them before Dr. Waldrop can get to them?"

A car pulls up to the curb. Lisanne gets out followed by Ilsa. "No, Lisanne, you cannot get involved here. Dr. Waldrop is planning to expel anyone who doesn't come in and go to classes. You can ill afford that."

"I want to be with my friends."

"No!"

"You can't make me go in there," she says.

Dr. Waldrop approaches Ilse and Lisanne. "We've decided to take a different tactic about this. She won't be punished if she joins them. We want to make this demonstration as safe as possible."

Ilse nods. "That is probably wise. Someone could get badly hurt by the police."

Lisanne runs over to Howie. "And I'm going to Howie's tomorrow," she says.

Ilse jets me an angry look, and I stare down at my cracked shoe straps. "Only the advanced placement kids got invited," Lisanne tells Ilse.

She shows me the peace sign. I return the gesture. Someone leads us in song. "We shall overcome," followed by "A change is going to come."

I find myself at the epicenter of something I only have a vague knowledge about. I join in "If I had a Hammer."

Someone with a guitar arrives and puts us into a better key.

The buses arrive—five with green-tinted windows. The drivers, fat guys in gray uniforms, open the doors and step out to allow the students to enter. "Go all the way to the back. Don't block the aisles."

We hear their commands echoing around us. Lisanne and I climb aboard the same bus under the gaze of Ilse, helpless to separate us this time. The doors close and the bus pulls out of its parking spot and follows the city streets to the ramp for the parkway. We see flames from the steel mill stacks in the distant sky as the driver steers up onto the ramp to the parkway—a system of clover leafs outdated before it even opened—another scar on the landscape of this filthy, old city. I look out onto the roads below us as the bus takes the curves. The bus driver takes his hands off the steering wheel and lights his cigarette. Minutes later, several kids, including Lisanne, light up and the bus fills with a nicotine haze. I crack the side-sliding window open a few inches and poke my nose through.

"Do you want me to put it out?" asks Lisanne.

I nod, coughing.

"It doesn't solve my problems anyway. I don't know why I do it."

We share some nervous laughter.

"I just wish it would all go away," I say. "Should we stand up at the demonstration and say we did it."

"My mother would send for the men in the white coats. People would think we were trying to be martyrs. It just wouldn't work."

We remain silent, watching the changing neighborhoods on the hills above the parkway.

The bus climbs onto an exit ramp. We have reached the downtown. Below us, business people and shoppers throng the sidewalks.

The old stone courthouse on Grant Street forms a horseshoe around an interior courtyard. We are told we have to demonstrate outside. I have never been to a demonstration but am familiar with the procedures from seeing the civil rights marches on television and on the newsreels. Cameras are aimed at us as we descend the bus and begin to take our places in the human chain. We are going to surround the building, an entire city block, but there just are not enough of us and the onlookers stare and go about their business. We shout about justice for

James and Aaron, sing more songs. Even the cameramen who greeted us enthusiastically as we descended from the busses have lost interest. The bus drivers loiter at a distance. None of the bystanders join us. People come and go from the courtyard entrance. In the distance, you can see prisoners marched over the "bridge of sighs" from the jail adjacent to the courthouse. Most of us are white skinned. The blacks pay us no mind. I'm powerless to stave off the empty and numb feelings coursing through my veins. We get back on the buses and are returned to school for the last two periods.

Chapter 30

According to Uncle Abe, Cy wants to make us an offer on the lake property. He's convinced my mother there's no harm in hearing Cy out.

My mother has her own motives. Maybe Cy will invest in her tile business. This she doesn't impart to Abe. She's determined to be the one making the offering.

Uncle Abe telephones for the third time. "Did she look at it yet?"

Our copy of an offer to buy our lake property sits half-folded on the dining room table on top of a heap of mail and old newspapers.

"She didn't say."

"Should be very straightforward. It will put a lot of cash into your pockets. Well, anyway, Cy's inviting her over to his happy hour thing tomorrow night."

I don't say anything. My mother with all these *hearing*?

"You there, Victory?"

"I'll go tell Ma."

"I've gotta go. Just tell your mother to be there at

five! Your come too, so you can translate. You'll hash over the details then. This is in her best interest."

സ്പ

At ten to five, we get off the bus at the corner of Roundhill Road. My mother puts the creased and folded bus schedule back into Aunt Shirley's old alligator bag. She wears her straight skirt and jacket with a fur collar— another hand-me-down from Aunt Shirley Mother's made over. I can see she's lost weight since my father died. That certain fullness she always had in her hips used to tug on the seams. Now the skirt seems loose the way Lisanne's mother would wear it. As usual, my mother is punctual. Because she does not drive, traveling for my mother is a matter of reading bus schedules and knowing the route far in advance. *"When I was your age, I took the wrong bus."*

"I know and you ended up in a bar on the south side and they had to call your father."

"Did I tell you already?"

I sigh. *"Every time we go somewhere."*

"It's very hard without your father, Victory."

"You should learn to drive, Ma."

She won't answer when I tell her that. Just shrugs. *"I wish your father was here."*

സ്പ

When I was little and she would take me to the zoo, we'd take three buses and manage to arrive as the big iron gates were being opened for the day. To get back to make my father's supper, we'd have to take the three o'clock bus to downtown and then trace the route backward.

Today she has figured out how to knock on the door just as her watch reads five o'clock.

Cy's house is the fifth from the corner and sits high on a green hill, guarded by a phalanx of closely planted poplar trees. Gravity seems to tug on us as we ascend past carefully edged beds of ivy.

I can see she's nervous.

"Don't be too impressed, Victory. Your uncle is too impressed by money. Green's the color of money. He's trying to impress us by having us come here. Then they'll try to take advantage. Your uncle Abe is in the palm of this Cy's hand."

I frown. *"Why do you always have to ruin everything by saying things like that?"*

"When you've had more experiences with hearing people you will understand."

"I am hearing people, Ma!" I sign, exasperated, even though, to her, I know I'm not. *"The Merlmans live in a park,"* I sign, not wanting to get into her ways of dividing up the world. *"It's green and shady."*

Two teenaged boys are sitting in jail because of me and I'm visiting a park.

She nods. *"Yes, it's very nice to have someone to take care of a yard."*

Even the shadiest corners are covered by well-chosen ground covers, trimmed myrtle, and pine scrub. The steep front lawn is terraced with richly mulched garden beds. The stumps of rose bushes have been cut back. in anticipation of the first frost, and covered in burlap hoods, like little monks at prayer.

"This isn't a very Jewish house," I sign.

It occurs to me for the first time just how white Nancy Drew is. In her books, all the crooks have "swarthy" skin. Carolyn Keene uses that word over and over again to connote unsavory people. My own skin is almost

swarthy—sallow, they call it. Not pink and freckled. I
don't think Nancy Drew would have figured out the mystery of the white paint, and she certainly was no prank-
ster. I notice another equestrian statue painted white, not
one of our doing. Cy has let Howie paint theirs. Lisanne
and I have given Howie a platform, and he has seized the
opportunity. Part of me wants to claim my rightful place
in this debacle for reasons other than justice for Jimmy
and Aaron.

At first view, the house is hidden by lush and mature
rhododendrons and seems to sink into the top of the hill.
A quiet secret, I think. Up close, however, its grandeur
and eminence become apparent—dark red brick and
floor-to-ceiling French windows leading out to a patio at
the side of the house. To the other side, the circular
driveway widens toward a triple-door garage before it
descends back to the street.

"*Where is the front door? You can't tell what door to
go to,*" my mother signs.

I can tell her worst fear is to take the wrong entrance.
"*I think you have to enter over here.*"

We're face to face with a massive door constructed
in heavy wood. Cross-slats separate wide empty spaces
where the wood grain swirls. I hesitate and put my hand
on the brass knocker. A lion's face leers above the heavy
metal ring clenched in its teeth.

My mother's eyes are wide with awe. "*Lift it.*"

"*They must have a hundred bedrooms.*"

She nods and takes my hand. The lion doesn't flinch
as I release the brass ring to strike a blow to the plate under its mouth. The sound reverberates. I flush with embarrassment but no one comes to the door.

"*The place is too big. They can't even hear their own
front door,*" she signs smugly.

A red convertible Mercedes comes to a halt at the

front door. An elderly man in tennis whites gets out. He's tanned, dry, and wrinkled. "Just walk in," he says. "Everyone just walks in. Once Cy gets going on those drinks of his, he forgets to answer the door. I'll let you in on a little secret—he lost three sets today. So he's gonna make the drinks extra strong. Watch out."

He pushes the door open and lets us enter into a marble foyer. Groups of people, mostly men, are crowded into a parlor beyond. I see Lisanne there with Howie. They wave hello. We take our time taking off our coats and hanging them on an oak coat rack, flanked with hooks and an umbrella holder filled with a bouquet of state-of-the-art tennis rackets. A carefully stacked pyramid of tennis ball cans sit on a ledge. In this house there seems to be more of everything. *"Uncle Abe says the only reason Cy sent Howie to public school is Jews are not welcome at the private schools,"* I sign, taking in the extent of luxury on display here.

"Uncle Abe likes to brag as if money could rub off on him like the geld around the mirror he looks into. You should see him at work. Every other minute combing the hair over his bald spot."

"Ma, they'll see us!" I'm suddenly feeling self-conscious about carrying on a sign conversation with my mother. I worry they'll know what it is she is saying.

"Usually they want to talk about why your father married me. For sex is all they think."

"Ma! What's wrong with you?"

"They can't hear us." It's a joke she likes to sign in public.

Cy sees us and comes forward. "Is this your mother, Victory?"

I sign to her that this is Cy Merlman. *"He was at our house during Shiva."*

"Come on in, Esther." He mouths his words carefully

as he shakes her hands. Then he puts his arm around my shoulders. I stiffen. "Relax! I don't bite."

"It's the bark you have to watch out for!" says the man in tennis whites. He hasn't figured out my mother can't hear a bark.

"Ha, ha!" says Cy, "Did you meet Artie?"

"I found them at the front door, looking kind of bewildered. Someday the wrong guy is going to walk through that front door of yours, Merlman."

"Shaw, you're going to die from worry! Come on in and let me make you a drink."

A trim-figured woman with dark hair bounces through a set of double doors. She has the build of a little girl but her face is leathery and wrinkled prematurely from the sun.

"Here she is!" says Cy. "Come on over here, Ellen. This here's Esther and Victory."

"*Is that his wife?*" my mother signs.

I finger-spell "*Ellen. Ellen is Cy's sister. Howie's mother is dead.*"

Cy Merlman has made hordes of money. He's self-made according to Uncle Abe, but never forgets his old buddies. "A shame about his wife Francie. Died so young leaving Cy to raise Howie. Never was a man so sought after by the widows in the community, but he seems to live now for his son," Abe says, intimating from the other side of his mouth that Cy is spoiling Howie.

Ellen plays hostess for Cy from time to time. Ellen's husband, Len, lounges lazily in an armchair. He picks at a tray of olives and celery sticks, looks up, and toasts Esther with what must be his second or third drink. Ellen glares at him and takes my mother's hand. She, too, mouths her words. "I'll be right back. I have to refill the crackers. Just let Cy get you a drink. He makes a great gin and tonic."

I translate as she flits off in the direction of the kitchen but is detained in the corner by the only other adult woman in the room. A buxom blonde in a tennis skirt and alligator shirt. My mother sees them whisper. It's funny how hearing people still whisper even in the presence of a deaf person. My mother interprets whispering as something directed toward her. In this case, she's right. Ellen is explaining that my mother is deaf. I see my mother losing some of her resolve.

"We're going straight in there to be taken advantage of. I don't trust these people. You use your ears and tell me what they really say."

"I'm not a spy, Ma!"

☙❧

We enter the huge parlor guided by Cy. Cy is a fairly small but muscular man with a big head, sunburned pate, hooked nose, and penetrating blue eyes. What's left of his hair is red mixed with gray. My mother and I gaze at a picture of a woman with a baby on a mantle.

"That was my wife Francie with Howie before she got sick," he states simply and I translate.

To look at Howie today, you can imagine Francie— thick curly, light brown hair. When Howie removes his glasses, he reveals a face much softer than Cy's.

Howie joins us from the other side of the room and takes me aside. "I was too young to remember my mother but part of me still misses her. Sometimes, when something is too difficult for me to do, I imagine what it would be like to do it for my mother, and I sail through it. She's there for me. Do you believe in spirits?"

"I felt my father's spirit the day he died. I know no one would ever believe that."

"And you have your father's paintings. Sometimes

my mother wrote poems. I'll show them to you. Do you ever write poems?"

"I write things in my diary that are almost like poems."

"You should work on them."

"I'm afraid they would make me too sad."

Cy has been watching us. "Enough said," he says. "This is a happy hour."

I'm both heartened that Howie spoke of his mother to me and relieved to forget the subject of death, even for a while.

"My dad means well," Howie whispers to me.

A Renoir hangs over the sofa plump with white slipcovers. The picture is in a very expensive frame, then I notice the plaque that says the picture is a reproduction. The room is big and two love seats—covered in the same bunchy white fabric and adjacent to the sofa but across from each other—form the basis for a seating arrangement. Other chairs have been brought in from other rooms. Someone brings one close to the coffee table for me. Everyone is crowded around, dipping chips into sour cream, munching salted nuts, and cutting off hunks of cheese.

"What are you drinking, Esther?"

"He wants to know what you want to drink, Ma."

She looks over at the tall glass in Cy's hand and nods her head.

He picks up the cigarette he's left on the wrought iron cart that he uses for a bar. "You don't have to speak the same language to ask for a drink. That's universal. Tell your mother she's made a good choice. I make great gin and tonics."

"Tell your mother to help herself to the kasseri!" says Uncle Abe. "We all schnorr off Cy." His forehead is glossy with moisture. He takes a handkerchief out of his trouser pocket. He seems fleshier than the other people in the room. The cord knit of his sleeveless undershirt shows under his white shirt. He's come from work not tennis.

"*No thank you,*" my mother signs. The room becomes silent as I translate.

"Pregnant pause," says Lisanne coming to the rescue. Laughter comes on like a change of channels. "We played tennis," she says.

"And she's not a bad little tennis player," says Cy.

"I'm sooo stiff. Cy's coz and this woman from Cy's office, we played doubles. Ellen won't play with Cy. She says Cy makes her nervous and she messes up her serve."

"If she could serve, she could play," Cy calls from across the room.

I don't know what to say so I say nothing.

"Is this the first time you've been here, Victory?" asks Lisanne.

I nod.

"Isn't this a wonderful house? Don't you wish it was yours?"

"It's really huge."

"Let me show you around. Howie, I'm going to show Victory your etchings." Howie doesn't seem particularly interested. "Howie and I are supposed to be working on a science project," Lisanne says.

"If you're going on the tour, could you come back with a box of Ritz crackers?" Cy asks Lisanne.

"If you tell me where I have to look," Lisanne says pertly.

"I thought you just became the tour guide."

"But I haven't been through all of your closets yet," Lisanne says. "When I have, I'll tell you what you ought to stock up on. I'm sure you're missing something essential."

"Don't you just love her?" Cy says to the roomful of people. "She's got guts to talk back to me."

Another facet of Lisanne has appeared. She's fearless in the face of adults. "You don't scare anyone, Cy. You just like to think you do," she says. "That's a joke," she says to me. "Cy's very neurotic about running out of things. It comes from growing up poor. So he has Ellen shopping day and night."

"She loves to shop," Cy says. "So do you!"

"I do not! I hate shopping. My mother buys everything in pieces. She made shrimp two nights ago and we drove to the fish store for twelve shrimp. I mean some people would buy a pound or a half pound or a quarter, even an eighth, but my mother has everything counted out—four carrots, three potatoes, two French fries. It's so European."

"Tell her to get a deep freeze," says Cy. "Ellen's got shrimp in five pound blocks in her deep freeze."

"She'll get away with murder," says Uncle Abe. "Did you see that Hitchcock? The dame kills the guy with a frozen leg of lamb. Then serves it."

"She's got ten legs of lamb frozen down there. Enough to kill off half of the room," Cy says.

"Every woman ought to keep a leg of lamb in the deep freeze just in case," Ellen says.

I look at my mother watching uncle Abe pull out his trump cards for his friend Cy.

"She'll be okay. Cy's got them all drunk. You've got to see the breakfast room," Lisanne says.

"I'll come right back, Ma."

Cy hands my mother a gin and tonic. She sits back and takes a long sip. Then, unable to join the conversation, she wanders into the solarium off the living room. She nods at the tropical plants, wrought iron furniture.

She notices cracked tile on the floor and stoops to pick one up.

I get up and follow Lisanne.

"Let's put some vodka in some ginger ale," Lisanne says. "They won't smell it on us. Vodka doesn't give you liquor breath." She looks at her watch. "My father is picking me up at seven-thirty."

The kitchen is gargantuan with two refrigerators. Lisanne takes out some bottles of Vernor's ginger ale and a bottle of vodka from the freezer and places them on a large stainless steel counter. She pours us drinks in metal milk glasses, hands me one, and we make a toast.

"To always be there for each other," I say.

"No matter what the adversity. We will get through this."

I'm thirsty and I drink quickly. The drink goes to my head almost immediately. The room spins around. Nothing is steady. I've never had anything more than a few sips of beer or Sabbath wine.

"We shall overcome," she says, leading me through the darkened plush living room and through the dining room with a long banquet table and a huge glass breakfront stacked with china and silver serving pieces.

When I stagger, she steadies me, as if the vodka has no effect on her. I put the glass on a side table, afraid to drink anymore.

I learn through Lisanne that everything in the Merlman house comes in quantities, whether it's tennis balls or toilet paper.

"Oh, you have to see the powder room, too."

She leads me to a heavy wooden door behind the staircase. Inside is a room larger than our living room with a settee and a mirrored vanity. Another door leads into a tiled inner sanctum with a toilet and large sink cabinet.

Lissanne opens the cabinet. "Enough toilet paper to last through an air raid. I told Howie he ought to put up a bomb shelter sign. He said he's going to steal one. Cy Merlman doesn't care what Howie does."

"Have your parents come over here?" I ask.

"Oh, yes. But they dropped me off and left. My mother wouldn't fit in. My father, however, could do with a drink."

When we come back to the gathering, my mother shows me the tile. "*I can make new one for floor,*" she signs. "*You tell him I'll fix.*"

Cy seems happy for an excuse to leave the group and guides Esther's elbow, insisting that Lisanne and I come along. We pass through at least five bathrooms on the second floor and my mother finds cracked and broken tiles in each one. "You can't buy those anymore," Cy says, nodding apologetically, and I translate.

"*But I can make them special. I know how to mix the glazes for the colors. Tell him.*"

"My mother can repair these for you." I explain her expertise in all things ceramic and I see a light bulb going off in Cy's face.

"Okay, you've got yourself a deal. No one fixes things anymore but I don't see why not. Don't tell your uncle. He'd advise me to cover everything in linoleum." He pumps her hand, she grins, and, when we return to the company, Cy announces his deal, much to Uncle Abe's consternation.

Konrad Glick has arrived to pick up Lisanne and is seated in an armchair next to Ellen, nursing a rather tall glass of scotch and water. I hear the phrase, "I guess it's all top secret or something," from Ellen.

He sees us with Lisanne and frowns. People don't seem to know what to say to him, and he doesn't seem to know what to say to them. There is a guarded quality

about him, and his accent is heavily German. He asks
Howie what he and Lisanne have been working on, and
it's plain to see that Lisanne has become a bit tipsy.

"Elementary particulars. And anti-mater," She says.
Then she burps and looks at Ellen. "Com—pli—mit—
ments to the chef," she says with a hiccup between each
syllable.

Konrad takes another slug of his drink and stands.
"Your mother will have dinner waiting. We will go."

Cy's guests are a bit shocked, but Cy seems to think
it is funny.

"You should have asked me before you went on the
house tour. Are you feeling no pain also, Victory."

I nod and lower my head.

"I don't think this is appropriate," Konrad Glick
says. "Let's go, Lisanne."

Chapter 31

Aunt Shirley calls at eight p.m. "Victory darling. It's Aunt Shirley."

She's using her banana-split voice, all gooey and sugary. I can just envision Uncle Abe pacing in the background. You can always tell when toady Shirley is determined to get something.

"How are you, love? I heard it was quite a happy hour over at Cy's. Did you ever see a house like that?"

I take a long silent breath.

"Are you there, Victory?"

"Yes." I'm reduced to monosyllables. My mother is signing, "*Who?*"

"*Aunt Shirley!*" I sign. "I just told Mom you're on the phone," I say to my aunt.

"Well anyway, I'll tell you why I'm calling. I haven't seen you and mother in a while. Tomorrow is Uncle Abe's poker night, and I thought I might take you and mother out for supper."

"I'll ask her."

"My treat! Rhoda's!" I hear the muffled sound of a hand covering the phone. "You see, Abie darling? Woman to woman. It's better that way."

CฺSCฺS

I meet my mother at the store and we walk up the street to Rhoda's. As we pass through the glassed-in vestibule, I notice Shirley ensconced in a booth, her reading glasses far down on her nose, reading the evening edition of the paper. *ARRAIGNED* shouts the headline over a picture of the two boys, Aaron and Jimmy, being arraigned before a white judge as their parents look somberly on. Butterflies form in my stomach, my pounding heart reverberates against the bones of my skull. My eyes keep glancing down as Shirley prattles on.

She places her hand on mine. "You can read about that ghastly business later. I've finished with the paper."

We order, my second giant corned beef sandwich in one week. We eat silently for a bit under Shirley's scrutiny. I peck at my sandwich. I can't get the boys out of my mind.

"Well, I wanted to speak with you about the store," she finally says.

My mother raises her eyebrows when I translate.

"If you could explain to mother that grandpa had a vision when he went into linoleum," Shirley continues. "It's contrary to grandpa's vision to go back to tile."

Loretta has lingered. "You know, Victory. Mrs. Gruber was saying how thrilled she was that you could match her bathroom tiles. Tell your mother that."

I repeat this in sign and it emboldens my mother. She grins. "*I already have many customers. It brings business into the store.*"

Shirley sighs. "That's very nice, but it takes away business from Abe because many people cover broken tiles with linoleum."

"*Well, they don't put it into swimming pools or showers.*"

"But they put it on bathroom floors. So you see the point, Esther, you are causing a conflict with Abe's business."

"But it is my business, too. I have my husband's interest and I need to make money. What Abe pays me is too little to live on, and I have more to offer than a file clerk does."

Shirley shakes her head. "I guess then that we are at an impasse."

Loretta gives us a thumbs-up sign behind Shirley's back.

"I've said all I'm going to say," Shirley continues. "But I hope I've given you some food for thought." She pauses to let us know she means business. "How's about desert?"

I groan.

"They have the best cheesecake in the world," Shirley says. "Even that place in New York City that's so famous can't compare, they say."

Chapter 32

Ilse has become more vigilant about preventing any interaction between me and Lisanne. She constantly enters Lisanne's bedroom and draws the drapes. Lisanne then opens them again so we can sign. She has fallen asleep at her desk with her head on a book. I signal with mirror and lights. She struggles to look up.

"*You look funny.*"

"*I'm just a little groggy,*" she replies.

"*We have to do something.*"

"*I know. I can't get it out of my mind.*"

"*The only thing we can do is go to the police and tell them the truth.*"

"*What if they don't believe us? And my mother won't let me out of her sight.*" The door to Lisanne's room opens again. "*See what I mean?*"

Ilse enters angrily and shuts the curtains. I know the address of the boy's parents because the *Post Gazette* published it. I find my mother's bus schedule. I'm not going to school in the morning, but I'm going to the Hill district to talk to Dr. Johnson, I've determined. I'll go by myself.

In the morning, a doctor, carrying a medical kit knocks on the Glicks' front door. Lisanne's curtains are still drawn. Shortly, the doctor, Ilse, and Konrad usher a very groggy Lisanne to the car. When she is in the back seat, Konrad goes into the house and returns with a suitcase. I watch them drive off with Lisanne slumped over in the back seat.

The doctor follows in his own car. The *Post Gazette* article is crumpled in my jacket pocket. My mother has already left for work, reminding me to dress warmly. There is a chill in the air. I catch the streetcar to downtown and ride with what my aunt and uncle would call the *hoi polloi*—maids, shop girls, the very elderly, the handicapped. At this hour, the students are already in school, so I am the only teenager on this ride and the subject of some staring as the streetcar clacks slowly along the rails, making frequent stops to allow more passengers to get on. It winds past the jail and the courthouse. Very few get off before downtown. There, I need to transfer to another streetcar. I get off at the Jenkins Arcade and wait in front of the candy store, redolent of caramel and popcorn, for the next car. A woman wearing a large apron and hair net pulls reams of taffy from a metal rod. I watch as it turns from a deep molasses color to an off white. I'm thinking about what I'm going to say when I get to Dr. Johnson's office.

I've decided there's no use in saying I did this deed with Lisanne. I wonder where they are taking her. There have been rumors over the years of recalcitrant teenagers being designated as mentally ill—children of the affluent usually. I'm afraid for my friend.

The Number Two to The Hill follows shortly and I ask the driver to tell me when we reach Wylie Avenue. I am the only young person on the bus and the only white girl among church ladies returning from night shift jobs. I

ignore their stares and gaze out of the window. We pass
buildings sagging at the foundations from years and years
of neglect. Children, too young for school, play in the
debris from razed buildings. Here and there are buildings
in good repair amongst those that have probably been
condemned, but not emptied of the inhabitants. Most of
the buildings sit right on the street. They were built for
waves of immigration, Irish, German, Jewish, before the
Negroes.

"Wylie Avenue, miss," I hear and clamber toward
the back entrance of the streetcar where I descend to the
cobblestone. Dr. Johnson's office is right there in a narrow brownstone. It has a quiet dignity. I ring the bell as a
patient exits and I enter a narrow hallway. To my right is
a reception area where a tall colored woman sits behind a
desk. To my left, pocket doors are closed. Patients, young
and old, occupy every seat in the busy waiting room.

"Can I help you, miss?"

I notice a mother holding three children on her lap. "I
need to see Dr. Johnson."

The receptionist looks at me curiously over the rims
of her reading glasses. "I don't think you've been here
before."

"No!"

"Well, miss, as you can see we are rather busy at the
moment."

"I can wait. It's very important."

"He usually makes a much longer appointment for a
new patient. I don't know how we're going to fit you in.
We're having short hours today because the doctor has
family matters to attend to."

"I'm not a patient."

"Then…"

"I won't take long. I just need to see him."

She hands me some paper forms. "I need you to fill these out. Is your mother with you, young lady?"

"No!"

"When was your last period?"

I must have looked very perplexed.

"You know the doctor doesn't do anything any other doctor in the town doesn't do."

"You think I'm..."

She nods her head in the affirmative.

"That's not why I came."

There is a rustling among the patient onlookers.

"Why did you come here?"

"I need to talk to Dr. Johnson."

"You live around here?"

"No, I live in Squirrel Hill."

She jets me a very hostile look, stands with hands firmly on her generous hips. "What business could you be on, miss, which brings you all the way from Squirrel Hill alone?"

"I need to talk to the doctor. Please, please. It's very important."

"I'll be glad to tell him anything you want."

Here I begin to cry. "It's really important. I need to see him."

"Okay, you wait here a minute. I'll get him." She goes into the inner office, returns just as quickly followed by Doctor Johnson, and beckons me toward them. The inner parlor contains the doctor's oak desk. Filing cabinets line the walls. They close the sliding doors. Dr. Johnson is a very tall man. He wears a white coat with pens in his pocket, a stethoscope slung around his neck. He looks at me and folds his arms. "I don't want to make it look like I'm pushing you in front of my patients but I don't think it is such a good idea for a white girl to be all alone up here in the Hill. There's a lot of bad feeling up here today. What do you have to tell me that's so important?"

"It's about your son and the other kid." I look at the woman. "She knows?"

"This is his mother. If it concerns our son, we both want to hear it."

"Well, I know he didn't paint the little statues."

"Uh huh! I know that and my wife knows that because our son was home all night. But how do you know that?"

I begin to cry again. "Because I did it!"

"You want to tell us that some little white girl ran all over Squirrel Hill in the middle of the night with a can of paint?" says Mrs. Johnson. "How old are you, anyway?"

"Fifteen. I thought it would be funny. I mean I think those statues are stupid and insulting. It never occurred to me that they would blame someone colored, I mean Negro."

Mrs. Johnson begins to cry. "Are you telling us the truth?"

I nod. "You don't know how sorry I am."

Dr. Johnson leers down at me, as if he considers putting his long hands around my neck. "Do you know what you put our boy and his friend through?"

"Yes."

"No, you couldn't know."

"Look, James, she's a brave girl. She came all the way here because she knew she made a bad mistake."

"If I can't believe you could do that all alone in the middle of the night, and I'm inclined not to believe that, how are the police going to believe you?"

"But it's true. I drove my father's car."

"You're just fifteen. What are they raising over there in Squirrel Hill? Are you going to tell this to the district attorney?"

I nod firmly.

"First thing is, we're going to call your mother and father."

"My father died and my mother is deaf. She's working in my uncle's store right now. My uncle will write for her." He shakes his head and picks up the telephone. I tell him the exchange and he dials.

I hear, "Povich Floors." My uncle has answered.

"I've got a young woman here. What did you say your name was anyway?"

"Victory. Victory Povich."

Dr. Johnson explains why I have come.

I hear through the receiver, "The Hill?" There is a pause during which he presumably has written for my mother. "She's okay, don't go hysterical on me. Now what could have been on her mind.? I'd better call Barney Ginsberg. Victory is going to need a lawyer."

From then on, the pace of time quickened. I remember a blur of the dark stone courthouse. This time, I am brought inside and into a courtroom flanked by my mother, uncle, and lawyer. I am brought before Judge Brody, and I tell him that I used my father's car and drove around with white paint. I hear Dr. and Mrs. Johnson sobbing. Aaron White's parents sit stone-faced. The boys come forward. They are bruised and battered. Aaron's arm is in a sling. Jimmy's forehead has a bandage that almost reaches over his right eye.

"James Johnson and Aaron White you are free to go," the judge says.

They sob in their parents' arms. The police have roughed them up for being the wrong race, and no one mentions if there will be an investigation into the police behavior. All avoid me but then, as an afterthought, Dr. Johnson breaks away from his wife and son. "I wish you good luck," he tells me, "and thank you."

I smile through my tears and once again say I am sorry.

"By the way," says Dr. Johnson. "So you know. Those jockeys have another meaning for some of us. They were placed at the entrances of the Underground Railroad so the escaping slaves would know where to enter. If it was safe, the jockey wore a green scarf and, if it wasn't, they'd tie a red scarf around its neck."

The judge is beginning to look impatient and Dr. Johnson returns quickly to his wife and son. They exit the courtroom.

Barney Ginsberg explains that we are going to go to the judge's chambers to finish this business. We are ushered into a back hall reached through the front of the courtroom.

"This is going to be very informal." Uncle Abe says. "The judge is a nice Jewish judge. We don't have to parade this in front of the *Goyim.*"

He leaves my mother and me in the hallway outside of the tall oak doors to the judge's chambers.

"Wait outside," the lawyer Barney Ginsburg says.

He points to a wooden bench next to the elevator on this floor of the once elegant courthouse. This high-ceilinged corridor seems to be a floor of offices. The ashtrays between the elevators overflow; and cigarette butts clutter the floor outside of every door—probably stomped out by nervous petitioners before entering a judge's inner sanctum.

Wait here? Why? I think, hearing murmurs through double oak doors that match the bench. The transom is open. I overhear. "We are on the record. In the matter of Victory Povich, a minor."

"I didn't understand...She's not deaf? No! It can skip a generation...You want to declare the mother incompetent?"

The doors open again. Ginsburg looks from my mother to me. "Come in, Victory, Mrs. Povich."

The judge's chamber is austere. It's his own room, his robe hangs from a coat tree in the corner, and the desk, oak and heavy, is not quite centered in the room.

"Your honor," says the lawyer, "This was a case of youthful indiscretion."

It was a word I've never signed so I finger spell.

"I've had a lengthy discussion with her uncle, Abraham Povich. Her mother is unable to raise a teenager without her husband. The child is failing at school."

"Is she running with a gang?" asks the judge.

Abe is about to answer but my mother interrupts with frantic signing. *"You tell judge I see what your uncle do. He not want me in the store."*

"Ma, he didn't say that."

"He says not there for you. Same thing."

The judge becomes impatient. "Mr. Ginsberg please impress upon your clients that everyone will have a say."

"Victory, I want the two of you to remain still."

"Then how do I know what is being said?" asks my mother.

"If I don't sign, then she doesn't know what you say."

"Tell her I will explain it all later."

My mother is becoming furious at the lawyer. *"Not fair! Not fair!"*

"Ma!"

The judge addresses me. "Victory, did you do this alone? What I can't understand is how you managed this on your own. No one else helped you carry the paint, nothing. You got in your father's car and drove? Has anybody taught you to drive?"

"No."

"It's crucial that we have all the truth."

"Yes."

"I find this hard to believe. You came up with the idea on your own?"

"Yes."

"Who are your friends?"

I shrug. "They were not with me."

"In a court, it is considered a crime not to tell the truth. It's called perjury. I need to know right now, young lady, did someone help you with it? Someone you are afraid to get into trouble?"

I burst into tears. "She's already in trouble for being my friend. Her parents took her away somewhere. They called a doctor and, when he came, he must have given her medicine. When they put her in the car, they had to hold her up. She was so groggy she couldn't walk. Her mother caught us coming back. We were painting her statue. We thought her mother was in New York."

"You have to tell the court who this person is."

I mumble Lisanne's name.

"You need to speak louder for the court reporter."

"Lisanne Glick. We just thought it would be funny."

"Outta the mouth of babes," says Abe, "Who would ever believe? And I thought she might be a good influence."

"I think we need a way to keep Victory out of trouble," Barney Ginsberg chimes in.

"I would like to hear what Lisanne and her mother have to say," says Judge Brody. "There was vandalism and, if their daughter participated, then she needs to make restitution as well."

"I'm going to suggest that uncle Abe be granted guardianship," says the lawyer.

"My mother is a good mother." I look down at the floor not wanting to look at my mother. I see the worn linoleum.

I imagine Abe thinking about the linoleum floor. Worn down to the tarpaper backing, leaving fudge colored cameo silhouettes of fanciful figures. I see a peacock, a bear, a woman carrying something on her head, the little liveries, me. Perhaps everything that comes into this court is carved into this flooring. Judge Brody looks from me to my mother.

"How is it you survive, Mrs. Povich?" I translate what the judge says.

"I'm a silent partner in the business," I translate for my mother.

Laughter.

"Please, please, everyone! How much do you draw each month?"

Abe rushes to interject. "Well, that depends on the business. Her needs are small."

"Is there property?"

Again, Abe answers. "A house, it's a half of a double on Sycamore Street and a cabin up at the lake. It's a privy, not much, your honor, but the land has some value I'm told. I'd like to see her set up with some income from it. But she won't sell. That's why I think she needs a guardian."

"Just because a person won't sell a property doesn't demonstrate the need for a guardian."

"Your honor, it's been one thing after another with her kid. Now with the police and the *schwartzies*—She's not up to it. Not without a husband."

"You've had your say," the judge tells Abe. "I'm going to let Victory and Mrs. Povich speak. Then I want to hear from Mrs. Kahn, the social worker."

Abe shifts on his feet and takes a seat with a pleading look at Barney Ginsburg.

"You father has been dead for half a year now," the judge continues. "Convey to your mother that she needs to make an arrangement for you after school so that you are not left to your own devices."

Abe interjects again. "In the past, your honor, she hasn't conveyed to her mother what was being said—"

The judge cuts him off. "Do you have homework every night? In high school, you have a lot of homework. I'm not so old I don't remember that."

I nod.

"How is she doing in school?"

Mrs. Kahn shuffles the papers in her social work file and shows them to the judge.

"Has your mother seen your report card?"

I lower my eyes to the floor.

"Does Mrs. Povich know when report cards are issued? We are going to start improving the family's channel of communication. Explain to your mother what has been discussed." He nods at the court reporter. "We will have a transcript of what is being said here. Do you understand, Victory? If you lie, she will know."

The radiator rattles and clangs in the stubborn silence. My uncle is glaring at me, too. I'm caught between four pairs of knowing eyes. No way to wiggle out of here. I wish I were in Lindy's woods, sitting on the cold ground talking the night away with Lisanne. I wish Lisanne was home practicing her sonata.

"My mother is a good mother," I repeat, relieved that they didn't drag the driving story out of me. I can see that my mother has relaxed a bit, probably also relieved the judge didn't drag the driving lesson story out of me.

"I'm going to take everything that has been said under consideration. Considering Victory's age and remorse at her lapse of judgment, there will be no criminal prosecution. But the court will act to see that she is properly supervised in the future, and that she doesn't drive until she turns sixteen. You will hear from me in a week."

Outside of the courthouse, news photographers try to snap our pictures.

"Say nothing to them," instructs the lawyer. "Victory, we're starting off on the right foot and taking you to school."

"*It is already two o'clock. The* winged victory *might have wings but it doesn't have a head.*"

My mother laughs at this bit of teenaged irony from me. Mr. Lane is going to call me a two o'clock scholar if he sees me. Traffic is heavy returning from downtown and I am saved by the bell. Kids are streaming out of every exit. I will have to contend with school tomorrow. Uncle Abe turns the car around and takes us to Sycamore Street. They let me off. My mother goes back to the store with him.

Suddenly alone, I feel like I have been away for a thousand years. Julie is on the porch when we drive up. I wave but she ignores me. "I just want you to know I'm not supposed to have anything to do with you," she says with her back to me as I climb the front stairs. "No offense."

"None taken. I won't miss you."

The next part of my greeting committee—Bill Rile— is riding his bike in circles on Sycamore Street in front of my house. "Hey, Pox, I guess the reform school wouldn't have you because you're contagious."

"Well then, there's a place for you."

"Hardyhawhaw. I'll get you again, bitch."

His threat makes me shiver. Julie goes inside slamming her door. I don't want to open mine. I'm afraid Bill Rile will follow me into the house. If I'm alone with him, he might do to me what he did to the mill girl in Lindy's woods.

The familiar tilts toward an unsafe place I don't know how to name. The loss of a best friend, the loss of a

not-so-best friend, all precipitated by the death of my father who left me way too soon. I see the living room curtain in the Glick house part momentarily. Ilse Glick must
be watching me. I'm going to go to the store to be with
my mother. I can't be here alone in this empty house.
When Bill Rile heads off on his bike in the opposite direction, I quickly walk to the other end of Sycamore
Street and turn off toward the shopping area. I am thirsty
and hungry. I didn't eat breakfast before my trek to the
hill and, in the subsequent court proceedings, forgot
about lunch, not that I could have digested it.

I buy some peanut butter crackers at Ben's.

"That's all you want?"

I nod.

"How about a few slices of bologna." He takes the
roll from the refrigerator case over to the slicer, slices
some for me, and wraps them in waxed paper. "And how
about a Vernors on the house?" He puts the drink and the
bologna into a paper bag and hands it to me. "I once
burned down my grandmother's barn. My cousin and I
wanted to see what would burn faster, hay or gasoline. I
had to make a confession. You did the right thing, sweetheart. You even improved the world a wee bit."

I smile through my tears. "Thank you, Ben."

"Anytime."

I step back out into the sunshine. The day is warm. I
walk to the store but it is closing time. Annette waits for
my mother with my dad's car. She's flushed and excited.
My mother comes and takes the car keys, a look of trepi-
dation on her face.

"*She's going to drive again. You want to come?*"

"*No!*" I sign. I can see that maybe it would be better
if I didn't.

"*You can get dinner in Rhoda's,*" my mother signs,
relieved. She hands me some money. "*We drive to the*

lake and back. Back by eight o'clock. You do homework tonight. I'll look at it when I get back."

"Okay."

"Okay?"

Berger is closing up his hardware store and I avoid him. I'm sure he has made the connection between the paint he sold us and what happened to the livery statues. In Rhoda's, I don't want to be seen and I take a booth way back. We call it Loretta's booth because when things are slow she sits there with her *Post Gazette* and watches the dining room. It's next to the WC, so people don't usually choose to sit there. I order matzoh ball soup from Loretta.

"Can I give you a hug, Victory? You look like you need more than matzoh balls. It was on the five o'clock news."

I embrace Loretta's round fat body and she holds me. "Where is your friend?"

I tell her what has happened to Lisanne.

"They will make her sick. That's too sad. It happened to two girls from the East End when I was growing up. Still there, last I heard. Hospital turned them into zombies."

I hear Uncle Abe enter with Cy and I hunch down low.

"How about you join me?" Abe says. "I've got some news about the lake property."

The place is relatively empty and their voices carry. I duck down as low as possible in the booth. My eyes plead with Loretta not to tell Uncle Abe I'm here.

"She wants us to buy it?" Cy asks.

"Well it's not that simple."

"I'm listening."

"It seems maybe the judge is putting me in charge of her affairs, you know, after, all that paint business... Well anyway, I want to set them up right, Cy."

"Well, you let me know how things transpire. I've got to go pick up Howie or I'd join you."

"Just for my information. What kind of price were you thinking of?"

"I'd have to run it by my group."

"When do you think you can get back to me? Idea is, I buy it myself and invest with you. That way they don't take the risk. I'll tell you, with all this paint business, I lost a lot of time this week."

"I see. Well, gotta run."

"Bye, Cy."

Abe takes a booth in the front and waves Loretta over.

"Pretty ingenious," she whispers to me when she passes my booth. "He don't take the risk and he stands to gain. He's been plotting about your mother's property for months now. Don't let her sell to him. I'll let you in on a little secret. Cy's a fair man. I've known him all my life. You can leave through the back if you want. Soup's on me."

She goes over to take Abe's order. I leave my mother's money down on the table and scoot past the ladies' and gents' for the back entrance.

When I turn onto Sycamore Street, there is Bill Rile standing on the corner and blowing smoke rings. It is dusk already.

"I owe you an apology."

I try to ignore him.

"I'm serious."

"That's a big change from an hour ago."

"I was jealous."

"Oh?"

"Well, aren't you going to accept my apology?"

"Sure Billy."

I begin to walk toward my house.

"That's no acceptance. In fact, there is more to my apology. I apologize for not doing this sooner."

The pain is staggering—a rock the size of a melon lands at my feet. I begin to limp home in agony.

"Sucker!" he screams.

I see the parted curtains close in the Glick living room as I climb our front stairs. I double lock the door and go to the back to make sure it hasn't been left unlocked. Inside and alone, I try to see my back in the hallway mirror. I find ice in the freezer and wrap the whole tray in a towel. I'm leaning back on it when I hear a key turn in the lock. But then the lights flicker and I know it is my mother returned from her driving lesson.

She looks at my tear-streaked face. "*Sick?*"

"*No.*"

"*What then?*"

I shrug but the pain is tremendous.

"*Something happened,*" my mother declares. "*What's wrong?*" She grabs the drippy ice from me and lifts my shirt. Frightened by the sight of my bruise, she covers her mouth. "*How?*"

"*No!*"

"*You tell how.*" She picks up the telephone and pushes it in my direction. "*You call Dr. Frank. Tell him come now.*"

I push the phone away. "No, Ma. I'm fine."

She grabs my hand and slams the phone into it. "*Call now, or I take you to hospital. Your choice.*"

Reluctantly, I dial Dr. Frank. "Dr. Frank, this is Victory," I say when he answers. "I hurt my back. I think I'm fine, but Mama insists that you come."

"Are you in a lot of pain?"

I sigh. "Yes, sort of."

He chuckles. "Sort of, huh? I'll be right there."

A little while later, he arrives.

"*You show doctor. Lean forward so he can see.*"

I do as she says and he begins to palpitate my spine. "I want you in the hospital for the night. This needs to be X-rayed."

I begin to sob heavily.

"How did this happen?"

"No one believes me anyway."

"I believe you and your mother believes you. This didn't happen by accident. Did someone hit you with something?"

I shake my head.

"Who was it? This was a vicious thing to do. Who are you afraid of?"

"Bill Rile. If he gets into trouble, he'll do it again."

"Has he done anything else?"

"In science class, he stabbed my thigh with his compass. When I screamed, Mr. Lane sent me to the principal. It was the day my father died. He gave me detention."

"Why didn't you tell Mr. Lane what really happened?"

"I did, but he wouldn't listen because I was late to school."

"Your father was very ill. What's wrong with Mr. Lane? I'm obligated by law to make a report. The police need to know about this."

⌇⌇⌇

I wait on a gurney in the hospital hallway. I've just come back from the X-ray room. My mother takes my hand and kisses my head. "*You can always tell me anything.*"

"*I didn't think you'd have any power.*"

"I only have power if you share the truth. He's a bully but he has a bully for a father. Like father like son. I know all about Ridgely Rile and his drunken habit, and his snooty wife and mother. Don't think I haven't had my own little encounters on that side of the street. I keep to my side when they are out there."

Double doors open, and Abe and Shirley rush over to us. "I heard from Dr. Frank."

My mother is clearly irked. *"Tell him we talk later. I talk to the doctor."*

"Victory's a minor, Esther," Shirley says when I translate.

"I'm mother."

My mother sees Dr. Frank before Abe does. He's waving X-ray pictures, and he has a smile on his face.

"You're a lucky girl. It's just a bad bruise. The police went to talk to Rile but it seems he's run away."

I translate this for my mother.

"His parents know," the doctor says. "I think they probably helped him. He was sighted hitch-hiking at the Monroe turnpike toll toward New York City. Let's hope he stays there."

I've always wanted to go to New York City but now I know I would always be looking over my shoulder for Bill Rile if I did. Loretta's brother was driving his truck from Harrisburg and stopped at the New Stanton service plaza. He saw Bill Rile get into a car. Someone must have made some arrangements for him. He got a ride from a tall blonde woman driving a wood-sided station wagon.

Tomorrow is Saturday. My mother says that we will go to the lake. *"I will drive,"* she tells me.

"I knew you could."

"Abe gave me some papers from the lawyer. I know what he's up to and I need to go up there."

We drive up early. My mother is at the wheel and I am in the front passenger seat. The day is foggy and sooty but it clears once we are out on the highway. We don't take the usual turn. A road from the town leads toward the other end of the lake.

"*I'm going to see the old hotel.*" she says, as if anticipating my puzzlement.

"*Does Cy know?*"

"*He invited me to see. He said walk around. One-hundred-thirty-five bathrooms and a swimming pool.*"

"*How can you do all that?*"

"*I talk to china factory.*"

We pull into a portico-covered driveway and park. Cy is in the entrance with Howie and Henry. He has hardhats for all of us. "Some of the floor boards are loose, so be careful."

The hotel's grandeur is apparent, despite the dilapidated condition—high ceilings with beams crossing far above a circular staircase. The rooms are full of discarded furniture.

Two parlors flank the grand entryway. One leads into a huge dining room with a solarium off to the side. Beyond the solarium, I see the massive empty swimming pool. The size of it would befit the Hearst Castle. A grand hotel in a town that has come and gone and is now coming back.

Cy consults his watch. "I told your uncle he could take the tour also. But I wanted to talk to you first. Do we have an agreement?"

I translate and my mother signs a huge "*Yes!*"

Cy and my mother shake hands.

Uncle Abe's Chrysler rounds the bend and stops under the portico. Abe gets out waving his papers. "Barney drew up all the paper work. Tell your mother we will get her into the investment, and she won't have to sign a thing."

"You know, Abe," Cy says. "I have a problem without Esther's signature."

"But this is for her protection."

"She can protect herself. In fact, she drives one hard bargain. I hired her to repair the tile in the hotel pool and she added on hundred and thirty-five bathrooms into the bargain. Am I a sucker or what?"

Abe looks from Cy to my mother, appearing dumbfounded at first, shocked, then miffed that he didn't get to broker any deal on behalf of my mother.

"*Don't worry, Abie, gotta have linoleum somewhere.*"

I translate and we all laugh.

ↄ∕ↄↄ∕ↄ

My mother keeps her agreement with Cy. While the hotel is under construction, it is one of our happiest years. We only wish my father had lived to see my mother blossom and flourish with her newfound independence. She radiates a new confidence—the gift of having her own business and using her artistic abilities. "*There is strength in adversity. You remember that, Victory,*" she tells me over, and over again.

Cy frequently comes to check my mother's progress in reproducing the tiles. He picks up her ruler and compares a leathery clay square with one of his samples. *Are you sure?* he scrawls on a tablet.

She scrawls back: *Shrink. You wait for bisque then you measure. I show you.* She leads him down our basement stairs and into her temporary work area. "*Dirty!*" she mimes, touching a surface and then rubbing her hands together as if brushing off grime.

She takes a pair of wire cutters, slices off a hunk from a twenty-five pound package of creamy porcelain, and begins to wedge it with the palms of her hands until she is satisfied. *No air*, she scrawls on her pad. She then puts it through an extruder and cranks the clay out in thick strips. These she cuts into squares. *Now bake*, she writes.

She picks up a tile already baked into bisque and lets Cy compare it to her newly extruded tile. She picks up her pad and pen again. *You let me work.*

He starts to climb the basement stairs. I am in the kitchen when he emerges. "It's quite a process," he says to me. "She's an expert. Are you helping her?"

"She shows me when she has patience," I say.

"She's got big orders to fill. I can let myself out."

When Cy is gone I go down to the basement. "*Ma, do you like Cy?*"

"*He's a good man but always in charge. He's like that with everything. Even his son! He will need to let him grow up.*"

No one I know has ever addressed the relationship between Howie and Cy as anything less than idyllic.

"*You can't make somebody something they aren't,*" she signs.

I begin to worry that she will lose the work. So many people we know depend on Cy for business. Nobody would dare cross Cy—certainly not my uncle Abe. Cy pulls so many purse strings. Yet he is considered a good, but very conniving man. If the synagogue needs a community room, they go to Cy.

"*Cy can pull money out of your pocket like a magician can pull rabbits out of a hat,*" Esther signs, laughing. "*I told him to stay away from my hard-earned money, and he laughed at me. They say if you want a contract with Cy's business, you have to turn your pockets inside out."*

I have visions of Uncle Abe's poorly tailored, turned-out pockets flapping out of his pants.

I frequently help at the store doing my homework between customers. We are so busy that we usually eat dinner at Rhoda's. In those meals, we are frequently joined by Cy, who insists on picking up the tab and instructing Howie to check on my homework.

"I'd rather read," I tell them.

I can't wait to get my hands on another book. Not Nancy Drew. I'm beginning to understand that these have been written to inculcate me and girls my age into thinking about people we don't have experience of as stereotypes that we must constantly reinforce with formulaic stories. I no longer want to be like Nancy—in fact, I've become angry at her shallow good will. There is something so pompous about always being on the right side of righteous. I want to read about people's foibles. I've segued into Wilke Collins. I've reread *Pride and Prejudice.* Now I snoop in my mother's book collection for DH Lawrence. I've got her copy of *Lady Chatterly's Lover* hidden under my mattress—a book recommended by Lisanne before our prank. Sex chapters from different adult books are scrawled on the bathroom doors in my school. Initials like *PP, Ch 1, book 6* for *Peyton Place.*

"You have to get the unexpurgated editions," Lisanne has always told me.

I marvel that my mother owns this edition. DH Lawrence's book was banned in England until 1960.

The book opens easily to the sex chapter. I read, aroused, late into the night, thinking about the boys I know. I can't imagine sex or even a kiss with Howie. I think he feels the same way. Nancy Drew's Ned is a knucklehead cartoon. Henry had always been silently attentive to Lisanne, not daring to make his feelings known. I have enjoyed this vicariously. Her brimming personality always engulfed his reserve. I think of him as her Mr. Darcy. Now that Lisanne has been put away, Henry's very, very quiet. He's suffering in silence while I am able to fill the pages of my diary.

I fill my pages now with thoughts of Lisanne, and I record everything that has happened since she was sent away. I'm saving it all for when she can return and I can share with her what she missed out on. I know she would love to know how well my mother is doing. Sometimes I write in letterform, letters I know I cannot send. Ilse and Konrad don't permit her to receive mail from any of us, and we are not sure where it ought to be sent. Howie says his father is working on some ideas, but is rather vague. We have, from time to time, followed Ilse on her morning peregrinations to the Giant Eagle, the drycleaner, and the butcher shop. Apparently, she seldom visits her daughter because the rest of her days are spent closed up in her house doing whatever it is she does as the Frau Doktor.

☙❧

Today Howie doesn't wait for us to finish work at the store.

I check my watch. It is almost time to close and Howie positively glows with excitement. "Cy saw Lisanne."

I cover my mouth.

"They're keeping her at Dixmont."

"Did he talk to her?"

"It was dicey. Come over to Rhoda's and I'll fill you in."

I leave the files, my homework, and the invoices I was supposed to file, grab my jacket from the coat tree, and follow Howie past my uncle, out of the store, and into Rhoda's where Loretta is seated in her booth. We join her.

"My father and Murray Schwartz were asked to bid on some construction for Dixmont," Howie says.

My heart is pounding. "What did he say about her?"

"He asked her to pretend she didn't know him. She was waiting tables in the doctor's dining room. They have the patients doing work therapy, so serving the doctors is their cure. She told him she shouldn't be there. He said he was going to try to help her. He told her how we all miss her, and she started to cry. She told him about this horrible medicine they give her, but she doesn't take it. She holds it between her cheek and gums and spits it out after the nurse leaves. She says she can't say anything.

"Everything she says, the staff there thinks is crazy. She asked Cy if he thought she was crazy, and he told her she wasn't. She never wants to go back to her parents. She can't understand how they could do this to her. Cy told her it was a knee-jerk reaction to what they perceived as bringing dishonor on their heads.

"He told her he thought they loved her and didn't know how. He told her to be patient. There are legal issues that have to be addressed. She asked if we could come and visit, but her parents have forbidden visits from friends," Howie explains. "The power of parents over their children is given to them by the state. It's very difficult to challenge a parent who abuses this power."

I suddenly understand that Lisanne is sentenced to jail, without a trial because her parents have the power to do this to her. Parents can put their children into institutions where they can put drugs into you and invade your brain. I saw Elizabeth Taylor in the film *Suddenly Last Summer* where she is put away and, in my last vi

Lisanne, she was catatonic and curled up into a fetal position in the back seat of her parents' car. I'm desperate to do anything to get her out of her parents' clutches.

"Cy says she still has her sense of humor intact. When he asked her what he could bring next time, she said, 'Maybe some good books. *Reader's over-digested* is the only thing you can find in the Dixmont patient library. Hey, maybe you could bring me some Kafka. Maybe I could wake up tomorrow as a giant cockroach and crawl out along the drainpipes.'"

We hear Henry's uneven gate before we look up and see him towering over us with a look of utter determination on his face. Howie takes off his glasses and wipes them on his shirt. Loretta hands him a napkin.

"So, do you think Cy will really do work for Dixmont?" I ask.

"He has to have his bid accepted by the directors," Howie says.

"So how does that work?" asks Henry.

"Yeah, explain what Cy is up to this time," Loretta says.

"How do you make a bid if you want to fix things up at Dixmont?" I ask.

"Well, Cy went out there with his construction partner Murray Schwartz. My dad's the money and Murray is the contractor. They were given a tour of the facilities. Then they went with the director to the doctor's dining room to talk ideas."

"That's where Cy saw Lisanne?" I ask.

"Yes."

"Do you think your dad will get the job?" asks Henry.

"My dad always outbids everyone else," Howie says.

"So when will we know?" I ask.

"Well, he brought home the plans for the facility to

study. He has to make a lot of cost calculations. He isn't in business to lose money."

"That's for sure," Loretta interjects. "That place is probably in need of a major overhaul. I remember when the state bought it. A lot of voters got miffed that it all happened behind closed doors."

"But if he wins the bid, he might see Lisanne some more?" I ask. "Can we see the plans?"

"Sure, Cy has them at home in his office."

"Well, what are we waiting for?" I ask. "I've never seen blueprints for a building but I think looking at them might put us closer to Lisanne."

We take the bus over to Howie's house where Cy has a huge home office. Howie says he does most of his real work from home on four or five telephones at once. No one is home when we get there. The housekeeper is gone for the day, and the huge home seems tomb-like in the fading daylight. Howie switches on the lights in the center hall, and we follow him back to Cy's study. Behind Cy's massive mahogany desk, floor-to-ceiling windows showcase a flagstone terrace with the manicured yard beyond. A cardboard tube containing Dixmont's blueprints stands in a corner.

"What if Cy comes home?" Henry asks.

"He's probably at Rhoda's right now. He was supposed to pick me up."

"So what are we waiting for?" I repeat.

Howie removes the metal cap from the tube and allows the blueprints to drop out onto the desktop. We help Howie unfurl them.

"Let me find the master," he says, pulling at the topmost sheet.

We hold its corners to keep it from curling back up. Howie gets books to weigh down the edges and we begin to pour over the drawings. It is very clear to me what I'm looking at: Most of the buildings are reached through the front gate, but a laundry facility and a machine shop are situated outside.

"What are these?" I indicate a series of blue-on-blue tracks that remind me of a monocolored Candy Land board. "They seem to connect to every building on the grounds and outside of the grounds."

"Tunnels!" Howie exclaims.

"Ohhh! Spooky! How do we get into them?" I ask.

"Keys," Howie says, opening up Cy's desk drawer and pulling out a massive keychain. "He has keys to the entire place."

"So we could borrow them?"

"Victory, are you thinking what I think you are thinking?"

I nod.

"I think you might be the real genius. What a great idea."

My adrenalin has begun to surge. "We have to figure out what connects to what."

"Well, look at this," says Henry. "The doctor's dining room connects to the laundry. The door says it leads to the kitchen pantry."

"So if we can get into the laundry, we don't have to worry about the guard at the front gate," I say. "Hardy Boys and Nancy Drew watch out. Here we come."

We are laughing our heads off and don't see Cy come into the room. "I guess I ought to learn to lock stuff up," he says.

"Dad, you didn't see anything," Howie says, his eyes pleading.

Cy throws up his hands and leaves the room. We all applaud and begin to make plans.

The planning session continues back at Rhoda's, where we take Loretta into our confidence. She's going to drive us but only to the bowling alley. So we'll have to walk a long way to get to Dixmont.

"We will need to cut school," I say. I'm already thinking about what to wear. Definitely, my Keds, in case we have to run out of there. "What if we get caught? What could they do to us?"

"We can't get caught, that's why we need to really plan this out," Howie says.

"We need to act when the doctors are eating. That's probably when she is freest," Henry says.

"But if we get caught," I insist. "Could we make it worse for her?"

"This is your most brilliant idea, Victory," Henry says. "Don't back out on us."

"You're right. And I can sign to her," I say. I'm feeling another infusion of adrenalin and my confidence returns. Action is the antidote to hopelessness.

"I'm not supposed to be hearing this," Loretta says. "They'll cook my goose with kidnapping charges. So you'ns play Hardy Boys or Nancy Drew or whatever. I'm getting you'ns some dinner. I recommend Rhoda's stuffed pepper special."

"I'm too excited to eat," I tell her.

"Don't get excited yet, kiddos. It's going to be a long haul. So ess mayn kind!"

"Where are we going to take Lisanne?" I ask.

"Her parents are going to bring the police to check on all of our houses," Henry says.

"She could stay at the lake. I don't think they know anything about our lake house."

"She's going to need a lawyer," Howie says.

"How do you get a lawyer? I sure wouldn't want my uncle Abe's lawyer. He told the judge that the Glicks had taken steps to discipline Lisanne."

"Let's get her out first," says Henry. "Let's do it tomorrow."

Loretta returns to our booth with plates of stuffed peppers and sides of mashed potatoes. She puts a plate in front of each of us. "You'uns is going to need all the strength you can get."

"Can you drive us tomorrow, Loretta?" I ask.

"If I say no, you'll go gallivanting off in your father's car, so I say, yes."

"Yey!" we all cheer.

"So let's make a pledge that no one will back out," Howie says. "Stack up all the hands."

We put our hands in the center of the table. I put my right hand out and Howie stacks his on top. Henry stacks his. Then I put my left hand on top of the stack. And they do the same. I feel the warmth from their hands and am energized with a newfound confidence.

"And we do solemnly pledge that we will not back out. We will free Lisanne," I say.

"I second the motion," Howie says.

"And I third it," Henry says. "Pledges cannot be broken."

"Never," we all agree.

Our plans are to enter the laundry at lunchtime and follow the tunnel to doctor's dining room.

My mother thinks I went to school. I wanted to wear jeans but then she would know I was cutting. Girls aren't allowed to wear jeans or pants to school. I'm wearing a red plaid pleated skirt and a matching sweater set with the Keds on my feet. I'm wearing knee socks and my legs are cold. I shiver. I also carry a bag of clothes for Lisanne, no books, no notebooks, but at least I have a sack, in case someone wonders. I get on the bus to Howie's house. That's where Loretta promised to pick us up so we don't have to pass the store or the school.

It is eleven a.m. when Loretta drops us off at Victory Lanes. "Your namesake," she says. "I picked it for good luck." She takes her bowling shoes out of a bag. "Well why not?" She gives us her best Loretta look to send us off. "Now you'ns be careful."

We walk along a winding highway for about a mile and a half. A Ford wagon passes us. "Look the other way!" I scream. "I think it was doctor and Mrs. Glick."

When we get to the Dixmont parking lot, we see a guard permit the Glicks to go through the front entrance. Dixmont was built in the nineteenth century and hasn't changed a lot. A circular entrance is paved in cobblestone like so many Pittsburgh streets. A half-circle of cars nuzzle up to the wrought iron fence on either side of a massive gate. The gate is topped with the name Dixmont in contrasting bronze. *It could say "Arbeit macht frei,"* I think as we scurry to hide among a group of white pines just outside of the grounds. We can see, through the wrought iron fence, the lush-green lawns and gardens of the grounds—filled with benches and statuary. Beyond is a greenhouse where flowers are grown. We can see patients tending to the plants through its glass panes. If it weren't for the ten-foot iron fencing topped with sharp finials, Dixmont would seem like a luxury spa. Cy said that Ridgely Rile was once sent there to dry out, but it obviously didn't work.

"I think we ought to let the air out of their tires," Henry says, indicating the Glick's Ford wagon. "Just in case they try to come after us."

"Be careful," I say.

Henry lopes over to the Ford. His lopsided gate prevents him from moving quickly. He gives us a thumbs-up as he crouches low and approaches the front passenger side. Nonchalantly, he uncaps the air valve, and we all hold our breaths as the tire sinks to the pavement—a surreal blob. When a delivery truck enters the lot, Henry walks slowly away, whistling. When he reaches us, we pull him into our midst. "Not bad for a cripple!" he says.

We watch while the deliveryman in a gray uniform unloads boxes of medical supplies and stacks them onto a dolly. When he wheels it through the gate and toward a ramp for Building B, we make a run for the laundry building.

All the washing machines are busy with mega-sized loads inside.

"They must run for an hour at a time," I say, catching the whiff of tobacco smoke. We see a man in a white uniform behind the laundry building, pulling on a cigarette and exhaling the smoke in a bored and lackadaisical manner. Probably waiting for the loads to finish. We duck low and go to the tunnel door.

Howie unlocks it. "That's how the linens, freshly laundered, are transported for the doctor's tables," he says.

The tunnel lacks spookiness—no dust, no cobwebs, no sign of ghosts. For me, its spookiness lays in its brightly sanitized, clinical sterility. Utilitarian convenience prevails. The Glicks must certainly approve of it. I shiver as the metal door closes behind us with a mechanical click of the lock. It's a soft click but with a finality to it. What if we can't unlock the doors at the other end, and what if we can't open the door behind us? I never liked going into the bank vault with my mother to open our safe deposit box, and I never liked taking a tour of the Klondike Factory with its gigantic freezer that could freeze you to death, in five minutes, if you get locked in. I look straight ahead at the cement-gray-painted floor and gray ceiling hung with fluorescent fixtures, several of which blink.

Maybe you could think those are haunted. I say a little prayer as we traipse deeper into subterranean Dixmont.

There is a junction where the tunnel branches off into other tunnels. We stay to the left. According to the blueprints, that is the tunnel that goes to the pantry for the doctor's dining room. This part of the tunnel is in disrepair. Water drips here and there from a leaky pipe, and we avoid pools of rusty water. Gray masonry walls are stained with blotches that remind me of cave paintings. I see a buffalo joined by dancing human figures. We whisper to each other, afraid that our voices might carry the length of the old pipes. Howie tosses a nickel against the wall and the sound echoes.

We reach the end. There is a metal door. Howie fumbles for the next key and opens it. I sigh with relief as we peer inside and see through the utilitarian pantry into a lavish dining room where Lisanne is covering a table with white cloths. We watch as she puts a vase of flowers from the greenhouse on the table.

My heart skips a beat. "We need to get her attention," I say.

Henry holds up his index finger to indicate that he has a solution to the problem. He pulls a bag of M&Ms out of his pocket, throws one into the air, and catches it in his mouth. Then he begins to a throw M&Ms at Lisanne. Several hit her in the back of her head, and she turns to see us peering into the pantry from the partly opened door. I'll never forget the look of total astonishment on her face that day.

I sign to her to finish setting the table and then slowly head toward us. She signs back that she understands, but then Dr. and Mrs. Glick enter the dining hall with an administrator—a tall gaunt woman of middle age. The Glicks wait at the entrance. The administrator first goes to speak with the dining room supervisor then comes over to Lisanne. She indicates that her parents are there.

We watch as Lisanne gestures that she needs to finish the table first.

We peer through a sliver opening of the tunnel door as Lisanne finishes setting another table and places a bouquet of red roses on it. She makes a ritual of adjusting the sides of the cloth to fit perfectly. When she is satisfied with the look of her setting, she turns to the pantry as if she is getting more linens.

""In *a few minutes. Complications!*" she signs to us.

The dining room supervisor sees Lisanne use the hand motions and just shrugs—all part of crazy behavior as far as she is concerned. Acting like she was going to set more tables, Lisanne goes over to the linen cart, brings a stack into the dining hall, and sets it on a sideboard. From the sideboard, she takes a tablecloth and covers a round table with it. Then she gives a very flustered look at Ilse. "Oh, dear, I forgot the napkins."

She returns to the cart in the pantry and backs up to where the tunnel door is just behind her. But the supervisor and the Glicks are watching now. There has to be a distraction I think. "Is anybody in the kitchen?" I whisper through the crack in the door.

Lisanne goes over to the kitchen and returns. "It's empty. The cook is in the bathroom. I think." She picks up a gallon can of cooking oil.

"What are you thinking of doing with that?"

"It's insurance! I'm going to burn the stew." Lisanne goes back to the kitchen where she turns the burner under a huge stew pot to the highest setting. Then she returns to the dining room with a stack of napkins and resumes table setting—fetching silverware and china from the sideboard. The tables are just about set to perfection. Several doctors wearing white coats enter and take their places at various tables. They look up in alarm as the smell of smoke begins to fill the air. There is a ruckus in the kitchen because the cook has returned. The supervisor goes into the kitchen to confront the cook. Lisanne comes over to the tunnel doorway, removes the lid from the oil, and topples it sideways onto the floor as she glides behind the tunnel door. We lock it from the inside. It will take them a while to think of the tunnel.

For a brief moment, the four of us embrace and rejoice. But we know we must act fast. Lisanne changes from patient clothes into clothes I brought for her. They are mine and are a bit too short for her—a gray wool skirt that doesn't close at the waist. She pulls a baggy blue sweater that was my mother's over her head. She can't go running around outside like a Dixmont escapee.

We hear Ilse demand to know where Lisanne is. Konrad is behind her. They are both calling, "Lisanne, Lisanne!"

"Maybe she went to the terlet," says a man's voice.

"Her parents have come to visit with her," says the supervisor.

"Do you want me to knock on the bathroom door?"

"No, give her a few minutes."

That's when we hear "clomp" and a groan. Someone has slipped in the cooking oil.

"Who spilled the oil?" asks the supervisor. "Cook! Cook!"

"Are you all right?"

"No, my clothes are ruined. Something is going on. Where could that girl have gone?"

"What do you mean 'where could that girl have gone?'" demands Ilse.

We all traipse as quickly and noiselessly as possible back to the laundry door suppressing giggles—but wary that we are not out yet. We are not prepared for a new unforeseen development. As we near the laundry side of the tunnel, we hear a clank, clank and a slam. A release of air as the laundry begins to turn in a dryer. We peek out. Daylight from the laundry hits moats of dust. The laundry man unloads the wash from the large machines into a huge dryer. He begins to fold laundry emptied from one of the dryers onto a cart. Ilse and Konrad sabotaged our schedule. We lost time waiting for Lisanne to make her exit. If the laundry man decides to push a loaded cart through the tunnel, we won't be able to hide.

"Run!" Howie hisses and the four of us run across the laundry and out of the door, followed by the laundry man.

"Hey, what's goan on?" He starts after us but we run like the devil is on our tails. My last vision is of the laundry man shouting in some kind of walkie-talkie. "Loonies on the loose."

Five minutes later, we hear sirens and a voice on a loudspeaker announcing, "This is a lock down."

We avoid the side of the highway and make our way slowly through a wooded gulch, littered with empty pop bottles, old mufflers, and tires, to the ear-blasting sirens of passing police cars. One car stops on the shoulder and four policemen run into the woods. We find a gully filled with debris from old cars and crouch low. They are close enough so that we hear.

"Shoot into the air and see if something moves."

We endure a barrage of gunfire but stay low on our bellies.

"Let's go! They ain't gone this way."

The policemen kick dirt and debris with their clod-hopper cop shoes and finally decide there is no one in this woods. We wait until they leave to poke our heads over the edge of the gulch. The way is clear. Our clothes are coated with automotive grease dumped along with the old auto parts. We finally reach the back entrance to Victory Lanes.

Loretta doesn't even change out of her bowling shoes but herds us out to her ancient Chevrolet. She drives off with the four of us crouching low with suppressed laughter. The Glicks are probably screaming at the hospital administrator, and we can only imagine what damning language they hurl at her before returning to their car to find the tire flat. Sometimes life gives great pleasures.

"Okay," Loretta says. "Where are we off to?"

"We can go to the lake," I say.

"But that's not practical. Yinz has to go to school or someone's gonna get very suspicious. And don't forget you're not supposed to drive, Miss Victory."

"It has to be a place the Glicks wouldn't think of," Howie says.

"They'll look first at your houses," Lisanne says.

"Well, they don't know me," Loretta says. "And I wouldn't mind some company."

Lisanne leans over the seat and throws her arms around Loretta. We all decide that Loretta's house on Montclair Street is probably the safest place to keep Lisanne. Cy now knows that we were able to spring Lisanne. Howie has called him and makes him promise to help keep her out of the mental hospital. She will leave the house only to visit Bob Blaustein, a lawyer Cy has found for her.

In the evening after our escape, the lawyer comes over to Loretta's house with Cy and asks a lot of questions. He's very young, doesn't look much older than Henry and Howie, but he wears a beard and jeans and doesn't look terribly lawyerly.

"I've come to see the fugitive," he says by way of introduction.

"Well, you've come to the right place," says Loretta.

"I have some questions for you, Lisanne," he says.

He's rather short on the preliminaries, I think.

"Are you up for that?" he asks.

"I am."

"Do you think you have a mental illness?" is the first thing he asks Lisanne.

"No, I don't," she says.

"Did you benefit from any therapy offered you at Dixmont?"

"Emphatic no."

"She'd be good on a witness stand," he quips. "Do you think you and Victory committed a crime?"

"We didn't intend to hurt anybody."

"But there was destruction of property?"

"We thought we were making a statement about equality."

"Are you remorseful?"

"I am. I'm also sorry my friend Victory had to shoulder the blame while I rotted away at Dixmont."

He looks at Cy. "Doesn't seem too crazy to me. Her friends took quite a risk for her so they must also believe she is sane. I'd like to take this on."

We all applaud.

"It's going to be a long process with no real guarantees. But I think we should begin some kind of negotiating process with your parents to get them to agree not to hospitalize you again. You'll come with Cy to my office in the morning, and we will lay out some plans."

Lisanne is in tears. "You don't know how much this means to me. All this support—Mr. Blaustein, Cy, Loretta, my good and dear friends."

We hug Lisanne and Loretta supplies her with some Kleenex to blow her nose then passes the box to me as I tear up, too.

After the lawyer leaves, Loretta allows the four of us to hang out there while she goes to work on her shift at Rhoda's. She leaves us a tub of potato salad, coleslaw, corned beef, pickles, Cleveland Rye, Vernor's Ginger ale, and chocolate cake for desert. She closes the blinds, warns us not to open the door to anyone, and leaves to work her shift. We load food onto paper plates and picnic around Loretta's coffee table.

Lisanne beams from one of us to another. "You saved me, you saved me," she keeps repeating over and over.

Loretta's big tom cat Chazer creeps on top of the plastic-covered sofa and down into our midst. Howie feeds him a slice of corned beef, and the fat tom keeps begging for another.

"I would be serving the doctors their dinner right now," Lisanne tells us. "Here's how I served them." She cuts a wedge from the cake, puts it on a plate, and carries it over to Howie with her thumb stuck through the icing and between the layers of cake. "I thought about saving my pills and putting them into their water pitcher. Give them a taste of their own medicine." Then she bursts out into tears. "It was so horrible. I know what it is like to lose your freedom. You can't even begin to imagine. They wanted to obliterate my personality. My parents never appreciated who I am."

We hug her and we hug each other. We tell her we will come back after school tomorrow.

I go home to find my mother painting bisque as usual, a sandwich at her side. She asks me if I am hungry and I tell her that Loretta fed us.

There is a knock on our front door. I see Dr. and Mrs. Glick watching from their porch. Three policemen stand on our porch—their hands feeling for their nightsticks. My mother comes and stands in front of me.

"Your neighbors are worried their daughter is staying with you," says a policeman.

My mother just looks mute and signs to me. *"Do you understand what they want?"*

"No," I sign, pretending to be deaf, too.

"Do you mind if we look around?" asks one of the policemen.

They enter before we can tell them not to. They divide the search and run throughout the house. Finding nothing, all three policemen return to the living room. "Look, if you should see that girl, give us a call. She's supposed to have a loose screw."

My mother and I both sign, looking perplexed. When the police are gone, I call Howie.

Howie tells me they have been to his house too. Cy told the police to get a warrant for his house and they left and never came back.

ℰↄℰↄ

Several days after the great escape, Bob Blaustein contacts the Glicks and asks them if they wanted to talk before he files his case on Lisanne's behalf. They refuse and more days pass by. Lisanne has now been at Loretta's for over a week. The Glicks are very stubborn. Mr. Blaustein suggests that Lisanne write her parents a letter describing what happened to her at Dixmont. She jumps at the suggestion and, while I'm at school, she's produces a very good letter. She reads it to me as we sit next to one another on Loretta's plastic-covered sofa. It crackles under us. I peer over Lisanne's shoulder as she reads out loud with vehemence.

"'To my dear but misguided parents:

"'Because my heart is generous, I offer you the benefit of the doubt. I don't believe you fully understand what you have set in motion regarding my life. It is my own to live, even at my age. You deprived me of my freedom. You have acted as my jailers rather than as my parents. I will be an adult in the not too distant future. Was it your intention to lock me up for life rather than prepare me for it? Is this "cure" you are subjecting me to open-ended? When do you pronounce me cured? When I have acquiesced to your every demand rather than have ideas of my own? What you see as defects in me are actually my strengths. How can I use my mind and be the smart person you expect me to be if I can't make mistakes, ever?

"'My lawyer tells me that, even if I were convicted of a misdemeanor for my prank, I would receive no jail time and, most probably, I would be asked to do community service. How can I grow up if I cannot be held accountable for my deeds? You drugged me and whisked me away to an institution, before I could make apologies to the boys who suffered for my actions.

"'Let me describe what life in a mental hospital is like: and you, in turn, must consider whether the punishment fits the crime. First and foremost, I was totally bored at Dixmont. I had no serious reading available to me and until I learned to only pretend that I had taken the medication, I could not have focused on a page. That's what Thorazine, the drug of choice, does to people's brains. I could have gone to the occupational therapy provided to the patients but that was making lanyard chains for hours and hours.

"'I had sessions with the psychiatrist Dr. Bland three times a week. In those sessions, I was allowed to ramble and talk in general while he stared at me in silence, watching for missteps. I was fearful that if I said the wrong thing that I would have to undergo more barbaric treatments like electro shock or even a lobotomy. So sometimes, I said nothing at all and fifteen or twenty minutes would pass. It was usually me who broke the silence for fear my lack of conversation would be interpreted as hostile.

"'The one other girl my age here at Dixmont has had a lobotomy and can't remember what she ate for breakfast. She will have to be cared for at Dixmont for life. She, also, has no clue what she did to get there.

"'After my first week at Dixmont, Dr. Bland decided on work therapy for my cure. It was my job, for no pay, to push a cart of laundry from building to building. I tried to tell you about this the last time you visited but you refused to listen to me. Pushing the cart, I saw patients lined up in a hallway to receive electro shock treatments. At the end of the line is a gurney. Each patient in turn lies down on the gurney and electrodes are attached to their heads. When the doctors administer the shock, you can see the patients convulse. One patient vomited, and I had to put the dirty sheet into the cart with my bare hands.

"'I requested a new job and was allowed to work as a waitress in the doctor's dining room. And you know the rest. So do you think that lobotomies, electro shock, work therapy, and Thorazine are acceptable punishment for someone—your own child—who has made a mistake and actually a funny mistake? And, by the way, there are many people who think that Victory and I did the right thing. As you know from Bob Blaustein, my lawyer, you will have no contact with me without an agreement not to send me back to any mental hospital. I don't have a mental illness. I am a normal, smart, and funny teenaged girl with great potential. Why would you want to change me?'"

And she signed it "with love from Lisanne." She despaired sending the letter. "Mother will probably correct my spelling. I'm a child suffering from my parents' pride. It is as if they worked backwards with me rather than forward. Radcliffe is the end of their line, and they don't have a thought beyond that stage—well, maybe another generation of Frau Doktors. I don't want to be a Frau Doktor."

"You can be anything you want to be," I say. "Even a real doctor."

"I've always felt so stifled by thoughts of my future. I want to be free to be whatever I want to be.

"And me, too."

"We both have to believe we can be whatever we want to be. But I want to take the long way to get there and enjoy life."

We hug.

"We won't let anything stop you," I promise.

"Do you think it's a good letter?"

"It's incredible."

The Glicks insist that Lisanne be there at the meeting but Mr. Blaustein tells them she will not appear. In addition to the letter, he would like them to hear from her friends. They refuse at first, according to Bob Blaustein, but Konrad prevails over Ilse and they agree to meet.

Howie, Henry, and I are already seated in Bob Blaustein's conference room when the Glicks arrive. It is clear that they, too, have suffered. Ilse looks years older—her blonde hair washed with more gray. And Konrad's already-pronounced stoop has worsened. A secretary offers them coffee or tea but they refuse. They don't say hello to us.

"I assume you helped her escape," is all Konrad says.

"Your daughter is very gifted and needs little help in any endeavor, it seems," Bob Blaustein says. "She just needs love with no strings attached."

"You know nothing," Ilse says.

"Did you ever engage in pranks, Dr. and Mrs. Glick?"

Ilse snorts. "There was no time for us to engage in pranks. We were fleeing the Nazis."

I look out at Pittsburgh from the lawyer's twelfth-floor window. It has begun to rain. The city seems like a motionless dragon—too exhausted to move. It's organs, struggling to maintain their life force, continue to belch and spit fires that darken the air we breathe. Heaving rain carries dirt from the air down in runnels on the walls of adjacent buildings.

"My parents, too, fled the Nazis," the lawyer tells them. "Do you want to punish your daughter for what you were denied?"

"It's not like that," Ilse says. "We were in a world gone mad. If you were defective in anyway, you were exterminated like a vermin. Our daughter has recently learned to sign like a deaf person. This would stigmatize her."

"So, instead, you burden your daughter with the stigma of mental illness. Forgive me, but your logic eludes me. Hitler sent the mentally ill to his ovens? This is America. It can't happen here."

"It can happen anywhere."

"Part of the purpose of filing this lawsuit is to prevent such things from happening, to prevent an over-intrusive state from abridging a child's freedom."

"When will we see our daughter?" Ilse asks.

"Your daughter will not meet with you until you guarantee that she will not be returned to Dixmont or any other institution. I've been retained to represent her in any proceedings."

"Who is paying you for this?" Dr. Glick asks.

"She has a generous benefactor who wishes to remain anonymous."

A sardonic Ilse snorts again. She is given to snorting when she is nervous. She keeps wringing her hands and refolding them into the lap of her grey wool suit skirt. A few hairs come loose from her bun and she brushes them off her forehead. "I can imagine who the benefactor is. One who serves drinks to minors.

"I had Shabbos wine growing up," Bob Blaustein retorts, "and sometimes I sneaked a little extra—my mother thought she drank it and kept refilling her glass."

We all laugh, except the Glicks.

"Let me just say this," he continues. "Even if there were no benefactor, I would pursue this case on my own. The institutionalization of children by their parents without grounds is that abhorrent to me. And I am prepared to take it to the supreme court, benefactor or not."

Ilse begins to cry. He ignores her and begins to pass out papers. "This is my preliminary motion."

I glance down and read the numbered paragraphs. It seems that lawyers spend a lot of time quoting. Each numbered paragraph is littered with copious footnotes.

"These are from the proposed new guidelines for commitment," the lawyer says. "You will have to present evidence that hospitalization is a more effective form of treatment." He engages in a staring contest with Dr. Glick.

"But we don't have to present any evidence," Konrad tells him, averting his eyes. "It is you who needs to change the law, as it is. Am I not correct?"

"You are correct. However, it will be a costly journey for you as well."

"And who wrote the letter?"

"Your daughter wrote the letter without any help."

"Just tell us where our daughter is," Dr. Glick says emphatically.

"I've promised my client that her whereabouts will remain secret for the moment," Bob Blaustein says.

Dr. Glick turns to us. "Kidnapping is a crime."

"You underestimate your daughter. She didn't need to be kidnapped," says the lawyer.

"And these young hoodlums?" Dr. Glick indicates us with a sweep of his hand.

"They are her friends—good friends."

"What kind of friend keeps a friend from getting medical attention?" Ilse asks, looking directly at me.

I don't answer.

"You can't answer, can you?"

I'm suddenly a cauldron of vehemence frothing over the edges. I lose my self-control and yell at Ilse. "We are friends and there is nothing you can do about it. You locked her up, and that didn't work. You make her hate everything she does, even if she does it well, like play the piano. She's been trying to tell you this. She's going to quit the piano because you forced it on her. I wish I had piano lessons. She's lucky, but instead of appreciating her music, you made her hate it."

"You know nothing. My whole life got interrupted. I played the piano well enough to pursue it as a career. We had to leave everything behind."

"Why don't you play again?" Henry asks her.

"Don't you see? It's because it is too late. By the time we settled, I was too old to resume serious studies."

"Maybe you could show Victory how to play," Howie says.

"Not a chance. Are you trying to worm your way into my good graces after you so callously abduct my daughter?"

"We didn't abduct your daughter." Howie leers into her face and Mr. Blaustein has to pull him away. "You abducted your daughter. You had a doctor drug her and lock her away where she was constantly under the threat of barbaric treatments."

"It is for us to decide our daughter's treatments," Dr. Glick says.

"We say otherwise," Bob Blaustein retorts. "I think that's enough for now. You know now where we stand. I have some papers here for you to look at. If you sign them, Lisanne will be present at the next meeting. These are her guarantees that you won't attempt to institutionalize her again. Take them and think about it."

Ilse Gluck rips them up.

"If you want another copy, just call my office."

"And suppose we acquiesce to this demand? What then?" asks Dr. Glick.

"We will schedule another meeting. And your daughter will be present."

"We will let you know," he says as he stands. "Ilse, let's go. We aren't accomplishing anything here."

The door slams behind them.

e/ɔe/ɔ

After seeing the lawyer, our foursome meets again at Loretta's house to tell Lisanne how the meeting went. Cy has brought over two pizzas from Mineo's. Mineo's is the new rage upstreet—the richest tomato sauce, thin crust, and copious cheese, baked in a brick oven. *Pittsburgh is a brick oven*, I think. *Always being stoked—burning embers and smoke were the constant by product of its industries. There is talk of filters on top of the smoke stacks but it won't happen until the steel industry is dying away.* I think about how my father's pain could have been eased if the air had been cleaner. Montclair Street is closer to the mills than our house on Sycamore Street.

Today Loretta runs a rag over her windowsills and comes up with dark soot. "Not worth it to hang out the laundry."

"Why don't you have some pizza, Loretta?" Howie says.

"Did Cy get me some pepperoni?"

"One pepperoni and one plain," I say.

"You can have my pepperonis," Lisanne says, pulling them off gingerly with her fingertips and putting them back in the pizza box.

She thinks she has gained a lot of weight eating the patient fare at Dixmont. We assure her that she looks just fine.

Loretta laughs and pinches Lisanne's waist. "Fat? Yinz has got to be kidding."

"Well, I just wish I wasn't cooped up in here. I need some exercise. Can I go for a walk?"

"Not yet. You have to be patient," I say.

She nods in acquiescence.

When I get home later, I find a note from my mother. "Gone to the movies," it reads. That's a first. In my entire life, my mother has never taken me to a movie. That was my father's job as a hearing man.

I begin my homework. Howie and Lisanne have been showing me how to solve algebra word problems. I'm also learning to factor. The math is like a vacancy I am filling in. No one ever made it fun and so now I am learning my timetables in order to do my work—baby stuff. It is clear to me what I missed out on when my father was sick. If I meet a little child whose mother or father is sick, I'll know the child is missing out and will somehow help. Howie, Henry, and Lisanne drill me like a little kid, and it can be annoying.

"Okay, Victory fifteen times eleven," Howie says every time I put food in my mouth. That was yesterday at Loretta's. "That's going further than anyone goes with timetables. I learned up to twelve," I protest but they keep on me.

"Prime numbers," Lisanne demands. "What are all the prime numbers from one to one hundred?"

My head is reeling. I just hope they won't start on my spelling. My old diary was filled from cover to cover, even the margins, and I left it with Lisanne with its less-than-perfect spelling. But I've learned that spelling isn't as important as getting my thoughts out onto the paper. She will now learn how I felt about her absence. I have a new diary on the stand beside my bed, and I open it to the first page. For ten minutes, I conduct an internal conversation with myself to the thrum of rain on my window. Just feelings I try to recapture—feelings about the last few days. What it feels like to do something really risky and get away with it. I'll read it tomorrow to see if it makes any sense. I'm supposed to write an essay on friendship. I would love to write about our pledge, but that will have to wait for many years to pass.

My mother returns from the movie as I am about to turn out the light and go to sleep. I keep the light on a few more minutes, in the hopes that she will look in on me. I am gazing out at Lisanne's now dark window, wishing we could converse in sign again. My mother comes into my room.

"*Why now you go to the movies?*" I ask.

"*Cy invited me. He knows I can't hear. He wrote not to worry, this time he couldn't either. We saw a French movie* Breathless *with Jean Paul Belmondo and we both read the subtitles. It was good. He invited me again for Saturday night. Kurosawa!*"

So my mother becomes a foreign film buff. I'm not ready to contemplate that she could be forming a relationship with Cy. She's a head taller than he is, for starters.

🙰

Dr. Frank and Cy have kept their promise to pressure the Pittsburgh police to bring back Bill Rile to face charges for his assaults on me. We have an appointment with the district attorney tomorrow, and I will have to miss school for that. School without Bill Rile has gotten tolerable for the most part. Mr. Lane allows me to answer questions. He has even let me hand in my paper on Madame Curie a semester late for extra credit. I love doing this paper. I read the biography by Eve Curie, her daughter. Next year I plan to take chemistry and the teacher is a woman, Dr. Mann, the only woman teaching science in my school.

Some of the kids have asked me to teach them sign language. We do it at lunchtime. The lunchroom teachers watch from a distance as a large group of kids forms around me. Twenty some kids crowd around a long lunch table. No talking allowed—only signing. Eating and signing is complicated for them. No one believes it is a real language. First, I teach them to finger spell then some simple phrases. They all want to learn how to cuss, of course, so now I probably have kids saying nasty things about their teachers. They have all exhausted talk about my exploits with Lisanne and *Radio-Free Sycamore Street*. I can't wait for Lisanne to come back to school, but she might not be able to for the remainder of the year, the lawyer says. There is talk of her being sent away from Pittsburgh until some agreement can be reached with her parents. Next year is her senior year because she skipped. She is supposed to graduate at sixteen as will Howie and Henry.

Aunt Shirley and Uncle Abe are suspicious that I somehow orchestrated Lisanne's miraculous escape. I run into Abe outside of Povich floors on the way to Rhoda's.

"So if you tell me where the little shickse is, I won't tell anyone," he says.

"But I don't know, Uncle Abe."

"You can't let me in on your little secret? Did Cy Merlman help you'ns out? No one just walks out of Dixmont without some help."

At another poker night dinner at Rhoda's with Aunt Shirley, my mother insists on paying the bill, saying that Shirley paid last time. It is difficult for Shirley to see my mother getting so independent. She no longer wears altered hand-me-downs from Shirley but has bought herself some very nice things from The Tweed Shop Upstreet, and a pair of madras Bermudas and a button-down oxford cloth blue shirt for me. We call our big shopping area near the Giant Eagle supermarket, and the big shoe store Upstreet. Rhoda's is actually located Upstreet as well as Povich Floors.

Chapter 33

A store has become available several doors down, and my mother has leased it. She and Annette have decided to become business partners. My mother invites Shirley and Abe to Rhoda's for cheesecake so she can tell them about it.

"What do you mean another shop?" Abe asks. "You're having beginners luck and you're going to over extend."

I translate this for my mother who laughs.

"I allowed you to start this tile thing in my store the least you owe me is a finder's fee. How would you have met Cy? Through me you met him."

"The store was mine, too. I'm letting you have the whole business."

Uncle Abe is livid with anger because he's decided the tile business is his as well. "After you cut into my business to start this tile thing? I have something invested in this tile, too."

Loretta is our spy hovering ever over everyone with her coffee pot. She's been privileged to all the machinations to keep my mother out of the tile business and now she's laughing her head off and cheering my mother's success.

Annette and my mother begin to ready the store. Because it is a tile store, Annette and my mother tile the floor. On Sunday when many businesses are closed, they can be seen on their hands and knees, gluing then grouting their own tiles.

During this period, my mother works out of the house. Sharing the space with Abe has become too uncomfortable. My mother and Annette not only repair tiles, they have designed a new line for the kitchen and bathroom, and they sell them as fast as they can make them. I came home from school one afternoon and my mother had pulled out all of the kitchen cabinets and tiled the walls behind with tiles depicting fruits and vegetables. She pulled off the old speckled Formica counters and uncle Abe's linoleum from the floor, and tiles are going down there also.

They are calling the business A&E Tile for Annette and Esther. We are going to have a ribbon cutting party run by the Pittsburgh Chamber of Commerce. We will serve champagne.

The day before the ribbon cutting ceremony, Howie, Henry, and I help my mother move into her store. My mother has had lights installed in the storefront window and glass shelves on the walls. We fill racks and shelves with tiles of all shapes, sizes, and colors.

All the merchants come after they close their shops. Everyone admires the new shop. Cy serves the champagne and there are Cy's signature hunks of cheese, salted mixed nuts, stuffed grape leaves, and plenty of crackers. Loretta brings over a tray of sandwiches from Rhoda's. I'm saddened that Lisanne can't be with us. I plan to go home with Loretta later and bring her some of the goodies.

A lot of gossip now circulates about Esther and Cy. Abe hasn't shut his mouth since Esther landed the deal. He even goes so far as to say that Esther is desecrating the memory of his brother, Loretta reports. We lost my father almost a year ago. He would not want my mother to be alone and miserable.

Abe hovers in a corner with Shirley. Povich floors never did anything with the front window. It was just extra storage for rolls of linoleum. You had to go through the front door even to see into the shop. Shirley now suggests to Abe that he do something with the window. "To draw the eye in."

"The second I make the shop fancy, that 'gonovim' landlord is going to raise our rent."

Loretta says Abe could have bought the building years ago and was too cheap to do it.

Chapter 34

Our meeting with the assistant district attorney took place a week after the store opened. It did not go well. We sat in his utilitarian office as he wrote on a yellow legal pad. ADA Hines had the air of an ex-military man, steel blue eyes, and salt and peppered hair. He looked a little like Mr. Lane in his navy gabardine suit. I could imagine him in a white coat. He was on his way into a trial, he told us impatiently thrumming the pencil on the pad.

"There were no witnesses to Billy's attack on you. It would be a difficult case to bring to trial. Besides, Bill Rile is still a minor."

I keep seeing the parting curtain across the street in my mind's eye but I don't say anything. If she saw something, Ilse would never come forward. We understand that Billy's grandmother found money for a lawyer, a cousin of Mr. Glock. We heard. Billy still hasn't returned to Sycamore Street.

The night after our meeting with the ADA, I am making some mashed potatoes to have with a Swiss steak for our dinner. The doorbell rings and that means the lights are flickering too. My mother wouldn't be home for another hour or so. Thursdays the stores Upstreet stay open late. Uncle Abe says that if little stores are going to compete with the big department stores they need to stay open late.

I put down the potato ricer, wipe my hands on the apron usually worn by my mother but not recently, and open the front door without thinking. Ridgly Rile puts his foot over the door jamb to prevent me from slamming it closed. I start to panic and look around for something to use as a weapon.

"I just came to talk. You're spreading dirty rumors about my boy."

Again, I notice the curtains across the street part.

He continues to rant, stinking of alcohol. His face is covered with blotches of broken veins. "Why do you want to get my boy into trouble?"

My hand slides down to the handle of an umbrella. If he comes closer, I pray I will be able to stab him with the pointed end. I want to scream "Why do you hurt him? It makes him hurt others." Instead, I say, "I'm going to scream for the police."

"I'm going to warn you. You're going to look like a fool in court. You're nothing but a little sexually over-active kike. I heard all about you. You asked for it."

"Go away!" I hear myself scream again. I grasp the umbrella handle more firmly and raise it. Ridgely Rile stumbles backward but begins to charge forward at me. I point the umbrella at him and holler for the cops as he reaches in toward me. I have the umbrella aimed at his heart. The thought of plunging the point into his flesh makes me hesitate.

Then I hear another voice: a man with a German accent. Dr. Glick has crossed the street. "It might be better if you go home, Mr. Rile." He helps Ridgly Rile down the steps and nods to me. "Lock your door."

When Rile staggers home, Dr. Glick goes back into his house. In fifteen minutes, my mother will be home. I shiver at the thought that I might have plunged the umbrella point into a man's heart. The spurting blood and release of air from the deep wound seems all too real to me.

The next day, I'm sitting in Loretta's booth at Rhoda's, eating a tuna fish salad sandwich. Loretta has finished waiting on the after school crowd, and it will be another hour before the supper crowd arrives. She sits down and sips a seltzer. She likes it warm and we always tease her about that. Howie says warm seltzer causes hot, wet farts. Loretta says someday he will outgrow scatology. I tell her about my visit from Ridgely Rile and how Dr. Glick intervened. How it is the first time any adult has intervened.

Loretta is thoughtful for a moment. "Why did you wait so many years to tell an adult about this business with the Rile boy?"

I shrug. "I have always found it so difficult to tell my mother things. I don't think my mother is real in a certain sense."

"It's because you think you are the mother here."

Loretta understands in an instant what no one else understood. With my mother and me, it was a reversal of our roles. I can now see it very clearly. If bad things happened to me, then the blame would fall on her, and I tried to spare her this pain. Layers of dishonesty were like a plaque on our relationship. Protecting her allowed me to control our lives—the lying about permission slips, grades, all of the things for which she depended on my father, put the power into my hands.

"So when you managed to botch things, you also

managed to allow the punishments to flow in the form of a Bill Rile or taunting kids."

Loretta blurts out the truth I have managed not to see. My little omissions and dishonest machinations brought things down on myself.

"That will be fifty dollars! And you don't even need a mental institution doctor to find it out."

I start to cry and Loretta hugs me. "Oh what children endure in this world."

At Cy's suggestion, we return to the district attorney's office with Bob Blaustein, who jumps at the chance for a bit of leverage over Lisanne's parents. He will demand to know what Ilse and Konrad might have witnessed and kept quiet about. With Bob Blaustein's help, I am able to paint a more complete picture of how I had been victimized by Bill Rile from the third grade on and why I live in constant fear of him. I also tell the district attorney about Mr. Rile's abusing Billy. Bill Rile lived in constant fear of his father and was humiliated in front of me. And I, in turn, lived in constant fear of Bill Rile. Only I never realized it wasn't normal to live in fear. Bob Blaustein makes it very clear that until Rile is prosecuted, I cannot be safe. I also tell the district attorney how Lisanne and I watched a rape scene in Lindy's woods. He would like a statement from Lisanne about this incident. We don't know the name of the girl who was raped.

ADA Hines is still skeptical. "Without testimony from the Glicks or a victim coming forward—" He shakes his head. "—there is no case."

In those days, victims didn't come forward. They were to blame.

Dr. Glick admits to the DA that he doesn't think it was appropriate for Mr. Rile to come to our door when my mother wasn't at home. But he doesn't say that anyone has seen attacks on me. He squirmed, according to

ADA Hines. I could just imagine a dialogue between Ilse and Konrad. She probably never told him what she saw. But there was no way to coerce more out of him. Bob Blaustein said that sins of omission might be unethical but are not crimes, as in committing perjury. You can't make someone see something they haven't seen. Even the parting of curtains doesn't necessarily mean she was watching me, although I knew she was.

ဆဝဆ

When my mother arrives at the store in the morning, the neighboring shopkeepers are clustered in front of her window. They part to let her view a jagged hole in the front window. Someone has thrown rocks through it during the night. It broke some of the glass shelving and one of the lighting fixtures. Tiles are scattered onto the floor and several in the display window are in fragments. There is no way, as usual, to prove who we think might have done the damage. The beautiful new store has been open less than a month. My mother and Annette cry in each other's arms.

We are in Loretta's living room after school and I think I see Bill Rile walk by.

"You've got to stop this, Victory," Henry says.

I've begun to see Bill Rile everywhere. Now that the principal and the teachers know what he did to me, I feel the safest when I'm there in school. I'm afraid to be alone in our house or out on the street. I make myself crazy with "what if's." What if he corners me near Ben's? What if he has been following me and biding his time until he can pounce? He's not one to learn a lesson. He is too damaged and his anger toward me has certainly escalated. We all agree about that.

We learn that Bill Rile has been sent to the Admiral

Putnam Military Academy, the very same that prepared Ridgely Rile to be an officer.

"It's not far from Dixmont," says Loretta, who never misses out on any little irony. She continues to be our eyes and ears. "They can always ship him over there if he misbehaves."

There is a pricey little market on the other side of Forbes Street called Randall's Fancy Foods. Randall's sells fancy fruit, meaning mealy red delicious apples, and non-kosher meats. That's where Mrs. Glock buys her chipped beef and canned asparagus. Randall's sells cheeses you can't find in the Giant Eagle. Cy owns the building and sends his sister Ellen in there for cheeses for his happy hours.

Ellen's ears perk up when Randall says, "Will that be all, Mrs. Glock?"

"Yes, thank you, Randall."

Randall seems reluctant to let her leave. "I wanted to ask you about the Rile boy. Terrible rumors circulating about him!"

"Well, you know who's responsible for the rumors."

"The little painter?"

"She now claims he has done nasty things to her since they were in the third grade together. My guess, having suffered them as neighbors, she made it all up. Poor boy has it rough with his father so debilitated from the war. They sent Bill off to Admiral Putnam Military. Lindy sees him when the schools have dances. In fact, her school is having its spring high school cotillion club dance with the boys from St. Andrews and Admiral Putnam.

"Lindy is certainly the young lady now!"

"Well, she's fifteen. Almost a debutante! Learning to volunteer for charity. Riding. Tennis. Never a dull moment."

"And your husband?"

"Work! Work! Work! But that goes along with the promotion."

"And your new house!"

"A gem! Roomy and so nice to finally have a place to entertain properly."

❧❧

The store window has been fixed and my mother puts her display together again. Howie and Henry help us set things right. When we are finished, we go over to Rhoda's. Loretta has packed up sandwiches and sodas for us and she ushers us out of the back door where Henry's father waits with his car to take us to Loretta's house. Dr. Frank has overcome his reluctance and has begun to get involved in what we are doing to help Lisanne. Poor Lisanne still hasn't been out of the house, except for lawyer visits, and she has to duck down on the floor of the car and enter the freight entrance of the law building.

The Glicks have hired a private detective to try to find Lisanne. We know this because he questioned all the shop owners to see if anyone had seen her. His name is Arnold Beamen—spelled like the chewing gum. *Good name for a gumshoe*, I think. I first noticed a Pontiac parked across from the Rile house with a fat man sitting in it for hours at a time. He changes parking spaces every hour, moving the car in front of the Lipmans' at the other end of the street. Sometimes he parks in front of the Kramers' house. I also noticed that when I climbed aboard the streetcar to go to school that the Pontiac followed me. I travel alone because Julie Kramer's parents still don't allow her to talk to me. I need to transfer from a streetcar to a bus to get to school. He waited for the bus a ways off as I waited and, again, followed as the bus wound down Shady Avenue to drop me off at school.

Once he followed my mother and me out to the lake. We saw a fat man peeing on a tree trunk a few properties away. We have gotten good at spotting him. He's slovenly and is always taking pictures with a Polaroid Land camera. Sometimes he comes into Rhoda's and orders a pastrami sandwich. One time, he ordered matzoh ball soup and Loretta put gefilte fish in it instead of matzoh balls. He told her that the matzoh balls didn't taste right.

"I assure you our matzoh balls are the best in the world," says Loretta.

We've peeked into his car. Pop bottles filled with pee roll on the floor along with White Castle, Klondike wrappers, and the backings to his Polaroid pictures. He has even followed Cy and Bob Blaustein.

We routinely let the air out of his tires whenever he leaves the car in front of Rhoda's.

"He's in there drinking coffee," Howie hisses.

I crouch down by the right front tire and Howie and Henry block me from view as I turn the valve causing the tire to deflate. We deflate all four tires. That's how we are able to escape by Rhoda's back door as Mr. Beamen gets out an air pump and begins to inflate them.

There has been no word from Lisanne's parents about signing any agreement. Things just don't seem to change, ever.

Henry has his arm around Lisanne and, whenever he thinks we aren't looking, he kisses her. Watching them makes me wish I felt that way about Howie. Howie wanted to try to kiss me but neither of us felt anything.

"I'm not sure what I'm supposed to feel," he told me and I didn't know what to say.

To me Bob Blaustein is cute and I get tongue-tied when he is around. *Someday I won't be too young for him*, I think. *I wish I were his client.*

"How can we make things happen?" Henry asks us as we unwrap our sandwiches.

We each have a half of a baloney and a half of a tuna fish. We peak into the other sandwiches, roast beef and egg salad, but we are too full to eat more. Howie and I go to put the rest into the refrigerator. I am about to return to the living room but Howie puts his finger over his mouth. We hear a rustling of Loretta's plastic sofa cover. Lisanne and Henry are necking so Howie and I stay in the kitchen and fill the percolator with coffee grounds and water, and sit at Loretta's kitchen table to give them some privacy. When we return to the living room, Henry and Lisanne are sitting upright holding hands.

"I would give anything to crash Lindy's school dance. I would trip Bill Rile for you," Lisanne says. "At least then one of our problems would be addressed."

She's given me an idea. "Suppose we send Rile a letter from a secret admirer that tells him she wants to meet him in Schenley Park the night of the dance," I say. "And when he gets to the spot in the park, we could terrorize him."

"Yes," Howie says.

"How would you terrorize him?" asks Henry.

"Assume he's probably going to get drunk at the dance so his reflexes are going to be off," Lisanne says.

"This has the makings of a good plot." I say.

"How do we get the invitation to him?" Henry asks.

"Pony express," Howie says.

"No, then they might smell a rat. Better he gets the note at the dance and is too plastered to think it through," Henry says.

"I like it," I say. *Revenge could be syrupy sweet*, I think. I remember Lisanne's astral celestial mirror trick when we first met and how it frightened me until I realized she was signing. We start to conjure up a ghostly display to greet Bill Rile at midnight in Schenley Park.

"How about we tar and feather him?" I suggest.

"How are you going to get tar?" Howie wants to know.

"Not real tar. Something sticky, yucky, and dark, like molasses."

"We could get a gallon of molasses from Rhoda's and get the feathers out of an old pillow," Lisanne says. "The plot thickens."

"Howie and I will canvas the park for the deepest and best-hidden thicket," Henry says. "In it, we will design our lair."

We plan to leave a trail for Rile to follow into it from the Park's entrance—a trail of garter belts, silk stockings, and bras—all Fredericks of Hollywood. The dance is at the Pittsburgh Athletic Club several blocks away from Schenley Park. No Jews allowed in the club. We will all dress up to look like supernatural creatures of the night. Imagination has no limit.

The first thing Bill Rile will find is a bottle of bourbon and, when he has had a considerable amount, we will come out of hiding, dump on the molasses and feathers when he passes out, and then wake him up to watch us perform our ghostly orations.

The cotillion ball is now two weeks away. We still haven't figured out how to get the note to Bill Rile at the dance. Lisanne suggests that she dress up like a debutante but we nix it. It is too dangerous. If she got caught, someone would call her parents.

"I want to be able to do this with you," she says.

Chapter 35

We are crowded into Loretta's tiny kitchen, eating bagels and lox and drinking fresh coffee. Henry once again has his arm around Lisanne and she leans into him. Howie moves in close to me and puts his arm around my shoulders, raising Loretta's eyebrows.

"I'll get yinz a bottle if yinz wants to spin it."

Howie takes his arm away and Loretta laughs.

We are expecting Bob Blaustein to come over with legal papers. He has suggested a writ of habeus corpus and, as I understand it, this is the way to force the Glicks and the doctors at Dixmont to say why Lisanne needs to be in a mental hospital. Blaustein says that he will also move for a termination of the Glick's parental rights.

This is very disturbing to Lisanne. "It's a damned conundrum," she says. She has sent them a counter offer that they will undoubtedly not agree to unless a miracle happens.

"So what are our arguments?" I say.

"She might lose a semester of school if she doesn't come back soon," Howie says.

"You'd think with all their emphasis on homework, they'd be concerned that you're not doing anything," I say. "Why don't we ask your teachers for your work?"

"I need a miracle," Lisanne says.

"What kind of miracle can we make happen?" I say, my mind drawing a blank after so much excitement. What could force the Glicks to acquiesce to a counteroffer from Lisanne?

Bob Blaustein arrives. I take his jacket and notice it gives off the scent of citrusy aftershave. I want to breathe it in. I hang the jacket on a hook in Loretta's hall closet and notice that it has patches on the elbows. I wonder who sewed on the patches. Maybe he is married, but he doesn't wear a wedding band. He follows me into the kitchen. I've grown at least an inch since the escape from Dixmont and wear a kahki straight skirt and button-down blue oxford cloth shirt my mother bought for me. I feel his eyes on my back and shiver.

Loretta gives Bob Blaustein a cup of coffee and fixes him a bagel with lox, the salty variety smeared with cream cheese. Nova Scotia salmon is a world away from our world.

He takes a bite and gets down to business. "The law here is rather thin, and we are skating on legal thin ice. I've talked to several psychiatrists who think there is a movement toward a doctrine of dangerousness for commitment, so if painting jockeys in the middle of the night constitutes dangerousness..." He lets this thought dangle then resumes. "Your parents will probably argue that you lacked reality when you went gallivanting off into the night with a can of paint. You are faced with people who will agree with them."

"So all this talk about the supreme court is hot air," Howie says.

"What we're faced with here is that there is no law to

challenge. There are protective agencies for children but, in a year, you will no longer be a child. You will be sixteen and, if you should desire to quit school and go to work, there is not much, short of the mental hospital, that your parents can do to you."

He hands Lisanne a letter from Ilse and Konrad. "They have suggested very strong terms in exchange for no mental hospital."

"It sounds like they want to bring the mental hospital home." Lisanne frowns as she reads it. "They are proposing a curfew fit for a two-year old."

"What does it say?" we all say in unison.

"I'll read it to you."

"'Dear Lisanne,'" she reads to us, mimicking their German accents.

"'We propose here a way for us to work out our concerns regarding your behavior. We will agree not to hospitalize you but you must agree to the rules of our house. We can't have you out roaming the streets at night with intent to do mischief. We felt the need to protect you from yourself. You will not attend adult cocktail hours. The drinking age in this country is twenty-one and, we see now, for very good reasons. The hours after school, you must fill with homework and study; and we expect you to continue to practice the piano. If you need to go to the library, one of us will accompany you there and see that you get home.

"'Let us know if this arrangement is agreeable to you.

"'With love from your parents,'

"And signed." She sighs. "That would certainly put a damper on further night antics, and I want to participate in the revenge plan and get Bill Rile, even if it means I have to hide out a while longer. Justice! Revenge! So sweet! I will write to tell them their terms are too harsh," she says. "Life is a negotiation. I'll say no curfew on weekends. And I will promise not to drink alcohol at Cy's happy hours, but I intend to go there with my friends. The alcohol didn't make me feel very well anyway. Especially when they followed it with a sedative. What could they have been thinking when they drugged me?"

"They were desperate to get you under control," I say.

"And I think I've fulfilled my mother's piano ambitions. She should work on it herself, already, and stop mourning about her past."

"So it is agreed that we serve the Glicks with a writ?" Bob Blaustein asks, and we all nod in agreement.

e⁄ɔe⁄ɔ

The lawyer served the Glicks with the writ the next day. They had no choice but to get a lawyer to represent them, and Bob Blaustein said that no lawyer was going to represent the Glicks without demanding a hefty retainer. And that's exactly what happened to end the stalemate. The lawyer wanted a two-thousand-dollar retainer and Ilse was horrified at the cost. They had already put up a considerable amount of money for the private detective.

The Glicks agreed to sign a guarantee that Lisanne would not be hospitalized. She agreed not to drink at adult parties but refused to have a curfew on the weekends. She has agreed to continue to practice the piano.

"It was my mother's cheapness that did it," Lisanne says, ebullient. "Remember how I told you how she shops—six shrimp, three carrots, and ten tiny peas. She's the cheapest woman on the face of the Earth, and she isn't going to pay my father's hard earned money out to a lawyer."

Chapter 36

Loretta drives us out to our lake house on Saturday, her day off. She brings along a line and a pole and sits on the end of the dock on a folding chair. We dig up some worms for her to put onto the hook. It is too early in the season for the bait shop to be open. The day is balmy. We are sitting on the dock, testing out the frigid water with our toes. It is still too cold to jump in. Lisanne is looking pale from her long confinement.

"Okay! Let's plot!" Howie says. "How's about Henry and I do the dutiful high school boy thing and shop some sexy underwear for Bill to follow into the thicket, and maybe we could strew hundreds of rubbers. Get his expectations up."

"As well as something else!" Henry says. "But coitus interruptus and bourbon will rule the night."

We are laughing so hard we don't notice that Loretta has returned with her pail.

"I caught you'uns some lunch." Little sunfish jar themselves against the sides of the pail and dive for the bottom. "Excepting it's lunch for a Liliputian. I want one of you'ns to row me out in the boat. I'm going to throw these guys back into the water."

We have to drag the rowboat out of the kiln shed, ease it onto the water, and tie it onto the dock. It's tight with five of us and we balance the weight with Loretta at the front end and Howie and Henry, each with an oar, in the middle. Lisanne and I sit at the back dragging our hands through the water and pulling up waterweeds. We tell Loretta what we are planning to do to Bill Rile.

"I always knew you were little geniuses—all four of you. I can get all the molasses you want and I'm sure Cy will supply the bourbon."

"He wouldn't miss it if I just took it from the bar," Howie says.

"No, but you have to ask," Loretta says. "He's not going to stand in your way."

"She's right, Howie," Lisanne says.

"There's another problem," I say. "Those girls are going to arrive at the cotillion with two escorts in chauf-feured cars. I've seen the how the chauffeurs line up with the cars to wait when there are events at the club. My father always said it was for the goyum. How are we going to get the note to him?"

"Someone needs to drive up in a limo," Howie says.

"And where do you suppose you'll get a limo, and who is going to deliver the note?" Lisanne asks.

"The only limo I've ever been in was from the funeral parlor," I retort. "I doubt they'll put it out on loan."

We all laugh. I must be getting some distance from my father's death because it takes me a few minutes now to tear up when I conjure the image of the limousine that brought us to the cemetery.

"Oh, we didn't mean to remind you." Lisanne hugs me and I laugh again.

"Hey, kiddos, scratch it all," Loretta says. "You're making it much more difficult than it has to be."

We stare at her.

"What do you mean, Loretta?" Howie asks.

"Who's in the message business?"

We all shake our heads.

"Western Union, geniuses! You could even send him a candy gram with a telegram attached, or even a singing telegram."

Henry sees the light. "That's what I call genius."

"That should whet his appetite," I say.

"There is a reason I was put on this Earth," says Loretta. "Common sense!"

We decide on the Candygram to sweeten Bill Rile's appetite for a tryst. Western Union will deliver it to the cotillion. Howie, Henry, and I walk from the Pittsburgh Athletic Club to Schenley Park where we find the perfect tryst spot, a thicket in Panther Hollow, lush with newly budded greenery and far enough off the main path so that our ghostly machinations won't be interrupted.

The day of the cotillion, we are busy with preparations for the night. Cy gave us a bottle of Bourbon and his blessings. My mother knows about this as well. Lisanne only told her parents that she would be staying at Loretta's.

In fact, they've decided that Loretta is a better influence than Mrs. Schmidt and let Lisanne stay at Loretta's when they went to another bomb-maker convention in New York. Loretta refused to let them pay her.

We have a blanket for the thicket floor, a box of "safes" to strew the length of the path, as well as several garter belts and bras. But, best of all, we have two gallons of viscous blackstrap molasses and four old pillows full of goose feather.

We send the telegram.

=Cadet William Rile=
=The Pittsburgh Athletic Club=
=meet me at ten o'clock in Panther Hollow =
= for a night to remember=
=marked the trail specially for you=
=your secret admirer=

It cost us thirty-five cents a word, plus the cost of the candy.

While the private school kids are arriving in their limos, we are setting up our tryst site in Panther Hollow. Henry and Howie leave a trail of condom packages and underwear leading in from the main trail to the thicket. Lisanne and I prepare the tryst site. We lay the blanket on the floor and hang paper red hearts from the branches. The bottle of bourbon we put in the middle of the blanket. Next, we all put on our costumes. Henry is the grim reaper and we are his helpers—with oversized black hoods and flared sleeves fringed at the edges. We wear skeleton masks left over from Halloween and carry cardboard scythes covered with foil. We've hidden the molasses behind the tree and make a last-minute decision to leave the pillows on the blanket for Rile's comfort. All we have to do now is wait. Scurrying animals give us several false starts. It is almost ten o'clock on Howie's watch. We hear footsteps and hide ourselves away behind the trees. A strange man wanders into our tryst site. He's a bit overweight and paunchy like uncle Abe. He picks up a package of condoms, pockets it. We watch as he takes in the tree cluttered with red hearts."

"How do we get rid of him?" Howie hisses as the man sees the bottle of bourbon on the blanket, picks it up, uncaps it, sniffs, and takes a swig.

That's when Bill Rile staggers into the thicket. He carries the red box of candy and a flask and he is in full military dress. He is already drunk and sits readily on the blanket. He notices the strange man. "Who are you?"

"Looks like you're planning a party. Can I come?

Rile pushes the man away. "No, you can leave before you ruin my evening."

The man pulls out a flashlight and shines it behind Bill Rile. The glare from the flashlight catches Henry, Howie, and me, sinister and lurking behind the brushes. The man emits a terrified howl and drops the flashlight.

Rile turns to look but the darkness hides us. Emboldened, he shoves the man again. "I'm meeting a girl here so why don't you bugger on out of here?"

Rile towers over him and jets him a menacing gaze.

The stranger begins to back out of the lair. "Have it your way."

"And if I catch you snooping around here, I'll break your fucking fat neck."

"I understand," says the now obsequious visitor as he backs out of the lair and breaks into a run.

When the fat figure recedes into the horizon, Rile sits back down on the blanket. He turns his flask upside down and despairs that it is empty. Then he notices the bourbon and removes the cap to take a swig.

"Come out, come out wherever you are!" he calls, slurring his words. "You're here, aren't you?"

It's all we can do not to laugh.

"I'm getting myself ready for you," Lisanne says in a disguised voice.

"Don't keep me waiting too long now!"

"The night is young! Have another drink," I say, disguising my voice to sound like hers.

"I know that voice," Rile says. "Where do I know it from?"

Howie covers my mouth with his hand and says in a falsetto voice, "In your dreams."

Rile takes another swig. Then another. Then he opens the box of candy and puts one into his mouth.

"Did you leave some for me?" Lisanne says.

Rile takes another swig.

"Did you save me a piece of chocolate, my sweet?" Howie asks.

"Shucks!"

"Not to worry. I have sweeter things in mind for you," Lisanne says. "Lie down on the blanket. I will only be a few more minutes. You can take off your trousers, if you like."

Rile fumbles for the zipper to his trousers and ends up having to remove the belted cadet jacket. "Hurry up! I'm cold."

"Wrap yourself in the blanket. You can take everything off if you like and shut your eyes. I've prepared something very, very warm for you."

The moon is out full. Bill is naked except for his gartered socks. He nestles down into the blanket. We see his erect penis go limp as he falls asleep. We begin to creep forward with our buckets of molasses but he stirs and sits up abruptly.

"Take another sip of bourbon to relax you," Lisanne says.

"You won't let me sleep the night away?"

"Oh, never. I have delicious plans for you."

He tries to stand up and has to grab onto the tree trunk. "I hope you are coming to me soon."

"Lie down and relax."

He does as we tell him and, when he has definitely passed out, I sneak up and take away his military uniform. We open the blanket and begin to coat his entire body in the molasses. He groans, shifts his weight, and tries once again to get up. We push him back down. His eyes focus for a second and he begins to lunge for us.

"Who are you? What are you trying to do?"

"You have plans with a lady from the netherworld," Howie says. "Don't you want to find out who she is, your mystery lady? She asked us to lead you to her."

Rile takes another swig in an effort to calm down. "She shoulda been here already. Who sent you?"

"You don't need to know that."

"The hell I don't." Rile tries to get up again but falls back, prostrate on the ground, and passes out.

With a penknife, Howie slits open both of the pillows. We eagerly grab handfuls of feathers. We dance around chanting and tossing the feathers onto Rile. We roll him over and put more molasses onto his back, followed by more feathers. We also place a placard around his neck: *I am a nasty, bullying jag off and your daughters aren't safe when I'm around.*

Next, we pull the blanket out from under him. That brings him into semi consciousness, and he shrieks when he sees us, the four grim reapers. He tries to get to his feet and falls down into the scrub. Pine needles and leaves attach to him, intensifying the effect of a huge, feathered beast. He gets up again and charges angrily toward us, but we elude him and make hooting sounds as we run away with his clothes and the blanket to the safety of the main trail where we watch what happens as Rile tries to get out of the park. He doesn't seem to know that he is stark naked. There is a chill in the air but he doesn't seem to notice. Maybe all that molasses and feather goo is insulating.

We follow him to Forbes Street. He is plain to see under the street lamps. People are coming out of the Syria Mosque where the opera has been playing. Students from Pitt crowd the street. Rile tries to talk to several people.

"You're covered in shit, man!" says a bystander.

Everybody on the sidewalk clears a big circle around Rile.

He looks down at his body and runs his hand through the molasses. He touches his penis, apparently realizes that he is naked from head to toe, and begins to scream for help. Someone calls the police from a payphone. When they arrive, they don't seem to know what to do. Rile begins to puke up chocolate candy and bourbon brown liquid.

"We can't put him in the backseat like that. What happened to you?"

Rile doesn't answer but passes out on the sidewalk. We hear the sirens of an ambulance and head up Forbes Street for the streetcar that will take us back to Montclair Street.

We spend the night at Loretta's, going over our prank, detail, by detail, while Rile's military uniform burns in a garbage can outside.

The high society pages of both the *Pittsburgh Press* and the *Pittsburgh Post Gazette* published pictures of the junior cotillion the next day—Lindy and her classmates lined up in flowing evening gowns, the boys in full dress uniform behind them. Everybody is named, including Linda Lynch Glock, the daughter of Mr. and Mrs. Edward Glock. The cotillion merited a full two-page spread but nowhere could we find a picture of Bill Rile.

Rile, however, merited the front page of both papers. The headline: *MILITARY SCHOOL STUDENT THE VICTIM OF A HAZING*

The article went on to describe how he had been found dazed, inebriated, and stark naked on Forbes Street, one of Pittsburgh's busiest thoroughfares. He told the police that a secret admirer had invited him to meet her in the park. He never found out her name. They questioned all the girls in Lindy's class. Lindy's headmistress made a statement to the press: "This is behavior unbecoming to a future debutante. I promise you, we will get to the bottom of it."

We hear later through Ellen, our Pittsburgh grapevine at Randall's, how the Western Union man delivered the Candygram to Rile right on the dance floor. It was a first for the cotillion. The dancers gathered around Rile, hoping to get a piece of his surprise but he refused to share his candy, saying that it was for later.

The military school officials became very alarmed when he didn't show up for the bus back to General Putnam after the dance. The hospital didn't learn his identity until he sobered up the next day. The school revoked all of Rile's privileges, and he was put on probation 1. That was the last I ever saw of Bill Rile. When the school year was over, we heard he joined the army. His father Ridgely succumbed to cirrhosis of the liver, and the two women are left to ramble alone in the big wreck of a house.

** భుఁ**

The Glicks never found out about how we terrorized Bill Rile.

"I'm going down to the Hill tomorrow to make my own apologies to Aaron and Jimmy," Lisanne says.

"I'll come with you."

"No, this I need to do this alone." And she did, telling her mother that she was at the library. A concerned Dr. Johnson drove her back to the library in time for Ilse to pick her up. Ilse continues her high demands on Lisanne, but Lisanne says, for one more year, she can live with it. They want her to apply to Radcliffe and she doesn't want to go. Lisanne and Henry now go steady and do their homework together every day. Ilse still thinks of Henry as one of Lisanne's kidnappers, but there is nothing she can do to stop their relationship. Henry's mother often has Lisanne for dinner. Henry and Lisanne plan to go to New York someday.

Cy invited Jimmy and Aaron and their parents to his next happy hour. He also invited the Glicks and served all the kids Shirley Temples with maraschino cherries and orange slices. No one dared sneak vodka into the Shirley Temples.

The Glicks sat there stiffly and ever vigilant while everyone else celebrated. Cy has hired Aaron's father as an architect on the hotel project and asked him to restore the building on the Hill that he lived in as a child.

I often find my mother with Cy when I come home. She usually puts him to work chopping vegetables for a meal. Tonight, a bottle of champagne sits in an improvised ice bucket. Cy takes out a cigarette and looks around for a match. My mother stays his hand, "*Not good for you*," she signs.

I translate.

Sheepish, he puts it away. "Just something to do with my hands."

"Maybe you should keep chopping," I say.

"Maybe you'll show me some of that sign language, too." Cy winks at me, "Where did Howie go?"

"He had a lab all afternoon," I answer,

"Cy looks at his watch, "I wish I had told him to come over."

"*He's capable of putting a TV dinner into the oven*," says my mother.

I translate. "He said he had a test tomorrow—coding theory," I add.

"That's my son," Cy says. "You ever put cheese into an omelet?"

"*We can*," Esther signs after I translate. She opens the fridge, "*Swiss, cheddar, Velveeta.*"

"I'll take Swiss. Velveeta's for the Goyim. Cheddar, I can take it or leave it."

She hands him a block of cheese and a triangular grater. *"Pour us some champagne,"* she signs.

Cy fills two glasses and, as an afterthought, a small one for me.

We toast, "L'chayim."

"I never saw your husband's paintings," he says to Esther, indicating a stack in a corner of the dining room.

They bring their Champagne glasses into the dining room and Esther begins to pull out paintings. She puts them wherever she can lean a canvass—on the sideboard, an easel, on chairs. She creates an exhibit. We haven't looked at his paintings in a long, long while—too much pain. Cy looks intently and says, "I'm no expert but I like them." He puts his arm around Esther. "He was an amazing painter."

e/se/s

The rest of the school year goes exceedingly well for me. The ten o'clock scholar, me, became a star student. Next year, I'm taking advanced placement courses and Howie, Henry, and Lisanne will graduate.

The year passes swiftly. My mother and I attend the graduation with Cy. Howie is the class valedictorian and makes a speech about how we need to control the proliferation of nuclear weapons. I watch Konrad Glick scratch his head throughout the entire tirade. When they call the names, the students come forward for their diplomas. We all clap.

When Lisanne Glick's name is called, she doesn't come forward. We look over at her seat. It is empty. On a sign post outside hangs a hat and gown.

I find a note under our front door telling me not to

worry. She is riding to New York City on the Greyhound Bus.

Once there, she gets a job as a sign interpreter and is thinking of going to college at night. She takes a room in the apartment of a singing teacher on New York's Upper Westside. Both Howie and Henry are going to Columbia University in the fall, and I can't wait to visit all of them. I'm thinking about school in New York, too. My mother and Cy continue to date. Howie thinks he will ask her to marry him. "Then we will both have a mother and a father," I say, "and I will have a brother.

"And I gain a sister."

We both hug. *He is my brother already*, I think.

About the Author

Sarah Levine Simon has enjoyed a dual career as a musician (opera singer) and writer. She has appeared as a soloist throughout the United States and Europe, singing difficult soprano repertory such as Bach Cantata No. 51, Lukas Foss's *Time Cycle*, and the lyric soprano operatic repertory. Writing began for the soprano as a way to access the literary texts she sang, and it led to her creating her own narratives.

Writing credits include: *Bernardo's Farewell* and *Mouse Music*, stories for actors and orchestra, produced with a grant from The National Endowment for the Arts, narrated by actress Tovah Feldshuh, among others. She has written two plays on commission for Plays for Living. *The Portrait* written as a radio play for National Public Radio in 1983 finally received a full production by the Ad Lib theater company at Theater 54 in New York City to critical acclaim in 2014. She wrote, produced, and sang as the "gourmet diva" in five musical videos to introduce classical music and have a little fun with it as well. https://www.youtube.com/watch?v=uSJs9EEzJnA.

In February of 2017, *The Dressmaker's Secret*, a play co-written by Mihai Grunfeld received a full production at Theater 59 in New York City. With *Winged Victory* and *Locked Out*, she makes her debut as a novelist.

CPSIA information can be obtained
at www.ICGtesting.com
Printed in the USA
FFOW02n1453050518
46452218-48368FF

9 781626 947078